Shot Off the Presses

An Avery Shaw Mystery
Book Four

By Amanda M. Lee

To my cousins, who give me fodder and laughs
without even trying.

Prologue

I'm not a bad person.

That's what I keep telling myself anyway.

I made a mistake. Everybody makes mistakes. That's the way of the world, the way of our world.

I don't think I should have to pay for that one mistake for the rest of my life? Do you? Of course not. You can understand that what happened, well, it wasn't even really my fault. I'm the victim here.

The fact that I have to do what I have to do now is just a fact of life. You might think I feel bad about it, but you would be wrong.

I'm a practical person, a logical person. And, logically speaking, this is my only course of action.

I've given it a lot of thought. The good of the many outweighs the good of the few, or the one. You see what I did there? I love science fiction movies. In fact, I know that Spock himself would not only understand what I was doing, but agree that it's the only way to rectify this situation.

It didn't take me long to come up with a solution. In fact, I got the idea from an episode of television. That's how I know it's a good idea. If it wasn't good, they wouldn't have aired it on television. That's a fact, Jack.

I don't know why I'm explaining this all to you. You'll either understand, or you won't. Besides, time is running short. I have a trigger to

*pull and an escape to make. Then I have more
research to do.*

*This isn't the first time I've done this – and
it won't be the last.*

*It's time. I've got to go. It's going to be rush
hour soon, and that will complicate my getaway.*

It's now or never.

One

If I could hunt down the person that invented satin shoes that can be dyed to match an ugly bridesmaid dress, I would kill them.

Okay, that's a little drastic. I would just rip off their arms and beat them with them until they lose consciousness. That wouldn't stop me from having to wear one of these horrific things, but I would probably feel better about it.

"You look ... adequate."

The voice of my best friend Carly's constant nightmares was currently trespassing on my present – and I hate the sound emitting from the abject evil standing behind me even more than Carly does right now.

"Thanks," I replied dryly.

"She looks great," Carly interrupted angrily, her thin features pinching into a hateful glare. Thankfully, that hateful glare was directed at her future mother-in-law and not me.

My name is Avery Shaw, and I'm a bridesmaid. Those words fill me with more fear than anything should – and I've almost been killed (a few times) this past year. I'm not really a professional bridesmaid. I'm a reporter for the local newspaper in Macomb County, Michigan. So, why am I in a wedding shop in downtown Mount Clemens? Because Carly has been planning the wedding from hell for the past year and a half – and the day is almost upon us.

"I'm not sure that this color really suits her," Harriet Profit sighed, tugging at the fabric on my bodice irritably. "It kind of washes her out."

Harriet Profit, in addition to being one of the most obnoxious people I've ever met, is the mother of Carly's soon-to-be husband, Kyle. I love Kyle. I cannot for the life of me figure out how a woman like Harriet gave birth to a great guy like Kyle. Carly can't either. She's become convinced that evil skips a generation and, when they have kids, she'll be giving birth to the one from *The Omen*.

"The color is fine," Carly snapped. "It's lavender. Everyone looks good in lavender. It's not like I picked red, like I initially wanted to. That would've really washed her out."

I glanced back into the full-length mirror in front of me and frowned. The simple shift dress, with the low-cut bodice and spaghetti straps, was supposed to be something I could wear again. Carly had promised. That's always a lie, though, and I know it. You can never wear a bridesmaid dress again. They're just too ugly. I'm fairly sure that's by design. This is the bride's day, after all. The bridesmaids are just window dressing.

Harriet reached up and gathered my shoulder-length blonde hair up and away from my face, pulling it back harshly. "She's going to have to wear her hair up. It will bring the look together. I hope, at least."

"What's wrong with my hair?" I whined.

"Nothing," Carly growled.

"It's just a little raggedy," Harriet said.

"Raggedy?" I was pretty sure that was an insult.

"I don't think you get regular conditioning treatments," Harriet pursed her thin little lips. "That might help. The wedding is too close, though. It's too late to do anything about that now."

I shifted my blue eyes to Carly and fought the urge to pinch her. It wouldn't accomplish anything, I reminded myself. It would just piss her off – even if it made me feel better for a few seconds.

"Her hair is not raggedy," Carly challenged Harriet. "I'm sick of you always insulting her."

"I'm not insulting her, dear," Harriet said evasively. "I'm just being honest. I don't want anything to ruin your special day."

"Then maybe you shouldn't come," I suggested brightly.

Harriet narrowed her eyes. "What did you say?"

"I said you look great," I lied.

Carly didn't even try to smother the giggle in her throat. When Harriet swung on her, though, Carly managed to wipe the wide grin off her face and look appropriately abashed. "She's just testy," Carly said hurriedly. "She doesn't like using her lunch time to do anything but eat."

"Is that why the dress is so tight?" Harriet countered. "Because she eats so much? I told you we should have put her on a diet."

"Hey!"

Carly put a reassuring hand on my arm. "She's not fat." Carly turned to me. "And the dress isn't too tight. You look great."

"I don't feel like I look great," I admitted. "I feel like I look like a big purple mermaid."

"Mermaids are beautiful," Carly waved off my concerns.

"Says who?"

"Walt Disney? Oh, just let it go," Carly grumbled. "It's too late to change the dress."

"You could call off the wedding," I interjected hopefully. "You haven't done that in weeks. Those were fun times."

"I'm not calling off the wedding," Carly said firmly. "I'm over that."

I couldn't help but notice that the glint of hope that had flashed through Harriet's eyes when I suggested calling off the wedding had fled just as quickly when Carly quashed the suggestion. She wasn't exactly thrilled with the prospect of uniting her family with Carly's.

"Can I take this off now?" I could think of nothing better than getting out of this dress – and especially these horrendous shoes – and back into something a little more comfortable.

"Yeah," Carly nodded. "Everything looks set with your dress for the wedding."

"Great."

I slipped back into the dressing room and stripped out of the lavender monstrosity – kicking the shoes under the bench as I did. I slipped back into my comfortable blue jeans and new Crystal Lake Killers hockey jersey – Geeky Jerseys, they're awesome – and pulled on my custom Batman Converse. I could hear Harriet and Carly sniping at each on the other side of the curtain and tried to push the voices out of my head. I only had a little more than a week to go, I reminded myself. Then it would be over. I could do this. No, I corrected myself, I had to do this. For Carly. She was my best friend, after all. As far as best friends go, she really was a good one – even if she was making me dress up for public ridicule in a few weeks.

I took a deep breath and slid the curtain open, slinging the dress over my arm and bending over to scoop up the shoes. "We're done here, right?"

"You've paid for the dress?" Harriet asked doubtfully.

"No, I thought I would just steal it," I replied sarcastically.

"I was just making sure," Harriet sniffed.

"Great."

Carly watched me zip the dress back up in its protective covering. She was quiet, but I could tell her mind was bursting with a myriad of thoughts. I had a feeling, given the fact that she was such a Type-A personality, that those thoughts were taking the form of to-do lists.

I glanced at my watch quickly, realizing that I still had twenty-five more minutes until I had to be to work. I could grab something to eat downtown if I hurried. "I'm going to go and grab a Coney."

"A Coney?" Harriet wrinkled her nose. "That can't be healthy."

"No," I agreed. "But it is yummy – and that's all I care about right now."

"Of course," Harriet said. "I should point out, though, that if you eat too many Coneys then your dress isn't going to fit the day of the wedding."

"Well, that would be a shame," I said with faux contrition. "I'll live with it, though."

"I'll go with you," Carly said. "I could use something to eat, too."

"A Coney?" Harriet looked scandalized. "I don't think that's a good idea."

"I was going to get a salad," Carly said sharply, pushing me toward the front door of the shop. "Now I'm going to have a Coney," I heard her mutter as we left the shop.

When we got to the Coney Island, we found a booth and ordered quickly. It only took the waitress a few minutes to bring us our order and I dove in happily. After a few bites, I realized that Carly wasn't eating. Instead, she was just pushing iceberg lettuce and big slabs of tomato around her plate – she had opted for the salad at the last minute.

"What's up?"

Carly glanced up in surprise. "Nothing. Why do you think something is up?'

"I know the salads here aren't very good, but you've eaten them before," I reminded her. "So, I ask again, what's up?"

"I'm nervous."

"Of course you're nervous," I laughed. "You're getting married. It's a big deal."

"You don't think I'm being crazy?"

I tilted my head to the side as I took a big bite of chili and onions and then shook my head as I swallowed. "I've seen you do a lot of crazy things,"

I said. "And for no reason. This is not an instance of that. I remember that time you decided to see if there was a car behind you by flooring the gas pedal in the dark. That was crazy. This is nowhere near crazy. It's normal to be nervous at a time like this."

"Do you really think so?" Carly looked at me hopefully.

"Are you worried you're getting cold feet?"

"Most of the time? No," Carly said. "After spending time with Harriet? Absolutely."

"You're not marrying Harriet," I reminded her. "You're marrying Kyle."

"She's his mother," Carly spit out. "I'm pretty sure she comes with the package."

"Yes," I agreed. "Her part of the package, though, lives in Chicago. That's six whole hours away."

"That's not that far," Carly said. "Not really, in the grand scheme of things."

"It's far enough that she can't just drop in," I said. "And when she does come to town, you can always come and stay at my place."

Carly brightened considerably when I made the offer. "That's true."

"Yeah," I took another bite of Coney. "You, me and Lexie, we'll have tons of fun."

Carly pressed her tongue to the roof of her mouth sympathetically. "Lexie is still staying with you?"

"Yes," I said, frowning as I thought about my cousin. "She's using all the money I gave her for the yoga studio, so she can't afford her own place right now."

"That's got to be annoying."

"It is," I agreed. "I've been spending most of my time over at Eliot's."

Carly's mouth widened into a full grin – the first genuine one I had seen all afternoon. Eliot Kane was my kind of new boyfriend. We'd spent months flirting and had just officially gotten together a few weeks ago. Things were still new – and they were still exciting – so staying at his apartment wasn't exactly a hardship. He's got a really great body and he's really pretty to look at. Yes, I'm shallow, sue me. He's got a good personality, too.

"I like him," Carly said. "Of course, I liked Jake, too," she added hurriedly. She was clearly hedging her bets.

Jake Farrell was, among other things – like being the county sheriff, my ex-boyfriend. We had spent our teenage years together before spending the next few apart. The fact that our paths now crossed on a regular basis – mostly because of our jobs – was a constant irritant to everyone involved.

"Why did you have to bring up Jake?" I groaned.

"Why not?" Carly looked confused.

"Eliot is still ... weird about him."

"Of course he is," Carly laughed. "Jake is his competition."

"Jake isn't his competition," I countered. "Jake is my past. Eliot is my present."

"Who is your future?"

I met Carly's curious eyes blankly. That was a weird question. Thankfully I didn't have to answer it because my cellphone was belting out the *Star Wars* theme from inside of my purse. I pulled the phone out and answered it. It was my boss, Fred Fish, and he had an assignment for me. After getting the details, I disconnected and turned to Carly apologetically.

"I have to go."

"A big story?"

"Pretty much," I said grimly. "There's been a freeway shooting on the north side of the city."

Two

It only took me about five minutes to get from downtown Mount Clemens to the scene of the crime. The directions my editor had given me indicated that the shooter had used the bridge over I-94 and Cass – which meant I could access the action by driving down Gratiot – a big highway with several lanes to ease unruly traffic congestion.

When I made the turn onto Cass, I was surprised to see the number of emergency vehicles congregating under the freeway bridge. Between the sheriff's department cars, two ambulances and three fire trucks – there weren't a lot of places to park. I pulled into the parking lot of the small Polish restaurant on my right, rummaged through my glove compartment for a reporter's notebook, and then exited my car.

I walked about five-hundred feet, until I got to the hastily erected police tape line, and glanced around. There was a group of people milling about on the same side of the tape as me – away from the action. Most of them looked appropriately horrified – and equally curious. Essentially, people feign horror at violent crimes, but they also want to know the gritty details.

The onlookers were focused on the bevy of police officers and emergency personnel who were working on extricating injured passengers and dazed drivers from no less than five crumpled vehicles. I turned to the woman next to me for answers.

"I thought this was a freeway shooter?"

"It was," the woman, a pretty brunette with a pixie cut, replied.

"Then why are there so many crashed vehicles?"

"I guess the driver of the car, the woman that was hit, crashed into one of the other vehicles and it caused several collisions."

"There was a woman driving?"

"Yeah," the brunette nodded. "I saw the ambulance load her up and take her away."

"Were you involved in this?" I asked, flipping my notebook open and jotting down a few notes.

The woman eyed my notebook curiously. "Are you a reporter?"

"Yeah, for The Monitor," I said. "I was downtown when I got the call to come out here. I'm still catching up."

"I wasn't in the accident," the woman bit her lower lip. "Can I still be in the paper?"

I didn't see why not. I took the information she had to give – which was unexpectedly plentiful.

"Can you describe where the female driver was hit?" I asked.

"It looked like it was her upper chest or shoulder," the woman replied. "That's the area they had bandaged when they loaded her into the ambulance. It was a mess, though. It's hard to be absolutely sure."

"Was she awake?"

"Yeah," the woman widened her brown eyes. "She kept asking about her kids."

"Her kids? I quirked my eyebrows in surprise. "She had kids in the car?"

"Yeah," the woman nodded. "They didn't look like they were injured, though. The sheriff's deputies loaded them in another ambulance and took them away. They were both screaming their heads off, but I think they were just scared. I don't think they wanted to keep them out here if they didn't have to."

That made sense.

"What about the injuries for the other drivers? I'm sure there were a lot of scrapes and bruises, but did you see anyone hurt really badly?"

"No," the woman shook her head. "They just seemed more angry and shook up than anything else."

I got the woman's name and then slipped underneath the police tape. The woman seemed impressed with my bravado, but I figured the cops had more to worry about than a reporter on the wrong side of the police tape. Or, maybe I just hoped that.

I moved closer to the accident scene, pulling my phone out of my purse to shoot some video as I did. I had gone unnoticed for a full ten minutes before I heard a voice behind me – and it wasn't a voice I was particularly glad to hear.

"Get your ass back behind the yellow tape!"

I swung around, plastered a fake smile on my face, and greeted my cousin Derrick with as much faux enthusiasm as I could muster. "It's so good to see you."

"You're such a liar," Derrick grunted, running his hand through his black hair angrily, when he saw me. Despite the fact that we had been practically inseparable as kids, we had taken different paths as adults. He had followed his heart into law enforcement and I had joined the one profession that made cops want to turn into violent criminals – a reporter.

"I don't think it's nice to call your favorite cousin a liar," I sang out jovially.

"Who says you're my favorite cousin?" Derrick countered.

"Of course, I'm your favorite cousin," I waved off his statement. "Who else would it be?"

"Mario," Derrick crossed his arms over his chest triumphantly and fixed me with a pointed stare.

"Mario? He's hilarious, I'll admit it, but he's not exactly someone you spend a lot of time with."

"I don't spend a lot of time with you either, thank God," Derrick pointed out. "At least I'm in a bowling league with Mario."

"You're in a bowling league? That's just embarrassing."

"How is that embarrassing?" Derrick narrowed his brown eyes. "You're trying to distract me."

"That's an ugly thing to say." Notice that I didn't say he was wrong.

"Get on the other side of the tape," Derrick ordered again.

"What? I'm not doing anything," I protested.

"You're bugging me," Derrick replied. "And this is my crime scene."

I pursed my lips. That could be both good and bad for me. "Well then, deputy, why don't you tell me what's going on here?"

"We'll have a press conference when we know more," Derrick said sternly.

"Oh, just give me something," I protested.

"I'll give you a fat lip," Derrick growled.

"You can't hit a civilian," I smiled widely.

"I can if she's my cousin," Derrick replied angrily. "Plus, you've earned it. Remember when you gave me a black eye when we were kids?"

"That was an accident," I pointed out. "You were the one that put your eye down to one end of a pipe that we were sliding a broom handle through to entertain ourselves. That was really your fault."

Derrick chewed the inside of his lip in aggravation. He knew I was right. He needed to let that black eye go. We were kids. Cripes. He had done equally horrible things to me. I was almost sure of it.

"I'm not telling you anything," Derrick finally said. "And because you're such a pain, I might even bar you from the press conference."

"You can't do that," I scoffed.

"I can so."

'You can't. I'll file a complaint."

Derrick looked incensed and he snorted through his ski-slope nose to indicate just how irritated he really was. He looked like an angry little bull and I was waving the red flag right in front of him. "You wouldn't dare."

"If you try to bar me from a press conference, you have no idea what I'm capable of," I warned him.

Derrick gripped my arm angrily. "I wouldn't advise that if I were you."

"Why? What are you going to do, tell my mom?"

Light glinted in Derrick's eye. That was precisely what he planned to do. I watched, fascinated and terrified at the same time, as he pulled his cell phone out of his pocket. I was still frozen in fear as he scrolled through his contacts and frowned when I saw him pull up my mother's name.

He smiled at me as his finger hovered over the little phone symbol that would connect him with my mother and her never-ending bag of grief. "If you do that, I'll call your mother and tell her you had sex with your high school girlfriend in her bed when she was out of town."

Derrick cocked his head and smirked. "She already knows. Lexie told her when she was mad at me a couple of years ago."

Crap.

"Did Lexie tell your mom about the time you stole her car when you were only fourteen and did donuts on the front lawn of the principal's house?"

I didn't have to ask the question because I knew the answer. No one knew about that. No one but me, that is. And how did I know? Technically I had been with him.

"That will get you in trouble, too," Derrick pointed out.

I considered the statement and then shrugged it off. "I don't care. I'll just tell my mom you made me go."

"She won't believe that."

He had a point. "Well, I don't care. I'll still tell on you."

Derrick blew out a frustrated sigh. "What do you want to know?"

"What do you have?"

"Not a lot," Derrick conceded. "We have a young mother and two small kids in the car. We have no idea if she was targeted or if she was just in the wrong place at the wrong time."

"Did anyone see the shooter?"

"No," Derrick shook his head. "Someone did see a white van parked on top of the bridge, though."

"License plate?"

"No, not even a partial."

"Any description of the driver of the van?"

"No."

"Man? Woman?"

"There was no description."

"What kind of a gun was used?"

"We'll have no idea about that until the doctors get the bullet out of the victim," Derrick said. "Even then, we probably won't make the caliber of weapon public."

"Was more than one shot fired?"

Derrick shrugged. "I honestly don't know. It's going to take us a long time to sort this mess out."

I glanced behind him and couldn't help but agree. "Anything else?"

Derrick wrinkled his nose. "No."

"When is the press conference?" I was enjoying messing with him.

"We'll send a press release to the paper when we decide." He liked messing with me, too.

He was done talking, though. That much was obvious. I didn't know what else he could give me anyway. "Thank you for your professionalism," I said snottily. "Have a nice day."

I started to walk away, back toward the area where my car was parked, but Derrick stopped me. "Are you going to family dinner tomorrow night?"

Crap. "Is it Thursday?" Time flies when you don't want to go to family dinner.

"Yep."

"Well, then I guess I'm going to family dinner tomorrow," I sighed. "I hate family dinner."

"Who doesn't?" Derrick didn't exactly look thrilled with the prospect of spending time with our relatives either.

"No way out of it, though," I said. "I think the only excuse is death – and I'm not sure if I'm willing to go that far."

"I guess I'll see you tomorrow," Derrick said.

"One way or the other," I agreed.

Three

      It only took me a few minutes to get back to the office. The Monitor is located on the outskirts of Mount Clemens – the county seat – and was erected on a piece of land that had once been a dump. It has a white trash flea market on one side and a series of low-income apartments on the other. A local river that slices throughout the county has beach access across the road, and one might think that would be a nice feature. Unfortunately, though, the river is so polluted that it sometimes smells like rotten fish (and the occasional dead body). Yeah, it's not a great area.

      When I entered the building, I used the fob on my keychain to access the departmental sections and offices behind the locked glass door that separated the reception area from the rest of the business. As I made my way to the editorial department, I cut through one of the conference rooms to get to the newsroom faster – and avoid the publisher's office. He wasn't a fan of the way I dressed and I wasn't a fan of just about anything he did.

      I made my way down reporters' row, dropping my new *The Walking Dead* purse in my cubicle and joining my co-workers as they gossiped in the middle of the aisle. When the cubicles were constructed, it was in an effort to cut down on our incessant chatter. That's why we had tall walls instead of short walls – like a normal newsroom. The effort was in vain. It just forced us to stand when we gossiped instead of sitting.

"What's up?"

Marvin Potts, one of my best friends at the paper, turned to me with a wide smile. "We're just talking about Duncan," he said.

"What did Duncan do?" I grimaced. Like everyone else in the building, I hated Duncan. He was the office tool. If you looked up douche on Wikipedia, you would find his photo. I'm not joking. I uploaded it myself.

"Duncan has taken it on himself to hold a seminar," Marvin replied giddily.

"On what?" I asked blithely. "How to be the office asshole and still keep your job?"

"No, but he should do that," Marvin agreed. "That's his only talent."

"Oh, come on," I replied. "He's also a pathological liar and emotionally vacant. He has a lot to offer to the journalism profession."

"There's that, too," Marvin agreed.

"What's he hosting a seminar on?"

"Cultivating contacts," Marvin said succinctly.

"Like he would know how to cultivate a contact," I scoffed. "He's alienated three police stations in as many weeks. He's got a personality like a rabid dog – only not as friendly."

"Don't tell him that," Marvin said. "He has no self-awareness. That's why he writes about bird diseases and historic speeches, stories that no one would ever want to read. He has no idea what real news is."

"He's just lazy," I countered. "He's a one-source wonder. He's incapable of writing an actual news story."

"So, I hear you got the freeway shooter?" Marvin changed the subject.

"Yeah."

"What did you get?"

"Not much. Mother shot with kids in the car. She's at the hospital. No one saw the shooter. There was a chain reaction crash after the initial gunshot. The investigation is ongoing."

"Is the sheriff's department having a press conference?"

"Yeah," I nodded. "I have no idea if it's going to be today or not, though."

I left Marvin to continue making fun of Duncan and wandered down to my editor's desk. Fred Fish is not what you expect when you envision an editor. Sure, he wears the tailor-made suits and the patent-leather shoes that go with being a successful businessman that has to be out in the public on a regular basis. He also wears enough jewelry to be confused with a pimp – or Burt Reynolds in the 1970s.

I leaned over his desk, trying to get a glimpse of what he was typing on his computer – just in case it was a memo about another dress code crackdown – and then waited for him to acknowledge me.

"What do you have?"

I told him about what I had witnessed at the scene and waited for further instructions. Fish glanced up at the clock and shrugged. "I doubt they're going to have a press conference today."

"No," I agreed. "It will most likely be tomorrow morning."

"This is yours," Fish said. "It's going to be a media circus."

We didn't get a lot of freeway shooters – only two that I could remember in my five-year tenure at the paper – but I knew he was right. "It's bound to drum up a lot of frantic people."

Fish grunted. "What else is new?"

"We should start outlining some angles now," I suggested.

"Meaning?"

"After we get the identification of the woman that was shot, we'll need to try and set up an interview with her or her family," I started. "If she dies, then we're going to need to do the puff piece on what a great person she is. We should also be prepared for all the gun control talk."

"Gun control?" Fish raised his eyebrow in query.

"It's bound to happen."

Fish nodded. "Yeah. We'll have to send someone out to the gun range and then talk to that anti-gun group out in Romeo."

"MAG?" I raised my eyebrows dubiously. "Mothers Against Guns? They could've thought of a better name."

"They're nuts."

I was surprised by the new voice interjecting itself into our conversation. I slid my face around and regarded one of The Monitor's newest employees – Brick Crosby – standing by the copy machine and regarding me coolly.

I didn't know a lot about Brick. He'd only been with the paper about two months. He worked nights, laying out the pages for the sports department. From what I had heard, he was kind of a weird guy. He brought a four-course meal into the paper every night to cook in the kitchenette – usually that included some sort of game animal as the main dish – and he was a rabid Pittsburgh Steelers fan. That was enough for me to dislike him without even speaking to him.

"You don't like MAG?" I directed the question to Brick warily. Seriously, what were his parents thinking when they named him Brick? I had to wonder if that was his real name. One of the other reporters had tried to adopt a penname of Turk a few months ago – but he was laughed at so much he had dropped it relatively quickly. Maybe Brick had done the same thing?

"That group's whole goal is to make sure that no self-respecting man can own a gun," Brick replied bitterly.

"Man? Or person?" I didn't like his tone.

"Does it matter?"

Apparently not to Brick. "I thought they were only against assault weapons and large magazines," I finally said, mostly to fill the uncomfortable silence. I wasn't sure what my stance on gun control was, and I wasn't really in the mood to discuss it with a guy named Brick.

"That's an invasion of my privacy," Brick said angrily. "I have a right to protect myself. The Second Amendment gives me that right."

"Do you have an assault weapon?"

Fish looked up curiously. "Yeah, Killer, do you have an assault weapon?"

"That's none of your business," Brick said coolly. "As a law-abiding citizen – and a veteran – I have the right to arm myself anyway I see fit."

I glanced down at Brick's camouflage pants and combat boots and then let my gaze wander up to his broad shoulders and aggressive stance. He was actually pretty short – only about two inches taller than me – which put him around five-foot-seven- inches tall. I had a feeling his aggressive people skills had something to do with Little Man's Syndrome. I was used to dealing with it when I interacted with Derrick, so I was familiar with the sudden fits of rage that accompanied the malady. I realized, pretty quickly I might add, that I had no inclination to argue with Brick – even if I thought he was probably a prime example of someone that shouldn't own a gun.

"Yeah, it's your right."

Fish smirked at me and then focused on Brick. "You said you were a veteran?"

"Yeah," Brick nodded. "Now you have a thing about veterans?"

"No," Fish shook his head quickly. He was clearly nervous around our new employee. It was interesting – and something I was going to file away for future reference (or blackmail material when I didn't want to cover a specific story). "I was just wondering if you know any snipers?"

"Why?" Brick was obviously a guy that didn't trust anyone. He had a certain air of paranoia wafting around him.

"Because someone just took a shot at a driver from a freeway bridge over on Cass," Fish said. "I'm assuming, with your knowledge of weapons, you would know how hard of a shot that was."

Brick visibly relaxed. "Oh, yeah, I would think that's a pretty hard shot. How open is the bridge?"

I described the area to him and waited.

"It's wide open?"

"Yeah."

"I guess it depends," Brick said finally.

"On what?"

"Whether it was a specific target or not."

That actually made sense. "Say it was a specific target. Say the shooter picked out a specific person in a specific vehicle."

"Then you're probably looking at someone that either has military training or has spent a lot of time practicing."

"What if it was random?"

"Then you probably only need someone with a basic knowledge of how a gun works and a little bit of luck," Brick replied matter-of-factly.

Well, that opened up the suspect pool drastically.

"So, basically, you're saying we need to know how many shots were fired," I sighed. "And how far away the shot really was."

Brick smiled smugly. "Yeah. I know it's probably hard for you, but you're going to have to get some actual information before you start going after gun owners."

I waited until Brick had disappeared back around the far side of the cubicles and turned to Fish. "Nice hire."

"He's not so bad," Fish said. "He brought me some venison jerky."

"Yum," I said sarcastically.

"It was really good. He's a master smoker."

"That's what she said."

"What?" Fish looked confused.

"Never mind."

I made my way back to my desk and booted up my computer. I Googled freeway shootings, hoping I would find some statistics, and was surprised to find that this wasn't the first freeway shooting in the area over the past few days. There had been one in Oakland County, too, less than a week ago. Now that I read the story, I vaguely remembered hearing something about it on the nightly news. The Oakland County police had attributed the shooting to bored teenagers – mostly because the shot was believed to have originated from a footbridge by a nearby park. It hadn't been solved, and the investigation had apparently stalled. Oakland County was notorious for hiding crime, though, so I had no idea where that investigation stood. I would have to try and reach out to a few reporters I knew across town – ones I could tolerate – which meant it was a short list. I printed out the story and took it to Fish's desk.

"What's that?"

I handed the story to him and waited for him to read it. When he was finished, he turned to me. "This could be a coincidence."

"It could be," I agreed. "We have no way of knowing yet if the two cases are related. One was a single businessman named Malcolm Hopper and one was a mother. They were in two different counties. It could be a copycat, too."

"It could be," Fish furrowed his brow. "Mention this shooting in your story, but don't focus on it. We don't want to create a panic if they're not related. That will just make us look like jerks."

Since the media was often regarded as jerks as it was, I didn't disagree with him. "I'll call over to the Oakland paper and see what they have. I'll dig into that shooting and see what else I can unearth."

"That's a good idea," Fish said. He glanced up at the wall clock. "You probably won't be able to get anyone until tomorrow, though."

"It's just another angle," I said absentmindedly.

"It's a good angle," Fish said. "Just don't press it yet. We don't want to do anything that's going to come back and bite us."

As a reporter that had witnessed many a story come back and bite me – or try to kill me – I had no problem acquiescing to his demands. I would wait. For now. I needed more information before I picked a direction to go.

Four

I placed a call to the sheriff's department and found out that a press conference had been scheduled for the next morning. Since no more information would be available tonight, I filed my story and headed home.

A few years ago, I had bought a small, two-bedroom home in Roseville. I loved the area because it boasted a bevy of restaurants and easy access to the freeway. It also had a high white trash population that alternately amused and irritated me. I pulled into my driveway and frowned when I saw that my hillbilly neighbors were out in their backyard grilling – without their shirts on. Maybe it's me, but I never think it's a good idea to be around an open flame with bare skin. Unfortunately, I would have no choice but to greet them – something I tried really hard to avoid most days.

The brothers had issues, there's no other way to put it. They lived in the two-bedroom house their mom had left them in her will – with one of the brother's wife and toddler. That was four people – three of whom liked to drink (a lot) – and a really shrill little girl. When the mood (and the forty-ounce beers) struck, the three adults liked to brawl in the front yard. The police were often called to break it up – and haul belligerent participants away. I liked to think of it as Neighborhood Theater, only entertaining.

Still, they weren't my least favorite neighbors. Sometimes that was the pot-addled slackers that lived across the road – but they were mostly harmless. Loud, but harmless. Right now, though, that honor belonged to the new family that had moved into the house on the corner. Sure, the bevy of toys that littered the yard – and blew across their driveway and into the middle of the road during storms – was a constant irritant. The rooster they had adopted and let walk around their yard and crow – at all hours of the day and night, no joke – was the current bane of my existence, though.

When I exited my car, I waved at my hillbilly neighbors and tried to scoot into the house as quickly as possible. Eliot's truck had been parked out at the curb and, while I was excited to see him, I was more excited to get away from Tweedle-Dumb and Tweedle-Dumber.

"Hey, Avery," the younger brother greeted me. His name was Larry. He had one of those little shriveled hands from a birth defect and I tried really hard not to stare at it when I was around him. Yes, I'm a terrible person, I'm aware of it.

I inwardly sighed. "Hey, Larry. How's it going?"

"Pretty good."

"Any prospects on the job front?"

Larry had been unemployed since I moved in. Secretly, I was pretty sure he was comfortable living on disability and drinking his days away. It was really none of my business, though.

"It's rough out there," Larry said.

"Yeah," I agreed. "Cooking dinner?" I hate people that ask obvious questions, but I didn't have a lot in common with Larry and his brother so I embraced the social nicety that I loathed to ease the conversation lull.

"Steaks," Larry said happily. "We're also discussing how to catch that chicken so we can barbecue it this weekend."

I mulled over the thought. I wasn't big on animal cruelty. In fact, I abhorred it. That damned rooster woke me up every day, though. "Don't bother," I blew out a sigh. "I already reported them to the city."

"You did?" Larry looked impressed.

"I tried to talk to the woman that lives over there," I admitted. "She told me to go ... well, she told me to go have a good time with myself, so I had a good time going and reporting them to code enforcement."

"How quick will they confiscate the chicken?" Larry asked eagerly.

"They've been given ten days," I replied.

"When was that?"

"About two days ago," I said. "Trust me, if the chicken isn't gone, I'll be reporting them again."

Fine, I'm a narc. Sue me.

I waved goodbye to Larry and then entered my house. The minute I closed the laundry room door behind me, a heavenly smell attacked my olfactory senses. Fajitas! Eliot was cooking.

I excitedly climbed the steps between the laundry room and kitchen and skidded to a halt on the linoleum floor.

Let me tell you, ladies, Eliot Kane is quite a sight. He's six feet of pure muscle and sex appeal. He has shoulder-length brown hair, bright brown eyes and just enough tattoos to make him sexy instead of trashy.

At the present moment, he had steak, green peppers and onions cooking on my George Foreman grill and he was busily chopping tomatoes at the counter. He lifted his head up when he sensed my presence and smiled at me seductively. "What's up, chickadee?"

"Chickadee?" I narrowed my eyes. "Is that a crack about the chicken?"

"It's still there," he laughed. "I saw it when I parked."

"It's the devil."

"Well, it won't be here long."

I moved to Eliot's side and exchanged a warm and flirty kiss with him – one that held a lot of promise for after-dinner activities – and then dropped my coat and purse on the kitchen floor.

Eliot eyed my discarded items. "You can't put those away?"

Here's the thing, Eliot is not a neat freak – but he's also not a fan of the unorganized chaos I usually embrace. Quite frankly, I'm a pig. Since Lexie had moved in, she did all the cleaning. Before that, I just lived in the mess. What? I need a maid. Since reporters make next to nothing, I can't afford one. It's an odd quandary. And no, I don't want to just clean my house and shut up. Trust me. I've heard that from my mother for years. Let's just say, it's not my thing.

I blew out a dramatic sigh and then picked up my coat and purse. After putting them away, I walked back into the kitchen to watch Eliot work. "Where's Lexie?"

"She's spending the night with whatever loser she's seeing these days," Eliot said briefly.

"Devontae," I supplied.

"What?"

"That's his name, Devontae." My cousin, Lexie, is pretty much the closest thing I have to a sister. I'm an only child, but I have a big extended family. My cousins and I are extremely close – probably too close – and we border on co-dependent on a regular basis.

On her best day, you could say Lexie is flaky. On her worst day, you could say she is reckless. Despite all that, I had spent a lot of time swooping in to save her from herself since she was a teenager. This was a fact that drove Eliot crazy. He was trying really hard not to badmouth her

Since she had completed a stint in rehab a couple weeks ago, Lexie had been pretty good. That didn't mean that her taste in men had gotten any better. Every man she was attracted to was black – which I understood. They were all smooth looking specimens of the male gender. Unfortunately, they often turned out to be dealers or shiftless losers, too. What can I say? She's got terrible taste in men.

"Is that a real name?" Eliot asked the question in a light tone, but I could see the muscle in his cheek ticking. Lexie wasn't his favorite person. The fact that she was partially responsible for him getting shot a few months ago had a lot to do with that – but the fact that he spent time with her (against his will) was also part of it.

.

I slipped my arms around Eliot's waist and rested my head against his muscular back. It was partially a stalling tactic. I also just liked the feel of him. "Can we not fight about Lexie?"

Eliot turned around and wrapped his arms around me, dropping a kiss on my forehead. "That sounds like a good idea."

I let Eliot finish the meal while I set the table in the dining room. The truth is, I'm not a great cook. My family owns a diner in northern Oakland County, but the cooking gene pretty much skipped me. My best dish is Stouffer's macaroni and beef. What? It's delicious.

Eliot and I settled down for dinner, exchanging stories about our day. We were pretty comfortable with each other at this point. I told him about my showdown with Derrick – a story that made him laugh out loud – and then told him about the freeway shooting in Oakland County.

"You think they're related?"

"Maybe," I said around a mouthful of fajita. "It could just be a copycat, though."

"You need more information," Eliot agreed. "Is the sheriff's department having a press conference?"

"Tomorrow at nine," I said. "This is really good. I knew I kept you around for a reason."

"I thought you were keeping me around for the sex," Eliot teased.

"Maybe I keep you around for a few things," I ceded.

Eliot smiled, flashing the dimple in his cheek in my direction. I practically melted when I saw it. He has a certain effect on me. That effect usually ends up with the two of us naked.

I didn't have a chance to let that thought take me over, though, because the next thing I heard was the backdoor slamming.

"Stupid assholes."

Lexie was home.

Lexie stormed into the dining room, all four-feet, and eleven inches of her. Her long brown hair was wild – and I doubted it was from the wind – and her brown eyes were on fire with rage.

"I hate men!"

I glanced across the table at Eliot. His jaw had clenched at the sound of Lexie's voice, but he was studying the meal on his plate instead of acknowledging her presence. That was probably a good thing, although I doubted it would last.

"What now?"

"Devontae says that I'm high maintenance," Lexie slid into the chair beside me and grabbed a piece of green pepper off my plate.

Eliot snorted. "And that's news?"

Lexie ignored him. "I am not high-maintenance." I took a bite of my fajita to delay answering her. That didn't dissuade her, though. "Am I high-maintenance?"

"No," I said hurriedly.

"Yes," Eliot said at the same time.

Lexie narrowed her eyes as she regarded Eliot. Despite the fact that he had saved her – several times – over the past few months, their relationship was getting more and more tempestuous.

"What does that mean?"

"It means that you're the most high-maintenance person I've ever met," Eliot answered honestly.

Lexie pursed her lips angrily. "That's not true." She turned to me expectantly. "Tell him that's not true."

I swallowed hard. "I promised I wouldn't lie to him," I said carefully. "I'm really trying to keep my promise." And I wasn't going to break it on something that held absolutely no benefit to me.

"What's that supposed to mean?" Lexie screeched.

"Oh, come on," I sighed. "You know you're high-maintenance. You get off on it."

"That's the meanest thing you've ever said to me," Lexie pouted.

"I once told you that we adopted you from a band of gypsies," I protested. "You cried for three straight weeks."

"I forgot about that," Lexie mused. "You've always been mean to me. I was five and I believed everything you told me. For the next two years I waited to grow fangs because you told me all gypsies eventually grew fangs."

Eliot looked incensed. "Mean? Didn't she just give you a bunch of money to start a yoga studio?" I guess he was just ignoring the gypsy thing. Despite the uncomfortable situation, it warmed my heart that he was standing up for me.

Lexie looked properly chagrined. "Yes, she did," Lexie agreed. "She's also a partner in that business. So, when it makes a lot of money, she's going to make a great profit."

"And, if it fails, she'll lose all that money," Eliot shot back.

I pinched the bridge of my nose to ward off the headache that was suddenly threatening to ruin the rest of the night. "Can we not fight?"

Lexie and Eliot both pretended they didn't hear me.

"It's not going to fail."

"You don't know that," Eliot scoffed. "You know absolutely nothing about running a business."

"That's why I partnered with Avery," Lexie shot back.

"Avery doesn't know anything about running a business either," Eliot replied. He shot an apologetic look in my direction. "No offense."

I couldn't really take offense since he was right.

"I guess that's why she's sleeping with you," Lexie said angrily. "You run a pawnshop, so you know everything about running a business."

"I run a private detective business, too," Eliot reminded her.

"Well, I guess all the pillow talk is about supply and demand then," Lexie was practically seething.

Eliot regarded Lexie coldly. "Good point," he said finally, getting to his feet. "And, with that, let's go to bed."

Eliot held his hand out to me. I took it, even though the gesture caused Lexie to frown.

"What about this mess?"

"You're living here rent-free," Eliot said. "Earn your keep."

Five

In general, I'm not a morning person. When I wake up next to a warm mass of muscles and tousled brown hair, though, I've been known to make exceptions. I blew out a sigh and snuggled into Eliot for a second, basking in the feel of his arms as they tightened around me.

"I can hear the gears in your mind working," Eliot mumbled sleepily.

"You must be a super hero to hear that," I replied teasingly.

"They sound rusty."

"You're funny," I said, starting to pull away from him in an attempt to get out of bed and start my day. Eliot pulled me back close to him.

"What were you thinking?"

"I was thinking I have to get ready for a press conference," I lied.

"That's not what you were thinking," Eliot challenged.

"Fine, I was thinking how pretty you are in the morning," I admitted.

"Pretty?" Eliot's brown eyes found mine in the early morning light. "I don't normally think of myself as pretty. Ruggedly handsome? Yes. Pretty? Not so much."

"Ruggedly handsome? You've given this some thought, I see." I shifted up into a sitting position, catching a glance at my disheveled blonde hair in the mirror across from the bed as I did. "I don't know how you do it," I complained.

"What?" Eliot was trailing his hand lazily down my arm, but he hadn't made a move to climb out of bed yet.

"Look so good in the morning," I said gloomily, running my hand through my snarled hair. "I think that's another one of your super hero abilities."

Eliot opened one of his brown eyes again, smiling as he took in my mussed hair. "I think you look cute in the morning."

"I'm starting to rethink that super hero vision thing," I said.

"Maybe you're the one that doesn't see things clearly," Eliot said. "Because what I see is cute."

I smiled at him as warmth rushed to my cheeks.

"And mouthy," Eliot added.

I scowled down at him. "You couldn't just leave it at cute?"

"You're not the only one that speaks before they think," Eliot admitted ruefully.

"And we're up," I grumbled.

After showering together – which involved a few wandering hands and lips – we made our way out into the living room and found Lexie doing yoga in front of the television. I had to admit that I was impressed at the contortions she managed to get her small body to conform to, even though it looked more like torture than exercise. I glanced over to see Eliot regarding her curiously. "What is she doing?"

"Yoga," I said simply.

"Why?"

"It's supposed to be fun."

"It doesn't look fun."

"Well, it is," Lexie shot back from her spot on the floor – where her knees were magically behind her ears. "You're distracting me."

"From what? Bending yourself into a human pretzel? I have a sudden urge to dump mustard over you."

"And then eat me?" Lexie asked haughtily.

Eliot looked suddenly uncomfortable. "This conversation took a turn I wasn't expecting."

"I know how that goes," I replied.

"I still don't understand what she's doing," Eliot continued. "That doesn't look like exercise to me."

Eliot was apparently spoiling for a fight. Since Lexie and I came from a gene pool that was always spoiling for a fight, she wasn't about to disappoint him.

"This is hard work," Lexie said primly.

"It looks like something little kids do when they're watching television and they're bored," Eliot countered.

I opened my mouth to stop the argument that I knew was about to blow up but moved toward the kitchen instead. What was the point? Lexie and Eliot were squabbling machines these days. They were going to find something to fight about, even if I tried to find a way to delay it.

I opened the cupboard to pick a cereal for breakfast, shoving Lexie's whole-grain wheat blend to the side and grabbing my box of Fruity Pebbles. I poured the cereal in a bowl, added milk, and then walked back into the archway between the kitchen and the main room of the house. Eliot hadn't moved, but Lexie was now standing in front of him, hands on hips, as she challenged him angrily. I had to give her credit. He had a foot and a half on her and yet she looked like the terrifying one in their standoff.

"This isn't your house, you know," she said. "This is Avery's house – and I don't have to take this in my cousin's house."

"You could leave," Eliot said blandly.

"You could leave," Lexie shot back.

"Oh, I'm not going to leave," Eliot replied angrily. "Not the way you want me to."

"Well, I'm not going to leave either," Lexie said snottily.

"That's because you don't have anywhere to go," Eliot continued. "Avery is the only one that will take you."

"That's not true," Lexie said "She likes having me here."

"Why would she?"

"What is that supposed to mean?" Lexie raised one of her perfectly arched eyebrows irritably.

"It means that you eat her food, live here rent-free and pretty much make a nuisance of yourself," Eliot answered. "Why would she want you around for that?"

Lexie swung on me angrily. "Are you going to let him talk to me like that?"

"Oh, yeah, run to Avery to protect you," Eliot mused. "Like you always do."

Eliot turned to me expectantly. "Aren't you going to say anything?"

I shoved another spoonful of Fruity Pebbles into my mouth and considered both sets of brown eyes as they regarded me – both looking for backup. I swallowed hard. "I have a press conference to get to."

I swung around quickly, dumped my bowl into the sink, and slid out the back door as quickly as my legs would take me. I didn't blow out a frustrated breath until I was next to my car. I needed to get Lexie out of my house – and not just because of Eliot. As an only child, I was used to my own space. I didn't do well when people were constantly pressing me for attention and trying to talk to me. I was perfectly happy spending three hours with my Kindle and Keurig in absolute silence. I hadn't had that in a really long time.

"Not quick enough."

I swung around and found Eliot standing in the driveway watching me.

"What?" I feigned ignorance.

"If you wanted to make a clean getaway, you should have gotten in your car and sped away."

"Would that have stopped you from tracking me down?"

"No."

"I don't know what you want me to do," I said wearily.

Eliot narrowed his eyes as he regarded me. "I know you're in a tough spot," he said finally. "I don't mean to make things harder for you."

"You're not," I protested.

"You can't tell me you want her to keep staying here," Eliot pressed. I think he was actually worried that, a year from now, the three of us would all be living together and he would have to blow his brains out to shut out Lexie's incessant chatter.

"No," I admitted. "I'm also not going to kick her out – at least not yet."

"Why not?"

"She's doing better," I started.

"Than what?"

"Than what she's been in the past," I ignored his pointed jab. "She'll get on her feet eventually. If I push her too quickly she could have a relapse."

"She guilts you and you fall for it," Eliot said harshly. "I find that interesting since you are usually the type of person that can't be guilted."

"That's not true," I replied.

"Really? That wasn't you at a family dinner two weeks ago that laughed when your mom cried, big crocodile tears with full sniffles, while trying to make you go to a baby shower for one of her friends?"

"Those weren't real tears," I grumbled. "And baby showers are like torture."

"That's not the point," Eliot said patiently. "You have a thing about protecting Lexie specifically."

I pursed my lips poutily. "It's just that …."

"It's a habit," Eliot supplied. "I know."

"You knew when you started dating me that I had a crazy family," I pointed out.

"There's crazy and then there's Lexie," Eliot muttered.

"I can't kick her out," I said finally. "I just can't. Not yet."

Eliot wrinkled his nose and pinched the bridge of it tiredly. "Fine. I don't expect you to kick her out. Until she's gone, though, how about we do sleepovers at my place instead of yours?"

I smiled, my first real smile since our shared shower an hour before, and nodded agreeably. "I think that's fair." What? He lived right next door to the best coffee place in town. That's not only avoiding stress but also finding Nirvana at the same time.

Eliot walked to me and lightly kissed me. "That's good," he agreed. "I don't think my blood pressure could take much more of cohabitating with the yoga Yoda – and I only see her once or twice a week as it is."

I smirked despite myself.

"What?" Eliot cocked an eyebrow.

"Yoga Yoda? I'm rubbing off on you."

"That's a terrifying thought."

He leaned in to kiss me more completely this time, but my cellphone interrupted his ministrations. I held up my finger to ask him to wait while I took the call. I saw from the caller ID that it was Fish.

"What's up?"

"That's the way you answer the phone?"

"I knew it was you."

"What if it was an anonymous source?" Fish grumbled.

"Calling from your phone? That would be quite the feat."

"No one has proper phone etiquette anymore," Fish continued. "It's a travesty."

This could go on forever. "So, why are you calling?"

"I'm sending Duncan to the press conference at the sheriff's department."

"What? Why?"

I glanced over when I saw Eliot smirk at my sudden whining.

"I need you to do something else," Fish replied breezily.

"What?" I asked suspiciously.

"Don't take that tone," Fish warned. "I hate it when you take that tone."

I adjusted my tone through gritted teeth. "What do you want me to do?"

"I've set up a meeting for you with the head of the air base."

I felt the air whoosh out of me. "Why?"

"What do you mean why? We're dealing with a freeway shooter. That means someone with possible military experience. We have an air base in this county. People are going to be naturally suspicious. We discussed this yesterday." Fish sounded frustrated.

"But why now?"

"They called us," Fish said simply.

"Who did?"

"The public affairs agent called me, at home I might add, this morning and said they wanted to set up a one-on-one interview about the situation as soon as possible," Fish supplied. "It took me by surprise, too."

"I don't understand," I said finally. "You don't think this sounds fishy?"

"I do," Fish said. I could practically see him nodding through the phone while twiddling his chunky gold wedding band. "That's why I'm sending you."

"Hmmm."

"I know you won't toe the government line," Fish filled in the silence. "You'll push past the bullshit – whatever bullshit they start shoveling our way. And, I'm telling you, I can just tell there's going to be a big stinking pile of bullshit."

"Thanks for the visual," I grumbled. "I think there was a compliment buried in there, though, so I'll let it go."

"Don't let it go to your head," Fish admonished me. "You have to be out there in forty-five minutes, so you should probably get going. It will take you twenty minutes to get through security. Don't wear anything inappropriate."

It was too late for that – and there was no way I was going to change now. I disconnected and turned to Eliot. "I guess I'm not going to a press conference at the sheriff's department."

"Why?" Eliot watched me curiously.

"Apparently I'm having a one-on-one interview with the base commander out at the air base," I answered. "He called and requested it."

"Leonard Turner?" Eliot asked, surprised etched on his handsome face.

"You know him?" I turned to him questioningly.

"Everyone knows about him," Eliot said. "He was all over the news when he came to town last year."

I felt a niggling suspicion that Eliot was hiding something from me. I couldn't press him on the subject, though, because I had to get out to the air base. "Yeah," I shrugged. "I guess I'll find out what he wants within the hour."

Eliot dropped another kiss on my mouth and started moving toward the curb where his truck was parked. I watched curiously as he stopped and turned around. "Be careful around Turner," he said finally. "He'll try to mislead you any chance he gets."

"How do you know that?"

Eliot turned back to his truck without answering. Well, this morning had taken quite a turn – quite a few turns, actually.

Six

Jefferson Air National Guard Base is one of Macomb County's most noteworthy facilities. It houses a branch of the National Guard and features an assortment of really big military planes. Yeah, I don't get the appeal, but there's a museum on the base that draws a big crowd every year – and the air show is always a big deal, even though there's usually some sort of catastrophe attached to it. We're talking plane crashes and people falling from various aircrafts to their death. Every single time they host one, something terrible happens – and yet they still keep hosting them. Yeah, I don't get it either.

The base is located in northern Macomb County, with one side facing Lake St. Clair, another facing the woods and a third facing one of the major highways that cuts across the industrial landscape to the east of one of the current shopping hubs.

I hopped on I-94 and took the freeway the entire way out to the base. At the gate, I was met by a stern-looking guard who proceeded to check my car from top to bottom – taking special care to frown at the *Star Wars* stickers on the back window – before he finished by shoving a stick with a mirror on it underneath the car.

"What's that for?"

"We're checking to make sure you aren't bringing a bomb onto the premises," the guard answered dully.

"Does that happen a lot?"

"Never. Because we check all vehicles for bombs."

"You don't get a lot of dates, do you?"

The guard fixed me with his icy blue eyes. "You're cleared for entry, Ms. Shaw. If you park in that lot right there, the public affairs officer will be out to pick you up in five minutes."

"You're kidding, right?"

The guard smiled. "No. It's standard procedure."

"What do you think people are going to try and do? Sneak in and steal the secrets to ... what do you guys even do out here? Do you have any secrets? I doubt it."

"Ma'am, if you will just pull your vehicle over there, someone will be with you shortly."

"Why did you take the time to check my car for a bomb if you're just going to make me park it in a field?"

"It's ...."

"Standard procedure, I know. This morning just sucks," I grumbled.

The guard ignored the statement, but I saw in the rearview mirror that he watched me until I pulled into the lot, put my car in park and turned off the engine.

The public affairs officer was prompt, and exactly what I expected: A middle-aged man in a pressed cotton shirt with perfectly ironed pleats in his pants and a bald spot on the back of his head. "I'm Sgt. Dan Harmon."

"Avery Shaw," I held out my hand.

"Please get in my vehicle and I'll take you to Commander Turner."

"I can't wait."

"Yes, he's very impressive," Dan nodded with a wide – and obviously fake – smile. He wanted me to think he was oblivious to sarcasm when he obviously wasn't. That didn't make me think he was charming, just suspicious.

"So, why am I out here?" I decided to press the situation.

"I'm sure I don't know what you mean," Sgt. Harmon said evasively. "You're out here for an interview with Commander Turner."

"Yeah, but you called my editor to request it," I pushed on. "That's not standard operating procedure."

"You'll have to ask Commander Turner about that."

"I can't wait."

"Yes, he's very impressive."

And they say military personnel don't make jokes.

Sgt. Harmon drove me to the center of the base, parking in front of a large and rectangular structure I had never seen before. I wracked my brain, trying to remember if I had ever been on the base for anything other than an air show, and came up empty. "What building is this?"

"This is the administration building."

"It doesn't have a fancy name?"

"It's the John F. Kennedy Administration Building."

Oh, good, another joke.

I followed Sgt. Harmon into the building, glancing around at the clean and well-pressed soldiers toiling silently around me. I realized, pretty quickly, that my jeans, simple black T-shirt and Darth Vader hoodie were probably out of place for an air base. Fish was right about wearing something inappropriate – although I would never admit that fact to him. I couldn't muster up a lot of worry about the situation, though. In fact, I was starting to wish I had worn a more colorful shirt to combat the dreariness of taupe that was starting to smother me.

Sgt. Harmon led me into a big, oval office where I was greeted by a severe-looking secretary with a bun that was so tight it looked like her skin was being stretched so hard it would snap like a rubber-band at any second.

"We're here to see Commander Turner," Dan announced.

"He's expecting you," the secretary said, running her eyes up and down my body – pausing at my *Thundercats* Converse – and then nodding toward the door. "Go right in."

I plastered a faux smile on my face and followed Dan through the door. Leonard Turner was not what I expected – well at least not entirely. Sure, he was dressed in the same dreary outfit everyone else on the base was wearing – though his was adorned with a lot more fancy jewelry (which I was sure was supposed to signify that he was some sort of military hero) – but he was leaning back lazily in his desk chair and smiling widely at me when I entered. There was something about his smile that bugged me, though, like I was the mouse and he was the cat.

"Commander Turner," I held out my hand in greeting.

I saw his green eyes run over my outfit – I really should have worn my *Keep Our Forests Green* Ewok shirt for shock value or, better yet, my *Shark Week Bite Me* shirt – and watched as his smile faltered. "You're Avery Shaw?"

"I am," I said amiably.

"I guess you weren't expecting to work today," Commander Turner frowned at my outfit.

"Oh, I was planning on working today," I said brightly. "I just didn't realize I was coming here."

"Oh, were you supposed to cover a comic convention or something?" Commander Turner apparently thought the way to get me on his side was to condescend to me.

"No, the press conference at the sheriff's department."

"Was it later and you didn't have time to change your outfit?"

"Nope."

"And your boss lets you dress like that?" Commander Turner was like a dog with a bone.

"Let? More like puts up with." I wasn't going to give an inch either(, though).

"And why would he do that?"

"I'm good at my job."

"And you're union," Commander Turner said finally, nodding his head like the answer to world peace had just occurred to him.

What was that supposed to mean?

"He can't fire you for your attire without the union being a pain," Commander Turner continued. "That makes sense."

Okay, now I was getting annoyed. I should have worn my *Keep Calm and STFU* shirt instead. That really would've gotten him going. Instead, I decided to focus on the task at hand. "What can I do for you?"

Commander Turner returned his gaze to my face. "I'm sorry."

"You called for this interview, so what do you want to talk about?"

I could tell he didn't like the sudden shift in the conversation. He didn't like anyone else to take control. "I figured that you would want this interview after the incident on the freeway yesterday, so I thought we would do you a favor."

Oh, a favor. "Why did you think that we would want an interview?" I decided to play dumb.

Commander Turner wrinkled his nose. "It's a freeway shooter."

"So?"

"That usually leads one to think of sharp shooters."

"And?"

"Sharp shooters are usually equated to the military," Commander Turner said carefully. "Even though that's a misnomer."

"Are you worried that someone from this base is out shooting someone?"

Sgt. Harmon's sharp intake of breath was my first hint that I'd probably gone a little too far.

"I didn't say that," Commander Turner argued. "I thought we would help you by dissuading you of just that possibility right from the get-go."

"And how are you going to dissuade me from that?"

"Well, it's just obvious that this is not a military person," Commander Turner said bitingly.

"How is that obvious?" I plowed on.

"What do you mean?"

"We don't know anything about anything yet," I said. "We don't know anything about the victim, whether she had enemies or not. We don't know anything about the type of gun used or how hard the shot really was, since we have no idea if the victim was purposely targeted or just a lucky get. So, essentially, we know nothing except that, according to you, it couldn't possibly be military related."

"Well," Commander Turner said stiffly. "I guess that you've got this in hand then."

"I do," I agreed. "However, I have to say, the fact that you called me out here to tell me that the military couldn't possibly be involved makes me believe that you think the military is involved for some reason."

Sgt. Harmon jumped to his feet hurriedly. "That's simply not true."

"Calm down, Esmeralda," I admonished him. I turned back to Commander Turner. "We're just feeling each other out here, aren't we?"

"Sgt. Harmon, why don't you leave Ms. Shaw and me alone for a chat," Turner answered harshly.

"I don't think that's a good idea," Sgt. Harmon said nervously.

"That's an order."

Sgt. Harmon cast one last look in my direction and then quietly slunk out of the room, closing the door behind him as he did.

"Alone at last," I smiled broadly, even though I was suddenly nervous.

"You have a certain reputation in this county, Ms. Shaw."

"I have a certain reputation in a lot of counties," I countered. "In Northern Oakland County, for example, I'm known as a sniper from the three-point line when playing street basketball. My height can be deceiving, I know, but I'm a raging cager."

Commander Turner ignored me. "You're known as a loose cannon."

"You're in the military; you like cannons."

"You're known for becoming a little too involved in your stories. That's not something a reporter is supposed to do, am I right?"

"I guess it depends," I said carefully. "I always tend to get my story, so I guess I'm given a lot of leeway."

"You've almost been killed, a couple of times, while getting these stories if I remember correctly."

It wasn't overtly a threat, but it felt like a threat.

"I have a certain effect on people," I replied. "I tend to drive them crazy."

"I can see that."

I pulled my notebook out of my *The Walking Dead* purse, flipped it open and looked back up to Commander Turner. "So, what statement do you want me to share with the public in this regard?"

Turner smiled – although it looked more like a snarl. "Only that this situation has nothing to do with Jefferson Air National Guard Base."

"And you would like me to base this statement on the basis of?"

Turner frowned. "It's the truth. "

"Of course," I started studiously writing in my notebook. "The military is not involved because Commander Turner said so. I got it."

The room fell silent, uncomfortably so. I was trying to find a way to gracefully exit without looking like I was running in fear when I heard raised voices from beyond the door to the outer office.

I glanced up at Turner and he looked equally baffled.

"He's in a meeting." It sounded like the secretary was trying to stop someone from entering the office.

"I'm sure he is, but it will have to wait."

I frowned when I recognized the other voice. I wasn't surprised when the door flew open and the county sheriff, Jake Farrell, strode into the room purposefully.

"Leonard."

"Jake."

"You haven't returned my calls," Jake said angrily, running a hand through his bird's nest black hair anxiously.

"I've been busy," Turner said quietly. "I'm busy right now, in fact."

"With what?" Jake glanced around the room and froze when he saw me sitting in the chair behind him. "What are you doing here?"

"Good to see you, too," I said evenly, although I was secretly glad to see him. His appearance would make my exit that much easier.

"Why are you here?" Jake repeated the question, his dark eyes focusing on me questioningly.

"Commander Turner requested an interview."

"I was doing you a favor," Turner frowned.

Jake glanced between us suspiciously. "Why would you request an interview?"

"Why would you just assume she's telling the truth?"

"Why would she lie about this?"

"You're saying she never lies? How would you know that? Oh, right, you have a past with her, don't you? Why doesn't that surprise me?"

Well this was getting ugly – uglier – pretty quick. I was definitely missing something here and I had a feeling that something had something to do with Eliot's weird reaction this morning.

Jake didn't rise to the bait. "Why wouldn't you return my calls?"

"I told you I was busy."

"With Avery?"

"Partly. I do run this base, in case you forgot. That's five thousand men under my command. I don't always have time to bend to the every whim of the county sheriff."

"Every whim?" Jake looked incredulous. He swung on me suddenly, hands on his narrow hips. "What did he say to you?"

I shrugged. "He just wanted to make it clear that the freeway shooter had nothing to do with the military base." I didn't see any reason to lie. Something suddenly dawned on me. "Hey, why aren't you at the press conference at the sheriff's department?"

"It was postponed until this afternoon."

"Why?"

"What do you mean why? Do I have to have a reason? I'm the sheriff."

"You usually do have a reason," I argued.

I could see Commander Turner watching us interact out of the corner of my eye. I didn't like it. "We're done, right?" I turned back to him.

"We are," he nodded. "I trust that I will find fair and balanced coverage in tomorrow's edition."

"Sure, whatever," I waved him off and turned to Jake. "What time is the new press conference?"

"After lunch."

"You're not going to tell me why it was postponed?"

Jake's eyes were fixed angrily on Commander Turner. He turned to me when he realized I was still there. "What?"

"Why was the press conference postponed?"

"The victim died. We needed more time to get the correct information together."

"She died?" That was sad, and enough to elevate his story from passing interest to all-out panic in certain motorist circles.

"Can we talk about this later?" Jake asked irritably. "I need to have a discussion with Leonard."

"It looks more like you're going to beat the crap out of each other," I said.

Jake shot me his death look. "I will talk to you later."

"Goodbye, Ms. Shaw," Leonard agreed.

I guess I'd been dismissed.

Seven

After an uncomfortable ride with Sgt. Harmon back to my car – one where we didn't say a single word to one another – I was back on the highway within five minutes and back at The Monitor within fifteen.

When I got to the office, I strode straight to Fish's desk purposely. "Well, that was fun, and I by fun I mean painful."

Fish didn't look up. "You're always so dramatic."

"I'm not dramatic."

"You are dramatic."

"I am not dramatic and I resent you saying I'm dramatic." Suddenly a memory from the previous night flashed in my mind, the one where Lexie said she wasn't high maintenance. I pushed the thought out as quickly as I let it in. Who needs that?

Fish finished typing whatever he was working on and finally glanced in my direction. "Please tell me you didn't go to the air base dressed like that."

"Funnily enough, you're less pissed off than Commander Turner was."

"What did he say?" Fish narrowed his eyes. It was one thing for him to pick on my outfit. It was quite another for someone else to do it.

"Let's just say he's not a big fan of the *Thundercats*."

"*Thundercats*?" Fish looked confused.

I gestured down to my black and orange cat-striped shoes, which featured a big-bosomed cat woman in all her glory. "She's got a nice rack," Fish said finally.

"She does," I agreed.

"So, what did he want?"

"He wanted to make sure we knew that the freeway shooter had nothing to do with the base."

Fish didn't look surprised. "I figured it was something like that. What do you think?"

"I think that he's trying really hard to distance the base from this shooting."

"And?"

"And? And that makes me think that he's knows something, or he's really worried about something. Or he's trying to misdirect us from something."

"Like?"

"How should I know? I was with the man for twenty minutes."

Fish smirked. "Something tells me you're going to find out what he's trying to hide."

"You make me sound petty."

"That's one of your virtues," Fish brushed off my petulance. "Just make sure you don't let your investigation into Turner get in the way of your coverage on this story."

"Like I would do that," I scoffed.

Fish rolled his eyes. "You always do that."

"It always works out," I countered.

"You do have a certain knack," Fish agreed.

"On that note," I started to move away. "The victim died."

"How do you know that?"

I told Fish about seeing Jake at Turner's office, omitting the parts about the antagonistic nature of their interaction. I wanted to keep that to myself – for now, at least.

"What was Farrell doing with Turner?" Fish asked curiously.

"Probably the same thing I was," I said. "Except he knows more about the shooting, which means that it was probably a pretty hard shot and that led him to the military."

"Well, Turner isn't going to like that," Fish mused.

"He didn't seem to."

Fish was quiet while he thought for a second and then turned back to me. "You're going to the press conference."

"Why? I thought I would be the one going to the family. You were going to send Duncan to the press conference."

"Now I'm sending you."

"Why?"

"Because you have better connections with the sheriff's department," Fish said succinctly.

"Jake? He's not exactly feeding me exclusives these days," I grumbled.

"And Derrick."

"He never feeds me exclusives," I shot back.

"They'll still talk to you. They still give you tips and hints. They don't do that with anyone else."

"And they won't talk to Duncan?" The minute I asked the question, I realized the stupidity of it. Duncan was the office tool for a reason.

"No one talks to Duncan twice," Fish agreed. "Once they've met him, it's pretty much over. You can't spend five minutes with the guy and not realize he's a total douche."

"So you think it's a good idea to send him to a grieving family?"

"I'll figure something out," Fish waved off my concerns. "I just know I want you at the press conference."

"Great," I muttered and wandered back to my desk. I found Marvin loitering in the walkway amongst the cubicles. "What's up with you?"

"Nothing," Marvin looked instantly guilty.

"Well, that was convincing."

Marvin glanced around the busy cubicles conspiratorially. "I've got a new mission in life."

Oh, good. I love Marvin, but he has a new mission in life every week. Last week it was to stop trolling AA meetings for women. He found out that, even though a lot of them were needy, they weren't willing to go out to his favorite bar every night like he wanted. And worse, when they did, they fell off the wagon hard and usually started stalking him. Yeah, he didn't really think that one through.

"What's your new mission? Are you going to get in shape with that mechanical belt you strap around your waist again?"

"No. I still maintain that was false advertising, though."

"Back to meditation in the park?"

"No. There are too many bugs there."

"So, what's your new mission?"

"I'm going to seize the day."

Huh, where to go with this, where to go with this? "I don't know what that means," I said finally.

"I almost died last night."

Oh, well, this wasn't new. Marvin is an outstanding reporter, but he's the biggest hypochondriac in the world. "How?"

"I was walking in the parking lot of the Roost last night." The Roost is his favorite bar. "And I was almost hit by a car."

"Were you drunk?"

"No."

"How close were you to the car?"

"It was like ten feet," Marvin said seriously.

"That's not very close."

"I saw my life flashing before my eyes."

"And what did you see?"

"It wasn't much," Marvin admitted. "It was a steady stream of women and drinks with nothing of substance attached to it."

Oh, good, he was feeling existential today. "So you're going to start going to that weird church again?"

"It wasn't weird. It was a real church."

"It was a motivational church," I corrected him. "Self-empowerment and all that. Chanting."

"That's still a thing."

"Fine," I conceded. "It's a thing. A thing with chanting."

"Anyway," Marvin was looking irritated now. "I realized I don't have anything to anchor me to this life."

"You want to be anchored to this life? Why?"

"I mean there's no one here who will remember me when I'm gone."

"I'll remember you," I said hurriedly. Like I could forget.

"Oh, please," Marvin said dismissively. "You'll die before I do. You live a reckless life."

"Nice."

"It's the truth."

Sadly, it was. "Where are you going to find this anchor?"

"I'm going to get married," Marvin boldly announced.

"To who?"

"I haven't decided yet, that's where you come in."

Uh-oh. "I'm not marrying you."

"Like I would want to marry you," Marvin scoffed. "You're mean."

"I'm not mean." Even as I said the words, I knew they weren't true. I idle at mean some days – and then I accelerate to evil when I have PMS.

"I need you to introduce me to someone."

"Someone to marry?"

"Yeah."

"I don't know anyone that would be right for you," I said carefully.

"What about that friend of yours? Carly?"

"She's already engaged," I reminded him.

"That means she's serious about marriage."

"Yeah," I agreed. "To Kyle, not you."

"Still, you could set it up."

"No, I couldn't," I argued.

"Please?" He looked so sad.

"No."

"Fine!" Marvin whirled and stalked back to his cubicle. "I told you that you were mean."

"Whatever."

"You guys argue like you're married."

I glanced up and saw Brick watching us with an amused – and somewhat disdainful – look on his face. "Brick."

"Avery."

"Can I do something for you?"

"I just heard you talking to Fish."

"Good?" I wasn't sure where he was going with this.

"I think it's typical that a liberal swine like yourself would naturally assume the military is involved in this."

"Why do you care?" I ignored the liberal swine remark. I couldn't muster the energy to be offended by a guy with the name of Brick.

"I'm a veteran."

"I think I already knew that," I pointed out. "That still doesn't explain why you've got your panties in a bunch about this."

"I don't wear panties," Brick looked incensed.

"I heard they were camouflage." Sometimes I like to poke angry little bears just for the hell of it.

"There's a reason why everyone in this office thinks you're an asshole," Brick shot back.

"Really? I was going for bitchy, not asshole. I'll adjust to get the outcome I want, though," I replied breezily.

Brick narrowed his angry brown eyes on me. "I can't believe someone hasn't shot you yet."

"I'll keep that in mind."

Marvin was back in the aisle and regarding Brick angrily. "You can't talk to her like that."

"Like what? You said she was mean," Brick reminded him.

"Yeah, but you're being a dick."

"I am not."

"You are, too."

This was spinning out of control. "I'm going to leave you girls to your hair-pulling fight," I said quickly. "I've got a press conference to get to."

"That's still hours away," Marvin said angrily.

"Yeah, well, waiting in a quiet room surrounded by cops sounds better than hanging out with you two right now."

I cast one last glance down the aisle as I left and found Marvin and Brick still eyeing each other reproachfully. There must be something in the air today. All the men in my world were going steadily crazy.

Eight

Once I got back out to the parking lot, I considered my next move. I had no intention of really going to the sheriff's department two hours prior to the actual event. Trust me, cops aren't generally fun party people. You don't want to spend any more time with them than you have to. Since I already knew Jake was in a terrible mood, I wanted to give him a chance to settle down before I started incessantly poking him for information.

That left Eliot.

I drove to downtown Mount Clemens and slid into a spot at the front of his pawnshop on Main Street. I killed the engine and sat back and watched him work from a safe distance.

He hadn't seen me yet, obviously, and I was enjoying the rare glimpse into his life when he wasn't aware anyone was watching him. He was a fine specimen of masculinity, all hard muscles, bright eyes and soft smiles. He was more, though. I watched as he helped a woman try to decide between two watches in his front display case, offering her an easy laugh and some little tidbit about one of the watches. The truth was, he was a genuinely nice guy. A genuinely nice guy that could snap your neck in three seconds flat, of course.

Eliot's past was murkier than his present. I didn't really know a lot about it frankly. It wasn't that he was especially tight-lipped; he just wasn't one of those guys that volunteered information out of the blue. And, the truth was, I hadn't pushed him too hard. I had wanted the relationship to grow organically. Of course, the fact that I kept finding myself in mortal peril – and crossing paths with my ex-boyfriend in the form of the county sheriff – could have something to do with that, too.

Eliot and Jake had a tortured past of their own. I knew they had been in a Special Forces unit of the military together – which I was starting to believe had caused both of them to have a few run-ins with Leonard Turner at some point in time – and that time together in Special Forces hadn't exactly bonded them. Jake thought Eliot was a bit of a loose cannon and, in turn, Eliot thought Jake was a bit of a tight ass. They both had a point.

Since Eliot had entered my orbit, the two men had started running into each other more frequently. A couple of times, they had even worked together to extricate me from some untenable situation that I had managed to get myself into. There was also an underlying sense of tension regarding my romantic entanglement with Eliot. Jake didn't come out and say he was jealous, but he acted that way occasionally. On the flip side, Eliot showed flashes of jealousy himself when he saw me interacting with Jake.

It was like a tower of cans that could topple at any second.

I was busy trying to decide how to approach Eliot about my suspicions regarding Turner when I heard a knock at my car window. I jumped, glancing up through the glass, and frowning when I saw Eliot standing there. How did I miss him leaving the store and heading this way?

I rolled down the car window and fixed a tight smile on my face as I greeted him. "What's up?"

"What are you doing?"

"Debating about getting coffee," I lied.

Eliot considered me for a second and then shook his head slightly. "How was your meeting with Turner?"

He knew me too well. "It was tense," I admitted, opening my door and climbing out of the car.

"Tense how?"

I told Eliot about my interview with Turner, including Jake's abrupt entrance and irritated countenance. I watched him carefully for his reaction. "That sounds about right," he said finally.

"Why do you say that?"

I saw the set of Eliot's jaw tighten. "Let's just say Jake and I both have had some dealings with Turner and leave it at that."

Like that was going to work. "You know I can't leave it at that."

"Well, you're going to have to," Eliot said stiffly.

I bit the inside of my lip and looked Eliot up and down. His usually affable demeanor had suddenly gone rigid. This probably wasn't the time to push him. I would gather some more information and then ambush him later tonight.

"Fine," I said finally. "I need to get some coffee and get to the press conference anyway."

"I thought the press conference was this morning?"

"It got postponed. The victim died."

"That's too bad," Eliot said. "So you're going to the sheriff's department?"

"Yup," I said breezily, starting to move toward the coffee shop that was next to Eliot's store. "I want to get there early. If you're not going to tell me the deal with Turner, I guess I'll just have to badger Jake until he does."

"You really think that will work? That Jake will just bow to your will and give you the information you want?" Eliot didn't look like he believed in my super power – which was a little disheartening.

"Yeah, well," I paused in the open door. "I know exactly what buttons to push on Jake to get what I want." With that parting shot, I flounced into the coffee shop. I risked one backwards glance to see Eliot's reaction and I was rewarded with an open scowl. Good. He deserved it.

I relaxed with a cup of coffee for a half an hour before I headed toward the sheriff's department. By the time I got there I was forty-five minutes early, but I figured that would give me a chance to push Derrick – and maybe Jake, too – for information before the other media vultures arrived.

I used the main entrance to the sheriff's department, traded barbed jibes with the officer behind the protective bubble, and then stuck out my tongue at him until he buzzed me into the inner hallway that led to the sheriff's conference room.

The officer behind the bubble, after telling me I was early, had admonished me to go straight to the conference room and not loiter in the hallway. I had promised I would, but that was a promise I had no intention of keeping.

I headed toward Derrick's small office first, not bothering to knock on the door, which was partially closed, and instead strode inside like I belonged there. Derrick was sitting at his desk working on paperwork. He glanced up when he saw me and then looked back down at his paperwork before shooting out of his desk chair when it registered who had actually entered his office. "Knock much?"

"Sure," I said gratingly. "Knock, knock."

Derrick slid back down into his chair and turned his attention back to his work, but not before shooting me his special brand of stink eye.

"You're supposed to ask who's there," I prodded Derrick.

"I'm not playing your games."

"You're a true joy to be around, has anyone ever told you that?"

"You just did."

I watched Derrick work for a few minutes, dropping a few well-timed sighs as I did. Since Derrick wasn't biting on the sighs, I decided to push the situation in my own way. Dangerous, yes, I know.

"So, what do you know about Jake's past with Leonard Turner?"

Derrick actually looked surprised at the question. He stopped what he was doing and raised his chocolate eyes to mine curiously. "Why would you ask that?"

I told Derrick about my run-in with both Turner and Jake earlier in the day and waited for his reaction. It wasn't what I was expecting.

"You're kidding."

"No," I shook my head. "Are you telling me you had no idea that Jake and Turner were trading verbal punches this morning?"

"I thought he went to the hospital to give his condolences to the shooting victim's family," Derrick said.

"Is that what he told you?"

"No, that's what he implied." Derrick realized – too late – that he had told me too much. I didn't let that dissuade me, though.

"So, don't you think it's funny that Jake went and orally pulled Turner's hair?"

"That's a nice visual," Derrick grumbled. "I honestly don't know anything about Turner and Jake. I had no idea they even knew each other."

Well, that was disappointing. "So, would it surprise you if I told you Eliot had sort of a negative reaction to finding out I was interviewing Turner, too?"

Derrick pursed his lips and considered the statement. "Surprise isn't the word. It is weird, though."

"Definitely weird."

"What did Eliot tell you?"

"He's being tight-lipped."

"Is that unusual for him? He doesn't strike me as the chatty type."

"He's not the hiding stuff type either, though," I pointed out. "Usually, if I ask him a direct question, he answers it."

"Did you ask him why he wouldn't answer it?"

"No," I shook my head. "I just started internally plotting how I was going to trick him into answering it."

"That sounds like a healthy relationship," Derrick scoffed.

"He's already irritated with the Lexie situation," I replied. "I'm scared to push things too far in case he snaps."

Derrick narrowed his eyes. Lexie was his baby sister and, while they didn't always get along, Derrick had found himself in the same rescuing situation with Lexie more times than he could count. "What did she do now?"

"Nothing," I said hurriedly. "She just drives Eliot nuts."

"She drives everyone nuts," he said. "Bonkers nuts. Almonds. Cashews. Peanuts. Nuts. Nuts. Nuts."

"She has a certain ability," I agreed. "That's her super power."

"Super power?"

"Eliot's is looking good in the morning. Mine is digging up dirt on people. Hers is driving people nuts."

"What's mine?" Derrick asked curiously.

I got to my feet and moved toward the door, glancing back at him teasingly. "Convincing people that you're tall enough to be a cop?"

I escaped out the door quickly, but not before I heard Derrick swear under his breath. At five-foot, five inches, Derrick wasn't exactly your stereotypical cop – a fact that drove him to distraction. It was also the scab on his psyche that I constantly picked at. Hey, that's what family is for.

I wandered into the conference room down the hall, helping myself to a cookie and glancing around to see what local news personalities had arrived. I recognized two print reporters from area weeklies, and one of the television reporters from Channel 4, Devon, who had unfortunately been dating Derrick for the past few months. Since she was only about five-feet, two inches tall, Derrick was actually taller than her. I figured that was the appeal.

Devon smiled warily at me. We had a tempestuous past – and it wasn't entirely based on the fact that print reporters and broadcast reporters generally loathe one another.

"Hi," Devon finally spoke.

"Hey."

"How are things?"

"Same old, same old."

"So, what do you think they're going to say at the press conference?"

I shrugged. "Press conference stuff?"

"Well, that's very helpful," Devon sniped. "Why do you always have to be such a pain?"

"I was born this way. Just ask my mom."

"Yeah, she does think you're a total pain in the ass."

I rolled my eyes. Devon's constant attempts to ingratiate herself with my family were something akin to nails on a chalkboard – or, more aptly, watered down whiskey. "Yes, well, you would know," I shot back. "You've known my family for a whole, what, four months now?"

"Six," Devon corrected me.

"It's been a long six months."

"It really has," Devon agreed.

I glanced up when I saw a figure standing in the doorway. If I weren't already irritated, the sight of the Channel 7 reporter – Shelly Waters – would've sent me right over the edge.

Shelly had only been in the area for a few weeks, but she was already my least favorite television reporter in the market – and that's saying something, especially since I detest all broadcast reporters on general principle. The fact that she had been dating Jake for several weeks only added to my hate.

"Avery," Shelly greeted me primly.

"Shelly," I grimaced.

"You're looking particularly ... casual today."

"You look like the same bitch I remember," I shot back happily.

Devon snorted behind me. The one thing we had in common was dislike of Shelly. It was our only bonding agent.

"You have a terrible attitude," Shelly said stiffly.

"News flash," Derrick said, stepping into the room behind Shelly. He was eyeing Shelly warily – he had seen us throw down a couple of times before and he looked ready to step in if things spiraled out of control. "She's had a terrible attitude since we were kids."

Shelly shot a flirtatious smile in Derrick's direction. "You poor dear, having to grow up with her. It must have been terrible for you."

Devon obviously didn't like the new direction of Shelly's attention because she stepped between the Channel 7 reporter and Derrick and gave him a brief hug in way of a greeting. "Hi."

"Hi," Derrick smiled sloppily.

Oh, jeez. "Shouldn't this be starting soon?"

"Jake is in his office getting his notes," Derrick replied.

"Oh, maybe I'll go say 'hi,'" Shelly said suddenly. I had heard, through the grapevine – yes, Derrick – that Jake had ended his dalliance with Shelly rather suddenly a few days ago.

"Yeah, there's nothing a man likes more than being stalked by his ex-girlfriend." I have been repeatedly warned to take three seconds to consider what I'm saying before I open my mouth, but apparently I'm incapable of doing just that.

Shelly turned on me venomously. "That's rich coming from you."

"What is that supposed to mean?"

"It means that you've been broken up with Jake since you were teenagers and you still run to him whenever you have a problem," Shelly seethed.

"Run to him? When do I run to him?"

"Oh, I don't know, a month ago he cancelled a date with me to race to your rescue up north."

"I was kidnapped by a madman," I reminded her.

"And whose fault was that?"

I instinctively took a step toward Shelly, visions of huge chunks of her hair in my balled-up fists dancing through my head, but Jake clearing his throat at the front of the room interrupted me. He had stepped up to the podium and was eyeing Shelly and me with moderate interest. "Let's get started."

I moved away from Shelly, not entirely of my own volition. Derrick's hand on my elbow was part of the moving away process.

Jake started the press conference by tacking a photo up of a young and smiling brunette to the board at the front of the room. "This is Carrie Washington. She's a mother-of-two from Chesterfield Township. She was driving a car along I-94 yesterday afternoon, with both of her children in the vehicle, when an unknown assailant fired a weapon from the Cass Street overpass into her vehicle."

Jake paused for dramatic effect before continuing.

"In the overnight hours, Mrs. Washington succumbed to her injuries and died. We'll have specifics on those injuries in a press release that you'll all be leaving with at the conclusion of this briefing."

"Has her family been informed?" I glanced over my shoulder and saw that one of the weekly reporters had asked the question.

"They have," Jake nodded.

"Have you identified the specific weapon?" I chimed in.

Jake met my gaze evenly. "We're still narrowing down a few things on that front. We do have a ballistics report, though, and it has brought up certain concerns regarding another shooting in Oakland County."

"I knew it!"

All eyes in the room turned to me. I glanced back up at Jake, silently urging him to pick the press conference back up and save me from being the center of attention.

Jake rolled his eyes in my direction and then turned back to the cameras, making sure he was presenting his best angles as he did. "The initial ballistics report seems to indicate that the same gun used in a freeway shooting in Oakland County was also used in our shooting yesterday."

Jake held up his hand to stave off the obvious next question. "We have no information about that victim at this time. We'll be coordinating with the Oakland County Sheriff's Department this afternoon and we will make that information available when we get it. We'll be having another press conference, a more expansive one, when we get that information."

"So what's the next step?" I asked.

"We're creating a task force," Jake said simply.

"Do you think there will be more shootings?"

"It's a possibility," Jake nodded solemnly.

"Have you ascertained if Mrs. Washington was targeted?"

"No," Jake said. "Right now, it's still a guessing game. We'll be delving into the backgrounds of both victims and moving forward from there. That's really all we have right now and I have to get going for a meeting with our new task force liaisons so I don't have time for questions."

I watched as Jake exited the podium and left the room. So much for questioning him about his association with Turner. I could've asked him at the press conference, but I didn't want to tip my hand to the other reporters. I'd have to pursue other avenues until I could get Jake alone – or I could verbally torture Eliot into giving up what he knew.

Decisions, decisions.

Nine

For many people, Friday nights are the apex of their week. For me, they're something akin to wading through a mud pit in ballet shoes.

Once I left the press conference, I returned to The Monitor long enough to bang out my story. Duncan had tried to pull me into a conference room to come up with a plan on how to coordinate our coverage of the case. Since I would rather deafen myself with Q-tips than coordinate anything with Duncan, I opted instead to pretend I didn't hear him. It drove him crazy, which was the point, and resulted in him stomping off amidst veiled threats of another complaint to Human Resources.

Once I was done, I called Eliot to see if he was coming to family dinner tonight. When he didn't pick up, I had a sneaking suspicion that he was screening my calls – which both infuriated me and filled me with a sense of empowerment at the same time. He could run, but he couldn't hide.

Once I was done at the office, I headed toward Oakland County and collected my thoughts for the duration of the ride. What did we know? Two dead people, two freeway shootings, one gun. That was pretty much the gist of it. Oh, and there was that air base commander acting all squirrely. That was an added distraction that I hadn't been prepared for, but I was no less focused on.

When I got to the family restaurant I was relieved to see a lot of vehicles I recognized. At least I wouldn't be the first one there. It was always a good thing when random family members served as a buffer between my mother's wrath and me. I had no doubt that, one look at my *Thundercats* shoes, and my mother's eyebrows would be lodged at her hairline for the rest of the evening in a mark of silent protest.

My family's restaurant is a throwback to the 1950s – maybe even the 1940s, who knows – and it has a real world nostalgia that has been built up over years and years of family snarkiness. The restaurant itself is separated into two sections, a dining room area with a full salad bar and a smaller coffee shop section with vinyl booths and a stretched counter.

The restaurant had been through two generations of family ownership – although my uncle Tim was currently running it under my grandfather's ever watchful eye, of course – and very little had changed over the years.

At the far side of the coffee shop section was the family table, a long rectangular booth with three tables interspersed through the seating. There was no sign to designate that it was a family booth, but everyone in town just seemed to know. That's one of the joys of small towns – or so I've been told.

The first person I saw when I entered the restaurant was my cousin, Mario. He's eight years younger than me and he's got the general attitude of most nineteen-year-olds these days: He thinks he knows everything. "What's up?"

"I'm trying to decide what classes to take next semester." Mario was studying a brochure from Oakland Community College as he spoke.

"I thought you were going to take over the restaurant from your dad when he was ready to retire? Shouldn't you be taking restaurant and business classes?"

"That won't be for like twenty years," Mario grumbled. "Business classes are boring."

"Yeah, but I thought you were working here in the interim." I slid into the booth next to him and glanced over his shoulder as he perused the brochure.

"Have you ever worked with your mother?" Mario asked suddenly.

"When I worked here as a teenager she was here, too," I said ruefully.

"Yeah, but you got out of that as soon as you could," Mario said. "I remember you doing a little dance when you got that job at the resort when you were eighteen. I think it was to *Born Free*."

"That was fun," I laughed at the memory.

"Yeah, you twerked before it was an actual thing," Mario agreed.

"Yeah, my mom didn't think it was so funny."

"Everyone else did, though," Mario laughed.

I pointed to one of the entries on Mario's brochure. "Interpretive dance sounds fun and just nutty enough to make your dad's head implode."

"Sold," Mario put a check next to it. "He's driving me crazy."

"That's a parent's prerogative."

"What's a parent's prerogative?"

I cringed when I heard the voice. There was a certain edge of disapproval that only a mother can properly convey – and she hadn't even seen my shoes yet. "Hi, mom."

"Avery, you look well."

"I am well."

"Did you have the day off?"

"No."

"You went to work dressed like that?"

"Yup."

"Do you think that's appropriate?"

"Hey, guess what? Mario is going to take an interpretive dance class next semester."

My mom turned her frown from me to Mario. "That sounds like a big waste of money."

Mario slid an angry glance in my direction. "Thanks."

"I've got a well-defined self-preservation instinct."

"Don't we all."

"It's the family way," I agreed.

My mom glanced between the two of us and shook her head dubiously. "I don't understand the younger generation today."

"Join the club," Mario said with a sly smile.

"What?" My mom looked confused.

"Stop toying with her, Mario," I admonished him. "It won't end well for either of us if you do."

"Duly noted."

"Where's Eliot?"

My mom can change a topic faster than a Kardashian can grab for unnecessary media attention.

"He had other things to do," I replied evasively. What? He could have other things to do.

"Did you two break up?"

"No."

"Are you sure? Maybe you're broken up and you don't know it?"

"I think I would know it."

"How would you know?"

"I think it would've come up between the time we got up this morning and the time I left for dinner."

Mario sucked in a breath as my mom's favorite frown came out to play again. She used to warn me my face would freeze that way when I was a kid. She didn't seem to think that little platitude applied to her, though. "That was ballsy," Mario whispered under his breath.

"It's been a long day," I conceded.

I was surprised when I felt the booth dip down next to me as Eliot slipped into the seat next to me. He gave me a perfunctory kiss. "Sorry I'm late."

"I thought you had things to do," my mom interjected.

"What?" Eliot furrowed his brow.

"Avery said you had things to do."

He glanced over at me curiously. "Why did you tell her that?"

"Because you didn't answer the phone when I called earlier."

"I was with a customer. You knew I was coming."

"I wasn't actually sure," I said carefully.

"Why?" Eliot leaned back in the booth, shifting uncomfortably.

"Yes, why?" My mom pressed. "Are you two fighting?"

"We're not fighting," I shot back irritably.

"Who's fighting?"

I had never been so happy to see Derrick enter a room – even if he did have Devon with him. "No one's fighting," I said quickly.

My mom greeted Devon with a warm smile and a quick hug – a gesture that irked me for some reason. "You look wonderful," my mom said happily. "See, Avery, this is how a reporter should dress for a day of work."

I glanced at Devon's black pencil skirt and matching blazer and blew out a very ladylike raspberry. I felt Eliot shake with silent laughter next to me, slipping an arm around me as he did. The crisis – at least temporarily – seemed to have passed. Crisis probably isn't the right word. It's more like a feeling of dread more than anything else.

"Well," my mom pursed her lips. "I can see where this conversation is going."

I was relieved when she slipped into the booth behind the center table and started talking to my Uncle Tim about some news item she had read in the paper today. Everyone ordered and chattered away. Derrick didn't seem to think Mario's interpretive dance plan was as good of an idea as I did.

"That sounds like a great big waste of money," Derrick said.

"I think it sounds fun," I argued.

"You would."

"You're just jealous because you have no rhythm."

"You have rhythm?" Derrick didn't look convinced.

Not so much. I changed the subject. "So, are you on the new task force?"

"What task force?"

My mom has ears like a cat. A really twitchy and judgmental cat.

"The task force for the freeway shootings," I supplied.

Derrick shot me a dirty look. "I am on the task force."

"Freeway shootings? Plural? I thought there was only one?"

"Not anymore."

Derrick told my mom about the ties between the two shootings with a cool detachment that I think must be taught in cop school. She handled it well.

"We're all going to die!"

"Who's going to die?" My grandfather plopped down at the far end of the booth, a plate full of onions and chili in front of him.

"There's a freeway shooter on the loose," my mom said, her tone now bordering on shrill.

"I saw it on the news," my grandfather said blandly, forking a mouthful of his dinner concoction into his mouth dubiously. "Why are you freaking out?"

"Because I don't want to get shot."

"You're not going to get shot," I scoffed.

"How do you know?" My mom narrowed her eyes dangerously. "Do you know who this maniac is targeting?"

"No," I said blithely. "I just think the odds are astronomical that you would be one of the victims."

"I'm sure that woman in the car with her kids thought the same thing," my mom said.

I hate it when she has a point. I opted to ignore the moment.

"This is why we need gun control," my mom blurted out suddenly.

Every eye at the table swung to her in surprise. My family is known for political arguments, but my mom usually tries to keep the harmony – at least until dessert. This was a possible powder keg of anger.

"It's our second amendment right to bear arms," Derrick said stiffly.

"Not guns that can kill people," my mom replied primly.

"All guns can kill people," Derrick replied.

"Then maybe all guns should be banned," Mario supplied.

I glanced at him questioningly.

"That is ridiculous," my Uncle Tim exploded next to him.

Ah, I get it now. Mario is all about driving his dad crazy. I recognized the gesture – and I applaud it.

"Why is it ridiculous?"

"Because it's part of the U.S. Constitution that we, as citizens of the United States of America, have the right to bear arms," Tim shot back.

"Well, if there were no guns then there would be no gun violence," Mario countered.

"That's so much crap," Derrick grumbled. "If good people stopped carrying guns that would just leave the criminals carrying guns. You think the criminals are going to follow the law? They're criminals. They're all about breaking the law."

"Maybe we should just arm everyone with tasers," Mario suggested. He looked like he was having a good time.

"That sounds dangerous," Eliot chimed in.

"Why?" Mario asked.

"Tasers aren't deadly, at least not in most cases. If everyone carried a taser, then there would be tasered people all over the place whenever an argument got out of hand."

Mario laughed. "You're just worried Avery will get mad at you and taser your balls."

"That would be unpleasant," Eliot agreed.

"I have a taser and it's a weapon, not a toy," Derrick interjected.

"You ever taser anyone?" Mario asked curiously.

"I haven't had the privilege yet," Derrick replied dryly. "It's still early, though, and you're more annoying than Avery tonight so, I guess, we'll have to wait and see."

"Let's change the subject," I said suddenly. "Let's talk about something happy."

"Like what?" My mom asked dubiously. "Although I do agree that any conversation about Eliot's balls is inappropriate."

"I don't know," I shrugged. "What's new with you, Grandpa?"

"I'm not going to jury duty," he boldly announced.

Huh!

"What do you mean you're not going to jury duty?" Derrick asked, his disappointment shifting from Mario to our grandfather.

"They summoned me for jury duty and I ignored the summons and now they're threatening to arrest me."

I glanced over to see Derrick swallow hard. If my grandfather got arrested for blowing off jury duty that would be a personal affront to him. "Why don't you want to go to jury duty?"

"It's stupid and I have better things to do," my grandpa said.

"It's not stupid," Derrick countered. "It's your civic duty."

"Well, I don't want to," my grandpa countered. "It will take up too much of my time."

"Just show up and tell them that you hate all cops," I suggested. "That's how I got out of jury duty a couple years ago."

"That's not true," Derrick corrected. "You got out of jury duty because of your bumper sticker."

I shushed him quickly.

"What bumper sticker?" My mom asked suspiciously.

"It doesn't matter," I said evasively. "I don't even have it anymore."

"What bumper sticker?" My mom turned to Derrick questioningly.

"I think it said *Mean People Kick Ass*," Derrick said smugly.

"Why would you have a sticker like that?"

I shrugged. "I don't know," I replied. "It just appealed to me."

"Why would that even come up at jury duty?" Mario asked.

"It was federal court," I said. "I have no idea. Let's go back to talking about gun control."

"It's our right as citizens!" My Uncle Tim was getting animated again.

Eliot turned to me with a small smile on his face. "Your family is never a disappointment."

"You don't share a gene pool with them."

Ten

The next morning was supposed to be a lackadaisical mixture of pajamas and Saturday morning cartoons. The minute I heard the annoying R2D2 beep of my cellphone – the one that signified an incoming text message – I knew that wasn't going to happen, though.

I groaned as I rolled over, reaching across Eliot to his nightstand, and grabbing my phone irritably. "I just know this is going to suck."

"Don't look at it," Eliot suggested, never opening his eyes, but trailing his hand down my back lazily. "I have a few ideas of other things we could do."

I glanced at the readout on my phone screen and scowled. "Crap."

"What?" Eliot asked, resigned.

"Fish just texted me the name of the Oakland County victim and he wants me to do some legwork on him today. He's authorized overtime."

"Is that good or bad?"

"I don't know," I blew out a sigh. "I could use the extra money. Converse just released some Black Sabbath shoes I really, really want."

"Who wouldn't?"

"I hate working on my day off, though." The truth was, I sometimes wasn't thrilled working on my scheduled days.

"Tell him no," Eliot replied, sliding his hand under the covers and pinching my ass suggestively.

"All I have to do is run over to some insurance office in Birmingham," I said. "I'll get paid for eight hours and it will probably only take me three. If I don't, that would mean I'm really lazy."

Eliot considered my statement for a second. "I'm not sure where I'm supposed to land on this, so I'm just going to let it go."

"That's probably wise."

"Do you want me to go with you?"

"To interview secretaries at an insurance office? I don't think I'm going to be in any danger."

"Do you only want me around when you're going to be in danger?" Eliot asked.

"No," I said hurriedly, I shoved him, though, when I saw the smile playing at the corner of his lips. "You're teasing me."

"It's easy in the mornings," Eliot agreed. "It takes you a good hour to be at your sarcastic best."

"Good to know.

AFTER a shower, a big breakfast at the local Coney Island, and a promise that Eliot could continue feeling me up in a couple of hours, I set out for Birmingham.

A lot of people picture all of Southeastern Michigan as one large appendage of Detroit. They would be wrong. The city has its problems, sure, but the suburbs are actually pretty nice.

While Macomb County is blessed with Lake St. Clair and quaintly idealistic northern communities, Oakland County is the money county.

And Birmingham? That's the supreme money town – of many money towns.

It took me about a half an hour to get to Birmingham – and another ten minutes to find the insurance company once I got there. I pulled into the mostly empty parking lot, it was a Saturday and they had limited hours, and I switched off the ignition of my car and sat and watched the business for a few minutes. I was trying to get a feel for it. If I thought I was going to get some magical insight into Malcolm Hopper, 55, though, I was sadly mistaken. It looked like any other insurance business – although the clientele was extremely well dressed. I shouldn't have been surprised, I guess, this was Birmingham, after all.

When I entered the building, I couldn't help but be a little impressed. Everything was in its place and ridiculously clean. I glanced around the office quietly. It was a weekend, so I didn't expect there to be many workers. It didn't take me long to realize that all of the workers in the office were women and – with the exception of the secretary at the front desk – unbelievably attractive. It looked like a model bomb had gone off here, with five tall, willowy blondes working at various stations across the office. That couldn't be a coincidence.

One of the blondes glanced in my direction, frowning when she saw my baggy canvas pants and *Kiss My Sass* sparkly Nike T-shirt. "Are you lost?"

"Not last time I checked," I said carefully. I wasn't a fan of the snotty attitude, but I needed information. I clearly wasn't going to get it from this woman, but if I threw her down on the ground and started pulling out her obviously fake hair tracks that probably wouldn't endear me to the rest of the office workers.

"What do you want then?" The woman's voice was impressively snooty.

"I'm just looking around," I said carefully. "I heard good things about you guys, I just wanted to see if you lived up to the hype."

"You heard good things about an insurance agency?" The woman didn't look like she believed me.

I glanced over her shoulder and saw the nameplate on her desk. "Yeah," I said jovially. "I heard everyone here but someone named Charlotte was really great and easy to work with."

So much for reining in the snotty.

The secretary, the only one that didn't look like she belonged on the pages of a Victoria's Secret catalog, snorted and buried her head in the paperwork she had been perusing when she saw Charlotte cast a biting look in her direction.

"Have a seat," Charlotte said. "Someone will be with you ... eventually."

"I can't wait."

I watched as Charlotte moved back to her desk and plastered a fake smile on her face for the woman sitting in front of her. Once I was sure that Charlotte was otherwise engaged, I sidled over to the secretary and shot a winning smile in her direction. "She's friendly."

The secretary, whose nameplate read Chelsea Princeton, glanced over her shoulder to make sure Charlotte wasn't looking toward us and then nodded her agreement. "She's a bitch."

"I'm guessing she's mean to you, too."

"Well, I don't look like her, do I?" There was bitterness to Chelsea's tone. I had a feeling that, at five feet, three inches tall, and a hundred-and-ninety pounds, she was the odd woman out in this particular nest. The shoulder-length bob and wide swath of bangs wasn't doing her any favors either. She was friendly to look at, though, which made me immediately gravitate toward her.

"She won't look like that forever," I said dismissively. "And once her looks go, no one will want to be around her because she's got the personality of a dirty ass."

Chelsea laughed openly this time, and I caught Charlotte raising her head and shooting a glare in our direction out of the corner of my eye. I opted to ignore it.

"So, what do you need?" Chelsea asked. "You need house insurance or something?"

"Actually, I'm looking for information on Malcolm Hopper."

Chelsea looked surprised. "Malcolm? Well, I hate to be the bearer of bad news, but Malcolm passed away."

"I know. He was killed in a freeway shooting," I said. "I'm a reporter over in Macomb County. We had a similar shooting over there the other day. I'm just trying to find out if Malcolm had any ties to our victim."

"I thought the police said that was a random shooting," Chelsea looked confused.

"The police don't know what to think right now," I replied airily. "My boss just wanted me to come over here and ask some questions about Malcolm. Personally, I think it's a waste of time. That's how I keep a roof over my head, though."

"What do you want to know?" Chelsea asked nervously.

"What was Malcolm like?"

"He liked young and pretty women," Chelsea said quietly, almost to herself. "He surrounded himself with them."

I knew she was the one to come to for information. "Are you saying the women here don't know how to do their jobs?"

"I'm sure they do," Chelsea replied. "I'm sure they knew exactly how to get their jobs, too."

That was pointed – and I knew which direction she was heading. "So, Malcolm slept with all the women here?"

Chelsea caught herself and shook her head. "I don't know that."

"You just have a feeling."

"He was a little ... handsy."

"With you?"

"No," Chelsea scoffed. "I'm not his type. Look around, why would he pick me when he could go after all of them?"

This was a woman in definite need of a self-esteem boost. "So, you're saying he goes for flash and no substance?"

Chelsea grinned and I couldn't help but think she had a nice smile. "I guess I am."

"Sounds like he wasn't too bright?"

"No," Chelsea shook her head. "I think he was really good at his job. I just think he had certain ... weaknesses."

"Most men do."

"Yeah, but not all," Chelsea smiled shyly. She clearly had a specific man on her mind with that smile. I noticed she didn't have a wedding ring on, so I figured she was referring to a boyfriend and not a husband.

"What happens to this office now?"

"What do you mean?"

"Malcolm owned it. Will it close now that he's gone?"

"No, his wife is keeping it open."

"He was married?"

"Yeah."

"And he was still getting handsy with the help?"

"Yeah, what a prince, huh?" Chelsea obviously didn't like Malcolm.

"If you hate it so much here, why do you stay?"

"It's Birmingham," she shrugged. "I make more as a secretary here than I would as an executive in Detroit."

She had a point. "Have the police came and questioned you guys?"

"Yeah, they did the day after it happened," Chelsea said.

"What did they want to know?"

Chelsea shrugged. "The standard. What kind of a boss was he? Did he have any enemies? Did we know of anyone that would want to hurt him?"

"Did he have any enemies?"

"Not that I know," Chelsea replied. "Like I said. He was good at his job. I think his only weakness was women. I mean, maybe one of them had a boyfriend or something."

"What about a woman named Carrie Washington? Did Malcolm have anything to do with her?"

Chelsea bit the inside of her lip while she considered the question. "I don't think so."

"Could she have been a customer here?"

Chelsea typed on her computer keyboard quickly, glancing at her screen after a few seconds and then shaking her head. "No. There's no one by that name that's a customer here."

"I didn't think so," I blew out a sigh. That would've been too easy.

"Who is she?"

"Who?"

"Carrie Washington."

"She's the young mother that was killed in Macomb County."

Chelsea's brown eyes filled with pity. "That's terrible. Do you think there's really a freeway shooter out there? Do you think we're all in danger from some crazy person?"

"It looks like it."

"Are you really a newspaper reporter?" Chelsea asked.

"I am."

"That sounds like a cool job. Where do you work?"

Everyone that has never been a reporter thinks it sounds like a cool job. The first time they found themselves with eighteen obits -- and a two-hour deadline -- they would realize it's not as glamorous as it sounds. "I work for The Monitor."

"Oh," Chelsea looked surprised. "I think a guy I went to high school with works there."

"Really? Who?"

"Oh, his name was Brandon. I think he's on the copy desk."

I shrugged. "I don't know anyone by that name," I said. "Maybe he used to work there or something. I've only been at the paper for about five years."

'Yeah, maybe," Chelsea said. "Maybe I heard wrong or something."

"Maybe."

I thanked Chelsea for the information, shot one last haughty look in Charlotte's direction, and then left the business. When I got to my car, I sent Fish a text to tell him I had found out some information, but nothing that tied Malcolm Hopper to Carrie Washington. I was waiting for his response when I saw Chelsea exit the front of the building and climb into a pickup truck that was idling in one of the parking spots.

I figured this was the special someone that she had been thinking of earlier. I watched the truck pull out in front of my car, straining my neck to get a gander at her boyfriend. I couldn't help but be curious.

I felt the air whoosh out of me when I saw the driver – and I recognized him. It was Brick.

"Holy crap!"

Eleven

I thought about following them – but I wasn't exactly trained for that. Who am I kidding? I can barely drive when I'm not distracted. Thinking about Brick laying pipe in a truck with Chelsea in the middle of the afternoon was enough to make me crash into a stop sign – or drive off a bridge – without noticing.

Instead, I drove back to Macomb County, and headed toward The Monitor. Someone there had to know something about Brick – like why his name was Brick and what he was doing with Chelsea in the middle of the day.

When I got to the paper, I fobbed my way into the building, and headed straight for the sports department. I didn't spend a lot of time with them – except for an ill-fated bowling league that made me realize that bowling was inherently stupid and I had subpar hand-eye coordination when it came to resin balls with holes in them. What I did know is that they were a unique group of guys that were mostly easygoing – which meant Brick would be the odd man out.

They were also gossipy – and I was banking on the fact that they would be chatty enough to give me the insight I was looking for.

The Monitor's newsroom is long and rectangular, with one half of the room boasting tall cubicles (the better, in theory, to cut down on our incessant chatter) and the other featuring shorter cubicles so the editors and copy desk could communicate with each other easier. The sports department was in the taller cubicles, with the reporters, and they were lodged one aisle over from where I sat.

I rounded the corner and ran into Steve Planter, the paper's Red Wings reporter first. "Hey."

If Steve was surprised to see me, he didn't let on. "What's up?"

"No Red Wings game today?"

"They're out of town," Steve said. We only cover the professional teams when they're in town – or deep in the playoffs.

"Bummer."

"It's fine," Steve said, waving off my concern. "It lets me catch up on some other stuff. What are you doing here, by the way? Big story breaking?"

"No," I shook my head. "I actually wanted to ask you something."

"Me?" Steve looked more alarmed than impressed. My reputation precedes me, I guess.

"Well, someone in sports," I corrected myself.

"You need tickets to a game or something?"

"No." Well, maybe. Eliot loved hockey. "I want to know about Brick."

"Brick Crosby?"

"Is that his last name?" Now that I thought about it, I guess I had heard that. It was just such a ridiculous name.

"Yeah." Steve wasn't looking impressed with my investigative reporter skills. I didn't blame him. "What do you want to know?"

"What do you have?"

"He's a little intense," Steve admitted.

"I got that, trust me."

"He's an avid hunter."

"The scary guy that constantly wears camouflage and expounds on a person's right to own forty guns likes to hunt? That doesn't really surprise me. Does he mostly kill deer?"

"And birds."

"What kind of birds? Like parrots?"

"I think more like turkeys and guinea hens."

Like I know anything about bird hunting. Although, on retrospect, the parrot comment probably did make me look stupid.

"What else?"

"I don't know him that well," Steve shrugged. "He's only been here for a few months. Maybe you should tell me what you're looking for."

"Okay, why is his name Brick?"

"Oh, that," Steve chuckled to himself. "His name is actually Brandon Richard. He just goes by Brick."

"Why?"

"Brandon Richard. B Rick. Brick."

Ah. Well, that was just stupid. "Did his parents give him that name?"

"No, we asked," Steve admitted. "He gave it to himself."

That made it even more ridiculous.

"Is he married?"

"Why? You're not interested in him, are you?"

"Not in the least," I said. "I'm just wondering about his personal life. I would think a guy that was getting sex on a regular basis would be a little less ... militant."

"Well, there is actually a story about that," Steve glanced around conspiratorially.

Finally.

Steve leaned in closer to me. "So, Brick is in the middle of a messy divorce."

"Someone really married him? I was just fishing for information."

"This is his second divorce."

"He found two women dumb enough to marry him?"

"His first ex is down in Tennessee," Steve said. "He has two daughters with her. They're both in high school."

"And the second wife?"

"She's living out in Romeo with her parents and the kids they had together," Steve continued. "He's living in the house that they bought together a few months ago in Marysville."

"Why did they buy a house together if their marriage was on the rocks?"

"I don't know," Steve shrugged. "I've never met her. I just know, according to Brick, she's a crazy bitch. He claims she tried to smother him in his sleep."

"I admire her restraint," I said. "I would've tried to stab him in his sleep."

"I guess she once said that woman that cut off her husband's penis while he was sleeping – and dumped it in a field while she was driving – was her hero," Steve said. "Brick said that was his first inclination that maybe their marriage was a little rocky."

"I bet."

"So they moved up here from Tennessee and immediately broke up?"

"Pretty much."

"Is he seeing anyone?"

Steve narrowed his eyes at me curiously. "Why do you want to know?"

"I just saw him with a woman," I hedged. I didn't want to tell Steve the whole story. The gossip mill at The Monitor is notorious – and by the time the rumor got around Brick would be doing her in the parking lot of the insurance agency. I didn't want to be responsible for that.

"What did she look like?"

"She was short, brown hair," I said.

"Were they in the parking lot?" Steve looked interested, like he wanted to go and check her out.

"It wasn't here," I said hurriedly. "It was in Oakland County. It just took me by surprise."

"Her name is Chelsea," Steve said. "They went to high school together."

Well, that was interesting, she really had known a Brandon in high school and he did, technically, work on our copy desk. "And they both just happened to end up here together?"

Steve looked confused. "Brick grew up here."

"I thought he was from Tennessee?"

"No, he just moved down there when he met his first wife. His parents are still here. He went to high school in Birmingham."

"Birmingham? He doesn't seem like a Birmingham native."

"No," Steve agreed.

"So he went to high school with this woman and just met up with her again?"

"Kind of," Steve said. "I think they reconnected on Facebook."

Huh. "Before or after his second marriage went south?" I asked.

"That is the question, isn't it?" Steve's blue eyes sparkled mischievously.

"What do you think?"

"I think that Brick was in contact with this woman on Facebook before he moved up here – and that's why he pushed to move back to Michigan," Steve said. "I think that his wife found out and that's when she moved out."

"Why do you think that?"

"I heard him screaming at her on his cellphone outside one day," Steve explained. "That's the way it sounded to me."

"So, it's not really a theory, you have actual knowledge of this?"

"I don't have any confirmation from his wife," Steve said.

"Still ..."

"Yeah," Steve nodded. "It sounds like Brick was at least emotionally cheating on his wife with this woman."

"And now he's actually involved with her?"

"She brings him a home-cooked meal every night."

"You're kidding. I thought he cooked?"

"He used to cook his own stuff every night. Now she brings huge meals to him. In Tupperware."

"Nice."

"Then they rendezvous in the parking lot for his fifteen-minute break before he brings the meal inside to eat."

Gross. "By rendezvous do you mean ..."

"Yeah, he's having sex with her in the parking lot." We were both as excited as teenagers. It really wasn't a ringing testimonial to our maturity level.

"How do you know that?"

"We might have spied," Steve admitted.

I was about to tell him that was both immature and disgusting, but then I realized I would've done exactly the same thing. "Do you know anything about this woman?"

"No," Steve replied. "I just know she thinks Brick is the greatest guy in the world."

"So, maybe she has brain damage?" I was joking – kind of.

"Brick seems happy," Steve said. "He's a lot easier to be around when he's happy. Trust me."

I didn't doubt that. I thanked Steve for the information and then dropped back by my desk. I checked my email to see if anything new had come in and then got back up. I didn't have enough for a new story, but I did have some interesting new leads. Now I just had to figure out what it all meant.

I was momentarily distracted by the sound of my cellphone going off. I glanced down and internally cringed when I saw Carly's phone number pop up on the screen. This couldn't be good.

"What's up?"

"I'm going to kill her!" Carly has been prone to dramatic outbursts since I met her. This wedding, though, was on the verge of tipping her over into a 48-hour involuntary psych hold.

"Who are we talking about?"

"Harriet, who do you think? And you call yourself an investigative reporter."

I could tell, by the shrill tone of Carly's voice, that things were about to explode in Chesterfield Township.

"What did she do now?"

"She wants the wedding moved to Chicago."

"Why?"

"Because she doesn't feel safe bringing her family to Detroit – where random people are getting shot on freeways," Carly seethed.

"They're getting shot in Chicago, too," I pointed out. "Chicago's murder rate is pretty much the same as Detroit's now."

"Not in the neighborhood they live in," Carly shot back snottily.

"Just tell her everything is already set," I replied pragmatically. "It's already paid for. You'll lose too much money."

"She says she's willing to cover the money."

"What does Kyle say?"

"Kyle doesn't want to upset anyone so he's just going golfing for fifteen hours a day. He's such a wimp."

That sounded like him. He was actually a good match for Carly, mostly because he tended to be even-tempered while she flew off the handle. However, that easy nature was also why he stretched prone on the ground and let his mother walk all over him whenever she felt like it.

"You're going to have to be firm with her," I replied. "Just tell her no."

"I can't," Carly whined. "If I'm too mean to her, things are going to get even worse than they are now. This woman is going to be a part of my life for years – unless I do get my wish and she's hit by a commuter train."

"Well, then move the wedding to Chicago," I said. "Just know I won't be there. I can't leave town with a big story brewing."

"I'm not moving the wedding."

"Then I don't know what you want me to do?"

"I want you to tell her."

"You want me to tell her what?"

"That we're not moving the wedding."

"Why me?" Now I was the one whining.

"Because you have no problem being mean to people," Carly replied. "And you don't have to ever see her again after the wedding if you don't want to."

She had a point. "Fine. Put her on the phone."

I listened as I heard Carly call for Harriet. After a lot of grumbling, I heard Harriet's voice through the phone. "Yes, Avery, what can I do for you?"

"The wedding isn't moving."

"What?" Harriet sounded surprised by my tone. I don't know why, it wasn't even the meanest tone I had utilized with her this week.

"The wedding is staying put."

"I really don't think that's any of your concern," Harriet said primly.

"Really? Because this is Carly's wedding and she wants it here. It's paid for. Stop trying to take things over. This isn't your wedding."

"I don't think I like the way you're talking to me," Harriet huffed.

"Well, I don't like talking to you," I said. "We both have our crosses to bear."

"You don't have a vote in this decision," Harriet reminded me.

"Neither do you," I shot back. "This is Carly and Kyle's wedding. She wants it here. You're not the boss of her. You're certainly not the boss of me and, quite frankly, I'm sick of your attitude. It's no wonder your son wanted to go to college and settle in another state. It was to get away from you."

Harriet was silent on the other end. I could hear some shuffling and then Carly was back on the line. "What did you say to her?"

"I told her to mind her own business."

"You made her cry." There was a bit of recrimination in Carly's voice.

"So?"

Carly was quiet for a second. "Yeah, you're right. She deserves it. You want to do something tomorrow?"

"I was going to check out Lexie's yoga studio."

"Okay, see you there at noon."

Another crisis averted.

Twelve

Sunday is my favorite day of the week – and that's not just because new episodes of *The Walking Dead* and *Sherlock* are starting soon. Mostly, just not entirely.

After a lazy breakfast with Eliot, I told him that I was meeting Carly at Lexie's yoga studio. He looked more amused than anything else.

"I thought you hated yoga."

"I'm not a big fan," I agreed.

"Then why are you going?"

"I promised Lexie I would check out the studio," I said, averting my gaze from Eliot's. I wasn't in the mood for another Lexie diatribe.

"And?"

"And Carly needs to chill out and there's no better way to chill out than to go through intense pain."

"Ah."

"She's just a little high strung right now," I said.

"I thought she was always a little high strung," Eliot sipped his coffee.

I narrowed my eyes in Eliot's direction. "You can't say that."

"You say it all the time," Eliot protested.

"I can," I argued. "She's my best friend."

"Is that a girl thing?"

"No, it's a loyalty thing," I corrected him. "I can say whatever I want about her. You cannot."

"That goes for Lexie, too, right?"

"Yes," I replied firmly.

"Good to know."

"It's a learning curve, I understand."

I got up to head to the bedroom and get dressed when Eliot stopped me with a look. "What?"

"I thought maybe we could take a quick shower together," he said suggestively. "You know, loosen you up for yoga."

"I'm not showering now."

"Why? Aren't you going out in public?"

"Yeah, but I'm going out in public to get all sweaty – without even the prospect of an orgasm. I'm not showering for that," I explained.

"I could handle the orgasm end of that for you."

I considered his offer for a second. "Okay," I said finally. "I'm still not showering before yoga, though."

I ROLLED into Lexie's new studio only fifteen minutes late. I had an excuse ready -- Eliot needed help at his store – but I found Lexie and Carly sitting at the juice bar gossiping when I came in. I guess an excuse wasn't necessary.

"Hey."

"You're late," Carly admonished me.

"Eliot needed help in his store."

"That's such crap." I was surprised when I saw Derrick straighten up from behind the bar. He had a hammer in his hand, so I guessed he was doing some sort of manual labor.

"It's not crap," I argued. "He needed help."

"Like Eliot would let you interact with the general public," Derrick scoffed. "He's a businessman. He knows better than that."

I stuck out my tongue at Derrick and then hopped onto the stool next to Carly. "So, how did things go with Harriet last night?"

"She cried and complained and begged Kyle to take her side."

"What did you do?"

"I told Kyle to call you and argue it out with you."

"Thanks."

"Yeah, well, if you make him cry I won't feel as bad as I would if I was the one that made him cry."

"Always glad to help."

I glanced around the yoga studio, taking it in for the first time. When Lexie rented the space in a Roseville storefront a few weeks before, I had been dubious. I had to admit, though, she had done a lot of work and it was starting to look pretty good. Lexie had painted the walls in a pleasing plum color. There were shelves on the walls – currently empty – but Lexie had said she planned on putting a variety of teas and apparel on the shelves over the next few weeks. The juice bar had been something she had found discarded on the street, but she had taken it in, refurbished it and fancied it up with some unique decoupage that made the juice bar look like a work of art instead of discarded garbage. The stools had come from the family restaurant and they were in pretty good shape.

"I thought you were doing classes?"

"Nothing scheduled," Lexie said. "We're doing a soft opening in two weeks. I'm just doing classes right now to get the word out. They're more spontaneous than anything else."

"Meaning she's doing them for free," Derrick said darkly. "What a great head for business she has."

"I think that's a good idea," Carly interjected.

"You do?" Derrick looked doubtful.

"Yeah," Carly said. "The whole point is to get people in here. To get people talking. The store isn't open yet. If she starts building up a clientele before it opens, even if it's by offering free classes that can only benefit her later on."

Derrick considered Carly's statement. "I guess you have a point," he said grudgingly.

"Of course I have a point," Carly said dismissively. "My business degree isn't just for show."

I smirked as Derrick scowled. "Now I see why you two are friends."

"Why?" Carly asked curiously.

"You're both condescending."

"Says the cop," Carly said knowingly.

"Excuse me."

"My dad is a cop," Carly reminded him. "I know how it goes."

"Cops are assholes," I agreed.

Derrick rolled his eyes. "Whatever."

"What are you doing here anyway?" I asked him.

"The floorboard is loose down here," Derrick said. "There was no reason for Lexie to pay for someone to come fix it when I could do it for free."

"Your mom made you come," I corrected him.

"It was strongly suggested," Derrick agreed.

"And he loves his baby sister," Lexie teased.

"That must be it," Derrick deadpanned.

I ignored him and turned to Lexie. "So, have you decided on a name?"

"Yeah," Lexie said excitedly. "I'm going with Yoga One That I Want."

Derrick groaned while Carly and I considered. "I like it."

"I do, too," Carly agreed.

"It's cute," I added.

"It's memorable," Carly chimed in.

"It's lame," Derrick grumbled.

"You are just a ball of bright sunshine this morning," I goaded him.

"That's what happens when my mom calls at seven in the morning and tells me to get my ass over to Lexie's yoga studio and act as a slave for a day," Derrick replied. "As if the other six days I worked this week didn't count for anything."

"Translation: You wanted to get lucky with Devon all day," I smirked.

"Like you wouldn't have done the same thing with Eliot," Derrick shot back.

"She already got lucky today," Carly said knowingly.

"How do you know that?" I asked suspiciously.

"You have a glow," Lexie interjected.

"Why couldn't the freeway shooter just shoot me?" Derrick lamented.

I glanced over at him. "Speaking of, anything new on that front?"

"No."

"No? Really? Or just no for me?"

"No for everyone."

"For Devon?"

"There's nothing new!"

"You liar," I challenged him. "There is something new, you've just been ordered not to tell anyone."

"Says you."

"That's why you didn't put up much of a fight when your mom made you come over here," I continued.

"Really?" Derrick looked nonplussed. "Have you ever said no to your mother?"

"All the time."

"Well, I'm a good son," Derrick replied.

"That way you don't have to put up with her trying to cajole information from you," I pushed on. "And I bet her methods of information extraction are a lot more ... personal than mine would be."

"Let's hope," Carly agreed.

"You're such a know-it-all," Derrick muttered. "It's really annoying."

"Especially when I'm right."

"You're never right."

"So, I'm wrong?" I mused evilly. "So, I guess if I called Devon and left a message for you with her, you know, thanking you for the news tip, then things would be just hunky dory with the two of you?"

"Things are never hunky dory when you use the term hunky dory," Carly pointed out.

"I'm tired," I apologized. "I'm not at my best."

"I hate you," Derrick grumbled as he moved away from the juice bar.

"There's another loose board in the other room," Lexie sang out. "Can you fix that before you go?"

"I hate you, too."

Whoever said spending time with your family on a lazy Sunday wasn't fun had never spent time with my family.

Thirteen

"Mondays suck."

"You have a way with words," Eliot chuckled, sliding a mug of coffee across his small kitchen table in my direction.

"Seriously," I grumbled. "How do you wake up looking so pretty?"

Eliot shook his head. "The word pretty makes me feel less manly. I told you to go with ruggedly handsome."

"Are you torturing me this morning for any specific reason?"

"I just like watching you in the morning," Eliot shrugged. "You're so cute when you're disheveled."

I cocked an eyebrow. "I don't think the word disheveled does much for my self-esteem."

"We'll file it next to the word pretty."

"In what? Our file of things we're not supposed to say to each other in the morning?"

"Pretty much."

"Great. We'll put it between 'the condom broke' and 'are you bloated for a reason.'"

Eliot barked out a laugh. "So, what's on your agenda today?"

"Press conference at the sheriff's department," I grumbled. "It's the first briefing from the new task force."

"You say task force like there should be air quotes around it."

"Derrick is on it. There should be."

"I think you're too hard on Derrick," Eliot said. "He's your family. You should be nicer to him. He's got a good reputation."

"You don't feel that way about Lexie," I reminded him.

"Lexie isn't family. She's a fluke."

"Her yoga studio is looking really good." I decided to change the subject.

"That's good." Eliot's tone was airy.

"It is," I agreed. "You should go see it."

"I'll pass."

"Fine."

"Fine."

A FULL hour later I made my way into the sheriff's department. The deputy behind the bubble was new – and he looked fresh off the police academy truck. I thought about messing with him, but I didn't have the energy. If it had been any other day of the week, I probably would've made sure I made an indelible impact on him. As it was, I just flashed my press pass and winked at him as I made my way into the inner sanctum.

Since I was running late, I headed straight for the conference room. I noticed, upon entering, that I was the last media representative to arrive. The television drones were grouped around the donut table chatting. The weekly reporters were doing their best to stay out of their way. A print reporter from one of the big Detroit dailies was also there, and he was doing his best to pretend he was above all of this while a woman in a black pencil skirt and matching blazer stood in the aisle and talked to him. I didn't recognize her. She didn't look like a reporter. Her ebony hair was swept back in a tight bun and her high cheekbones were colored with just a smidgen of makeup. She obviously wasn't with the television crews.

The woman saw me looking at her and took a step toward me. "And you are?"

"Who are you?"

The woman pursed her lips at my evasion but then extended her hand toward me. "My name is Christine Brady. I'm the new media liaison for the sheriff's department."

"Which sheriff's department? Oakland's?"

"No," Christine shook her head. "I was just hired by Sheriff Farrell."

"Why?"

"To be the face of the department," Christine said blankly.

"He's the face of the department."

"Yes, but he can't handle every little inquiry, can he? That would be just silly."

He had so far. "I don't understand."

"The county board feels that Sheriff Farrell is spending too much time with individual media representatives, time that should be focused on his job," Christine continued. "I'm here to make his job easier so he can focus on actual law enforcement."

"So the county actually hired you," I said knowingly. I had a feeling I knew which county board members had made this decision – the ones that Jake was constantly butting heads with. She was a spy.

"The county made the decision to hire me," Christine said primly. "Sheriff Farrell agreed on my selection."

"I just bet he did." Whoops. Did I say that out loud?

"I'm sorry, who are you?" Christine was eyeing me curiously.

"Avery Shaw," I said succinctly. "I'm from the ..."

"The Monitor, yes," Christine frowned. I had a feeling I was one of the media representatives the county commissioners had been worried about.

"I see my reputation precedes me," I joked lamely.

"It certainly does," Christine agreed.

"Why? What have you heard?" There was an edge to my voice. I heard it. I knew she did, too.

"I've heard that you're tenacious," Christine said. "That you're a hard worker and you always get your story."

Well, that wasn't so bad.

"You're also known for getting yourself personally involved in stories and your personal relationships with Sheriff Farrell and another deputy have become cause for concern."

And that was more akin to what I expected.

"You mean my cousin Derrick? And I don't have a personal relationship with Jake. We went to high school together."

"And yet he's often seen in public with you," Christine pressed.

"Define seen."

"Okay," Christine said primly. "On occasion, Sheriff Farrell has been seen at your home."

"Only when I've been threatened."

"And does that happen a lot?"

Too often for comfort. "Not really."

"There have also been times when local police have been called to assist you and Sheriff Farrell has shown up and infringed on local investigations," Christine continued.

"He just wanted to make sure I was okay," I protested.

"He doesn't do that for any other media in the area," Christine pointed out.

"I guess I'm special."

"That is one of the problems, yes," Christine agreed. "You seem to need a lot of Sheriff Farrell's special attention – and that's not really fair to the other media, now is it?"

I didn't give a shit about fair. "Now you listen a second … ."

I felt a hand on my arm pulling me away from Christine. I didn't have to look to know it was Derrick. "Why don't you come over here and have a donut," he warned.

"Deputy Johnson," Christine nodded at Derrick. "Why am I not surprised that you're stepping in?"

"I don't know," Derrick said coldly. "Why don't you go and discuss that with Commissioner Ludington."

"Oh, I knew it," I groaned. "I knew Tad was behind this."

Tad Ludington was a guy I dated briefly in college. He was brief about everything, just FYI. He had been elected to the Macomb County Board of Commissioners about a year before – and he had been irritating me on the political front ever since.

"Commissioner Ludington is a great man," Christine said. "You could learn a lot from him."

"Thanks, I don't need to know how to brush my hair to cover up a bald spot," I shot back.

Derrick choked back a laugh. As much as I irritated him, he got a kick out of watching me irritate others. That is the way of family, after all.

"You have a bad attitude," Christine said.

"That's going to be engraved on my tombstone," I replied.

I glanced up at the conference room door when I saw Jake enter the room. He didn't look happy. When his glance fell on Christine, Derrick, and I, his jaw set grimly. He moved toward us purposefully.

"Christine," he said ominously. "I thought you were going to wait to introduce yourself to everyone at the press conference?"

"I thought I would get a jump on it," Christine replied airily. "I didn't think it would be a big deal."

"Well, have you met everyone?"

"Mostly," Christine said. "I was just getting to know Ms. Shaw here."

"It's always a pleasure," Jake said sarcastically. "Unfortunately, it often ends with prodigious swearing and veiled threats of physical harm."

"I don't swear," Christine said.

"I wasn't talking about you."

Christine took the hint and moved away, making her way to the television reporters. Shelly greeted her with a fake smile and faux enthusiasm, while Devon looked a little unsure of herself. Once she was gone, I swung on Jake. "What the hell?"

"I don't have a choice," Jake said stiffly.

"Flipping Tad," I muttered. "I'm going to FOI every single campaign contribution document in his file."

"Do you think it's good to poke the angry bear?" Jake asked.

"If it gets the angry bear ousted, what do you think?"

Jake considered the statement for a second. "Go nuts."

"Really?" I watched him suspiciously. "You usually try to dissuade me when I go all vengeful."

"Yeah? Well, Ludington has it coming. I figure he deserves you on his ass."

"Like a really big pimple," Derrick chimed in.

"Thanks."

"Just trying to be helpful."

Fourteen

If a press conference with one group of cops is uncomfortable, a press conference with two groups of cops is unbearable. I knew going into it that the briefing would be a pain, but I had no idea just how torturous it really would be.

You had two sheriffs – both trying to one-up one another. Then you had eight deputies – four from each department – trying to make sure they would get their media face time at the podium. And then there was Christine, the really obnoxious media whore, who managed to step on everyone's toes.

When the press conference was over – without one new tidbit, I might add – I couldn't get out of the sheriff's department quick enough. I escaped out the back door, the one by the courtroom at the back of the building, and took the long way back to my car. I didn't want to see any other media personalities – especially Shelly – and I didn't want to risk running into Christine either (especially without a car to flatten her with).

When I got out to my car, I was surprised to find Jake leaning against it. "What are you doing here?"

"Waiting for you."

"I would've thought you would be jockeying for air time with the three network stooges."

"There are plenty of other people in there to do that," Jake replied.

"Yeah, it's a regular media extravaganza," I agreed.

Jake was shuffling in front of my vehicle, his gaze latched to his own shoes. I could tell he wanted to tell me something but he didn't know how to do it. I figured I would help him. What? He looked miserable.

"You don't have to worry," I started. "Christine already told me I wouldn't be getting special treatment anymore."

Jake lifted his head. He looked angry. "I have to be careful."

"I know."

"I'm not happy about this situation."

"I know."

"Stop being so easy to get along with!" Jake practically exploded.

"What do you want me to do? Rant and rave? Act like a baby?"

"That would make me feel better, yes," Jake admitted. "I don't like having my hands tied like this."

"It won't be for long," I said honestly. "You're too good at your job."

"Christine is going to be a pain." Jake ran his hands through his already messy hair. He was more worked up than I could remember in recent weeks.

"Don't worry," I said cagily. "I plan on running some background on her, too."

"Really?"

"Oh, yeah."

"Be careful how you do it," Jake warned. "They'll be expecting you to do something."

"Yeah, I'm predictable that way," I agreed. "It's better for you, though, that they're already aware that I'm ridiculously vindictive."

"If anyone can find something, it would be you."

"I think that's the nicest thing you've ever said to me."

Jake looked uncomfortable with both my statement and wry smile. He started to move away and then turned back around. "Those stickers on your car are ridiculous."

"And we're back to normal."

WHEN I got back to the office, I found Marvin holding court in the center of the aisle with a handful of my co-workers grouped around him. He was entertaining, even if he drove everyone nuts at one time or another.

"I'm telling you, I'm a hundred percent sure this time," Marvin said.

"A hundred percent sure about what?" I asked.

"Marvin is in love," one of the city reporters answered.

"With who? His hand?"

Everyone chuckled appreciatively. Nothing made reporters laugh more than a pointed jab at someone's manhood – especially if it wasn't directed at them.

"No," Marvin said snidely. "With a woman."

"Stripper?"

"No."

"I'm sorry, I mean exotic dancer."

"No, and they're people, too, you know?" Marvin was scowling at me.

"I do know," I nodded, dropping my notebook on my desk. "You've told me repeatedly."

"Well, you seem to forget."

"Sorry. So, you met another exotic dancer?"

"No," Marvin said. "She is not an exotic dancer. She has a respectable career."

"Really? Like a nurse? You do like women in uniform. Especially in the service industry."

"She's not a nurse."

"I'm starting to lose interest," I admitted.

"She's a bartender at The Roost."

Cripes. "Well, it sounds like a great career. What's her name?"

"Ariel."

"Like the mermaid?"

"Yes."

"Just checking. Go on. You're in love with Ariel." I couldn't really get worked up about another Marvin love story. He wrote a new one every week. Okay, that was unfair. Sometimes they lasted as long as a month.

"She's an angel," Marvin sighed.

"I thought she was a mermaid."

"If you're going to be a pain, I'm not going to tell you about her."

I knew he meant it as a threat, but I was really considering taking him up on the offer. I had some research to do – and it wasn't all tied to the freeway shooter. Still, Marvin was a good friend. If listening to his most recent romantic exploit made him happy, it was really the least I could do. "I'm sorry. Ariel is an angel. Go on."

"She gave me a double shot and only charged me for a single shot," Marvin nodded smugly.

"That is love."

"Then she sat and talked to me for the entire night. Just the two of us. She's fascinated by the news business."

Most people usually were. They had no idea how tedious it could be.

"There's just one thing," Marvin hedged.

And here it comes. "What would that be? Is she married? Because you said you were going to stay away from married women after that whole weird threesome thing?"

"She's not married," Marvin said hurriedly. "And you promised you wouldn't bring that up again."

"Sorry. What's the problem?"

"Well, when I was walking behind her, I kind of put my hand on her back."

"So? She doesn't have another arm back there does she?"

"No," Marvin shook his head vehemently. "Her back is just sort of ... sweaty."

I considered the statement. He never ceased to amaze me. "I don't know what that means."

"She has a sweaty back."

"So? Wasn't she working?"

"Yeah, but once I knew it was sweaty, that was all I could think about."

"You're never going to find a woman if you keep fixating on these ridiculous little things."

"A sweaty back is not a little thing," Marvin countered.

"I think most people would think it's a minor thing." I glanced around at the other reporters for support. I wasn't surprised, though, when they all avoided my gaze. "Like you guys are some big prizes."

"Yeah, but we don't have sweaty backs," the court reporter said.

"You have ear hair that is long enough to braid."

"That's just cosmetic," he countered.

"And a sweaty back is a high crime?"

"You can't talk to a woman," Marvin said.

The other reporters agreed and then quietly dispersed, casting frustrated glances in my direction.

I quickly cranked out my story, sending Fish an email that it was in, and then turned to the county's website. All the financial documents for political representatives throughout the county – no matter the position – are available online. The problem is, most of these politicians have thousands of donors. Hitting on the right one – one that might put the pressure on Tad – was going to be a chore. I was up to it, though, because I was totally pissed off – and when I'm pissed off, I tend to get petty.

After a few hours of looking through financial documents, I found what I was looking for. The Giannone family. He had not one but two checks from them. The Giannone family has ties to organized crime. While the two individuals listed on the checks had never been arrested for anything, the name was enough to give me a starting point.

Once I was done, I closed my computer and left for the day. I was at a standstill on the freeway shooting and there was only one place to look right now: Eliot. I needed to know what he knew about Leonard Turner. And now was as good a time as any to press him on the subject.

Or maybe I just hoped that. Either way, I was spoiling for a fight.

Fifteen

I stopped at the coffee shop next to Eliot's store to calm myself before confronting him. I knew he was going to be evasive, but I was ready to deal with it.

When I entered his store, I found him working behind the counter. The store was empty, and he was busy balancing the books for the day. He looked up when he heard the bell over the door jangle and smiled when he saw me. "You're early."

"There was no new information at the press conference," I admitted.

"So, what did they talk about?"

"We got to meet the new media liaison."

"For who? The task force?"

"No, the sheriff's department."

"Why would they have a media liaison? I thought Farrell liked to do that stuff himself?" Eliot looked confused.

"He does. The county commissioners thought he needed a media liaison so he didn't get distracted by certain members of the press and give them special treatment."

Eliot was quiet for a beat. "Meaning that they think you're getting too much favoritism."

"Pretty much."

"What's he like?"

"She. Her name is Christine. And she's the devil."

Eliot chuckled. "Sounds like the two of you are going to get along swell."

"Don't say swell. It makes me think of what she would look like if I popped her in the eye."

"I take it things didn't go well," Eliot said sagely.

"Not well at all," I agreed, peering into one of his cases as I moved around the store restlessly. "She did let it slip that Tad Ludington was the one behind her hiring, though."

Eliot's face clouded. "That guy is a douche."

"Yeah, I've already started his payback," I said.

"How?"

"I pulled his financials from the most recent election."

"Isn't that a lot of work?"

"It is," I agreed. "However, the next election is going to cut the board in half because of that whole county executive thing. That means that a lot of these districts are going to be overlapping."

"And he won't have a walkover in the election this year," Eliot supplied.

"Exactly."

"Did you find anything?"

"A couple of checks from the Giannone family."

"Really?" Eliot looked surprised. "What are you going to do with that?"

"I haven't decided yet," I admitted. "It's just a beginning."

"Well, I pity the fool that would take you on," Eliot smiled sweetly. "If you need any help, I'm up for doing some legwork to bring him down, too."

"Really? I didn't see you as the type of guy that would want to help Jake?" It was a pointed question.

"Jake and I have issues," Eliot agreed. "He's good at his job, though. And Ludington is a total ass."

"He is definitely an ass."

Eliot watched me move around his store curiously. He went back to balancing the register, but I could feel his eyes periodically move back up to me as the silence enveloped us both. Finally, he couldn't take it anymore – which was just the reaction I was going for. "What do you want?"

"What makes you think I want anything?" I asked innocently.

"Because you're not very stealthy," Eliot replied.

I blew out a sigh and turned to him. "I want to know about Leonard Turner."

Eliot's previously amused eyes immediately clouded over. "I don't know what you're taking about."

"Eliot, I know that you're hiding something from me," I said. "I don't want to know any of your covert ops information that I shouldn't know. I just want to know why you don't like Turner."

Eliot groaned. "I knew you weren't going to just let this go."

"I think I've been very good about letting you have your space on this," I countered.

"Space? You're in here grilling me about him right now?"

"This isn't grilling," I argued. "When I'm grilling you, you'll know it."

"Fine," Eliot said.

"Really?"

"You seem surprised."

"I thought I was going to have to be a lot more persuasive than this," I admitted. "I thought it might involve sexual favors with outfits."

"Let's just say I don't want this hanging over us and leave it at that," Eliot looked resigned. "I might take you up on the outfits, though."

"Okay," I agreed.

"Lock the door," Eliot instructed me.

"Is this one of those you can tell me but then you have to kill me conversations?" I asked nervously. "Because I'm not sure if I want to know that badly."

"Lock the door."

I did as I was told and then followed Eliot to the back of the store. I sat down at the small table in the back room and watched as he rooted around the refrigerator. When he came to the table, he slid a Diet Coke across the table toward me and then popped the top on his own can. "Where do you want me to start?"

"When did you meet Turner?"

"About a year after I was promoted to Special Forces."

"Was he your commander?"

"No," Eliot scoffed. "He was just a newbie."

"You didn't like him?"

"You could tell there was something wrong with the guy the minute you met him."

"Wrong how?"

"He was just off. He lied whenever he spoke – like saying that he played cards with the president the week before he came to Special Forces. He also liked to try and play people against each other, tell one guy that another guy was ogling pictures of his wife, really juvenile stuff."

"How did he get promoted?"

"The rumor was that he was promoted because his dad was a general."

"Do you believe that rumor?"

"Yeah," Eliot said dejectedly. "I didn't want to at first, but there was no way that guy could pass the psych profile without a little help."

"He was crazy?"

"Crazy is a subjective word," Eliot countered. "He was uneven. He was all over the place. He was blood thirsty, too. He wanted to go out on missions that he thought would have a high body count – and he didn't care if kids were involved in that body count."

"You're kidding."

"No," Eliot said grimly. "He was a jackass."

"How long did you serve together?"

"Only six months."

"And Jake was there, too?"

"Yeah," Eliot said. "In fact, Turner is the reason Jake and I don't get along."

I didn't like where this was going. I had to know, though. "What happened?"

"I can't give you the specifics," Eliot warned. "I can tell you we had a mission to extract a high level Hamas operative from a small village. It was just supposed to be a snatch and grab."

I waited quietly, letting Eliot tell the story in his own time.

"When we got to the village, it was really quiet," Eliot continued. "We went to the house where we were told he would be and we entered. I went in the front with Turner and Jake went around the back with another guy from our team."

Eliot's face looked pained.

"Turner went in first. I didn't even see what happened. I just heard him start firing. I raced in behind him, but it was already too late. There were two people in the room, and they were both dead."

"So you lost your Hamas contact," I said.

Eliot shook his head. "He wasn't there. I don't know if he was ever there. The only two people in the room were an elderly woman and a young girl, her granddaughter."

I covered my mouth in both horror and surprise. "Were they armed?"

Eliot shook his head. "No."

"Why did he shoot them?"

"You'll have to ask him."

"What happened then?"

"Jake raced in from the back and I had to stop Turner from shooting him," Eliot said. "He was like a rabid dog. It was like he couldn't differentiate between the enemy and anyone else."

"What happened?"

"Jake was pissed, I mean really pissed," Eliot said. "I didn't blame him. I was pissed, too."

"He attacked him." I didn't know how I knew, I just knew.

"You could say that," Eliot said. "I just know that it took everything I had to wrestle Jake off of him. When it was over, Turner had a broken arm, a black eye and a bloody nose."

"Sounds like he had it coming."

"He did."

"So he was removed from Special Forces?"

"Not exactly," Eliot shook his head.

"How could they keep him on?"

"They weren't going to do anything, at first," Eliot said. "Jake made a formal complaint, though. I told him he was stupid to do it, which was a mistake on my part."

"Why did you tell him that?" I was honestly curious.

"I was worried," Eliot admitted. "Turner's father had a lot of juice. I knew he did. I thought Jake was painting a target on his own back."

"So you didn't file a complaint."

"No," Eliot conceded. "In retrospect, I wish I did. I'll never forget Turner looking at me, when it was all said and done, and telling me that what happened in the field stayed in the field. I wanted to punch him myself."

"But you didn't."

"No, I didn't. One of the great mistakes of a life that has had a lot of mistakes."

"And Jake thinks you betrayed him?"

"He would be right," Eliot said miserably.

I was at a loss. Eliot looked so sad. I got to my feet and walked over to him, wrapping my arms around his shoulders. "It was a long time ago. You shouldn't beat yourself up over it."

"Those people were innocent."

"And Turner was the one that was guilty."

"Yeah," Eliot agreed reluctantly, running his hand up and down my arm. "He was guilty."

"What happened then?"

"Well, instead of getting brought up on war charges and being drummed out of the military, Turner was transferred to a cushy office job overseas – complete with a raise."

"That's unbelievable."

"It is, what it is," Eliot sighed.

"That's why Jake went to confront Turner," I said thoughtfully. "He thought that Turner was bloodthirsty enough to shoot someone from a freeway bridge."

"He would be right," Eliot agreed.

"Do you think he did it?"

Eliot looked genuinely torn. "I don't know enough about the shooting to say either way."

"This sucks."

"It definitely sucks," Eliot agreed.

I tightened my arms around his neck. "Thank you for telling me."

"What are you going to do?"

"I have no idea," I admitted. "It's not like I have a source in the military that can give me information without anyone knowing."

"And the information on Turner is going to be buried. Deep."

"I need to give it some thought," I said finally. "If I wasn't already suspicious of Turner, though, I would be now."

"Stay away from him," Eliot warned. "He'll have no problem going after you. And, given your ties to both Jake and me, he probably would enjoy it. I have a feeling you weren't exactly respectful when he called you into his office."

"Why would you say that?" I asked with faux outrage.

"I've met you."

"Oh, that."

I pressed a comforting kiss to Eliot's temple and then pressed my forehead against his for a second. "We'll figure this out."

"What?"

"Getting Turner," I said easily.

"Getting him? You're going to go after him?"

"I'll just add him to my list."

"That list is getting long," Eliot said.

"You have no idea."

Our close moment was interrupted when my cell phone beeped with an incoming text message. I sighed as I pulled away and fished my cell phone from my purse. I frowned when I read the text display.

"What is it?"

"There's been another shooting."

"Where?"

"The 12 Mile and I-94 overpass. Right by my house."

Eliot looked grim. "Let's go."

Sixteen

I let Eliot drive while I busily texted Fish during the ten-minute ride.

"Take Gratiot down, not I-94," I instructed him.

"I'm not an idiot," Eliot clenched his jaw.

"I didn't say you were," I said irritably. "It's just that you're not used to driving to a crime scene."

"I'm a private investigator on the side," Eliot reminded me.

"You go to a lot of crime scenes in your capacity as a private investigator on the side?" He was starting to wear on me – or maybe it was just the situation. Either way, I was pretty much teetering on a precipice with the possibility of tumbling over into bitchy at any second.

"More since I met you," Eliot replied grimly. I had a feeling I was starting to irritate him, too, which was completely ridiculous.

Once we got down to 12 Mile and Gratiot, Eliot glanced around. "Where do you want me to park?"

"Are you being sarcastic?"

"No, I really want to know where I should park."

"There should be some form of command center being set up," I said, leaning forward to glance around the area. "Park in that liquor store's parking lot."

"Is that because you feel like drinking?"

"Maybe in a little bit," I conceded. "You're driving me to it."

"Right back at you."

Eliot maneuvered into the parking lot and killed his engine. He turned to me expectantly. "Now what?"

"Now? Now I wander over there to see if I can see down."

"Won't that piss the cops off?"

"It's what I live for."

"Don't I know it."

"You don't have to come," I reminded Eliot. "You can wait here."

"I'm coming."

I couldn't figure out why Eliot was so adamant about the situation, but he clearly wasn't going to give on this particular subject. I shrugged. I didn't really care either way.

Eliot followed me across the exit ramp from the freeway to 12 Mile, which had been shut down at the source by the sheriff's department – with a little assist from the Michigan State Police, if I had to guess. I led Eliot to the sidewalk on top of the bridge. I could see a myriad of lights flashing below me, but I couldn't quite make out what was happening down below because it was too dark.

"You see anything?"

"No, it's too dark," I grumbled. "I can see one of the photographer's cars down there, though," I pointed toward the median. "At least we'll get some decent pictures."

"There's two ambulances down there, too," Eliot said. "It doesn't look like they're in any big hurry. Maybe no one was hurt."

"Or the victim is already dead."

"You're a pessimist."

"I'm a realist."

"You dress up and play *Star Wars* games on your Kinect. That's not a lifestyle based in realism."

"Why are you riding me?"

Eliot looked surprised – and then chagrined – by the question. "Sorry. It's just been a weird couple of hours."

"You don't have to be here," I reminded him.

"I already told you I'm staying," he snapped.

"Fine."

"Fine."

"Excuse me, the two of you are going to have to move along. This is a crime scene."

I swung around and frowned at the sheriff's deputy standing in the empty exit ramp behind me. "We're just looking."

"This is a crime scene," the deputy repeated.

"Really? I hadn't noticed."

"Ma'am, you need to move along."

"We're not hurting anyone," I shot back.

"I've been ordered to clear the scene." The deputy was using what I'm sure he considered his sternest voice. I wasn't impressed.

"The scene is down there," I pointed. "Go nuts."

"We're searching the area up here, too."

"For what? Shell casings?"

The deputy narrowed his eyes. "Why would you ask that question?"

"Because I'm a reporter for The Monitor and this is the third serial shooting in the last few weeks," I answered honestly.

"They're setting up a media area down in the parking lot at the corner of Gratiot and 12 Mile," the deputy said briskly.

"Great. I'll alert the media."

The deputy took a step toward us, but I noticed a figure move in behind him and stop him with a hand on his arm. Even though it was dark, I recognized the silhouette.

"I'll handle Ms. Shaw, Deputy Bryson," Jake said calmly. "Why don't you go and see if you can find any witnesses at the liquor store."

"Yes, sir," the deputy actually clapped the heels of his shoes together and then moved away – but not before he shot me an angry look.

"Made a new friend I see," Jake said dryly.

"That's a daily occurrence, what can I say?"

Jake stepped forward, nodding at Eliot as he did. "Kane."

"Sheriff Farrell," Eliot nodded back.

"You're now going out on stories with Avery?" There was a coldness to Jake's voice.

"We were together when she got the tip," Eliot shrugged easily. "I figured she would be safer if I brought her."

"Safer from what?" Jake asked.

"Herself," Eliot responded.

Jake smiled, despite the effort he was exerting to remain stone faced. "That's probably a good idea."

"You know I can hear the two of you, right?"

"Hear? Yes," Jake said. "Listen? That's a whole other thing."

"Who is the victim?" I decided to change the subject.

"I'll give you his name, but I don't expect you to publish it for at least three hours," Jake cautioned.

"Agreed."

"His name is Lance Plimpton, standard spelling. He's a 17-year-old senior from Roseville High School."

I gulped. "Is he dead?"

"Yes."

"Shot?"

"Yes."

"Is it the same shooter?" It was a stupid question, but it had to be asked.

"It's the same caliber of bullet," Jake sighed. "We won't be able to confirm that for sure until tomorrow."

"It would be a heck of a coincidence to have another freeway shooter in this area," Eliot mused.

"Not necessarily," I said. "Sometimes freeway shootings like this become a rash of crimes."

"Like one shooting inspires someone else to do the same thing?" Eliot asked.

"Yeah."

"Do you think that's what happened here?" Eliot turned to Jake.

"No," Jake shook his head. "It doesn't feel like that."

We all heard the staccato sound of a woman's heels on a hard surface before we saw the figure moving from the neon lights of the liquor store parking lot to the muted dark of the highway overpass. I noticed Jake stiffen when he realized who was coming.

"Sheriff Farrell, I've been looking for you," Christine Brady said as she stepped up on the sidewalk. "I thought you were going to keep me informed?"

When Christine realized Jake wasn't alone, she plastered a fake smile on her face. When she saw just who he was talking to, that smile faded pretty quickly. "Ms. Shaw, why am I not surprised?"

"Because if you actually changed your facial expression it would cause lines on your face and you would need Botox?" Seriously, I can't explain why I do it either. It's a sickness.

Christine wrinkled her nose. "Sheriff Farrell, I thought everyone was on the same page about certain media representatives getting special treatment?" The woman's tone was brittle.

"He wasn't giving me special treatment," I shot back. "He was trying to clear me from the scene – and I was putting up a fight. I'm bitchy like that."

If Eliot was surprised by my lie, he didn't show it. Instead, he nodded in agreement. "Sheriff Farrell just asked us to vacate the scene."

Jake cast a sidelong glance in Eliot's direction. He seemed surprised at the backup. "I told them that we were creating a media hub down the street in the parking lot of the strip mall."

Christine glanced at all three of us dubiously. "Why don't I believe you?"

"Because then you wouldn't be able to ask questions like that out loud in an attempt to make others think you have some keen insight into the human psyche," I interjected. Yes, it's a sickness, I tell you.

"Perhaps you should make your way down to the media staging center," Christine suggested coldly.

I should have done what she told me to, but something stopped me. "You're not a cop," I reminded her.

"So?"

"You have no authority over me," I added.

"No, but Sheriff Farrell does."

Jake sighed. He was being pushed into a corner here. Eliot didn't allow me to make that corner any tighter. "I'll take her down there," he said, gripping my elbow and pulling me back toward the liquor store.

Christine focused on Eliot for the first time. "And you are?"

"Eliot Kane," he held out his hand in greeting, never removing his other hand from my elbow.

Christine took it, never moving her eyes from Eliot's handsome face. "And why are you here?"

"I drove Avery," Eliot replied easily.

"Why?"

"Because she was at my place when we got the news." Eliot's tone was affable and yet standoffish at the same time. It was quite a feat.

"So, you're involved with Ms. Shaw?" Christine pressed.

"I don't see how that's any of your business," Eliot answered coolly.

"I'm just curious about Ms. Shaw," Christine said carefully. "She seems to have no limit of men willing to jump in and protect her." With those words, Christine cast a knowing glance in Jake's direction.

To his credit, Eliot didn't take the bait. "She's does have a certain something about her. It's like a weird mix of snark, humor and childishness."

"Hey!"

"Don't forget the hints of loyalty, the constant fashion fails and the never ending need to prove that she's right," Jake supplied.

"That, too," Eliot agreed.

Christine looked irritated by the exchange more than anything else. "I guess you have to be a man to see these wonderful traits."

"I guess so," Eliot agreed.

Thankfully, for all four of us, a tow truck traveling down the exit ramp caught all of our attention. I felt Eliot stiffen beside me when the car that Lance Plimpton had been driving came into view.

The front end was mangled from running into the base of the bridge after Plimpton had been shot. The windshield was intact, except for a round bullet hole about a foot up on the driver's side. Even in the dark, I could see the dark stain on the gray fabric of the seat where Plimpton had been sitting.

"I knew it," Eliot swore furiously.

Jake turned to him in surprise. "Knew what?"

"That's a black Ford Focus," Eliot said.

Jake's face hardened. "You're saying ..."

"What?" I was starting to get annoyed. The fact that Eliot had figured out something important that I had missed was both impressive and infuriating.

"I knew the location wasn't going to be coincidence," Eliot said. "I just had a feeling."

"This is the exit she would use," Jake nodded.

"Who would use?" They were both bugging the shit out of me now.

"You," Eliot said simply.

"Me?" I still didn't get it.

"It's the same car you drive, Avery," Jake pointed out. "The same color. The kid was shot at the same time you should have been coming home from work."

"Wait you're saying ..."

"You were probably the intended target," Jake supplied harshly.

"Who would anyone want to shoot me?"

"Who wouldn't?" Christine replied, quickly looking away when Jake shot her a dark look.

"Who have you interviewed in the last few days?" Jake asked the question.

"I'm not telling you that," I scoffed, although I wasn't feeling as sure about myself as my voice implied.

"She went over and talked to some secretary at that insurance office where the first victim worked on Saturday," Eliot replied.

"Tattletale."

"And then, of course, there's Turner," Eliot added.

Jake's face looked like it had been carved out of granite it was so hard. "Yeah, I know."

"Or," Eliot blew out a sigh. "It could just be because she's been the one writing the stories. She doesn't necessarily have to have pissed someone off in person."

"Yeah, she pisses people off just by existing," Jake agreed. "She shouldn't be left alone."

"Yeah, I got it," Eliot nodded. "Protecting her is like a second job these days."

"That's another one of her special personality traits," Jake agreed, trying for a wry smile that came off as more of a grimace than anything else.

"I'm standing right here!"

They both ignored me.

"We can't be sure that the car was targeted because someone thought it was her," Jake said.

"No," Eliot agreed. "We can't be sure that the car wasn't targeted because of her either."

"No."

We couldn't be sure of anything. But, it was a possibility, that a high school student could have been killed because he was driving the same kind of car I had.

"I think I'm going to be sick."

Seventeen

Eliot stayed close – too close – to me for the duration of the evening. He stood directly behind me at the press briefing, casting suspicious looks in a bevy of directions. While the gesture was sweet, it was also stifling.

After the press briefing was over, I took the opportunity to pull Derrick aside while Eliot was busy staring down a van he didn't like at the gas station in the parking lot. "Tell him you're going to give me a ride."

"What?" Derrick looked confused.

"He's driving me crazy."

"How?"

I told Derrick about what had transpired with Jake, Eliot, Christine and me – including the revelation about Lance Plimpton's car – and then waited for his response. "You're shitting me?"

"No – and I don't get that saying."

"Why didn't Jake tell me about this?"

"It just happened," I said. "I think he wants to get away from Christine first."

"Yeah, she's a real ... piece of work."

"She's going to be a pain until we can get rid of her," I agreed.

"Get rid of her?" Derrick quirked an eyebrow in my direction.

"Not like the mob," I said quickly. "More like digging up dirt on her or Tad so I can pressure the situation until it's back the way I like it."

"For once that spoiled rotten thing you have about not wanting to share your toys is going to benefit the greater good," Derrick said.

"I'll take that as a compliment."

"You should."

"So, you'll take me?"

"Yeah," Derrick blew out a sigh. "I'll take you. If you're going to go after Christine, I guess I owe you."

"Good," I said, catching a glimpse of Eliot moving toward us. "You tell him you need me to ride with you because you want to question me."

"What?" Derrick looked flummoxed.

"He won't believe it if it comes from me."

"He's not going to believe it coming from me either."

"Yeah, but he'll be less likely to call you a liar," I replied.

"Fine," Derrick muttered irritably. "Hey, Eliot."

"Derrick," Eliot nodded. "What were you two talking about?"

"Global warming," I said quickly. I'm bad at thinking of lies sometimes.

Derrick rolled his eyes and shook his head. "I was telling Avery that I'm concerned our grandfather was going to be arrested if he kept ignoring his jury duty summons."

Yeah, that was a much better lie.

"Do you think he will? Maybe he's just looking for attention," Eliot suggested.

"He does like his attention, but this is going to get him a whole heap of crappy attention," Derrick said.

"Well, if he gets arrested, you'll have another fun family story to tell," Eliot said breezily.

"Yeah, those fun family stories are still painful at times," Derrick said.

"Yeah," I agreed. "Like the time we were sneaking into the pool and found him sleeping naked on the trampoline."

Eliot barked out a laugh.

"It's a funny story," Derrick agreed. "It's a scarring memory, though."

"He claimed he could tell time when the sun rose, like he was a sundial," I explained.

Eliot thought about it a minute and then cracked the first true smile of the evening. "Ah, I get it."

"Sometimes it takes a while," I said.

"Are you ready to go?" Eliot asked.

I turned to Derrick expectantly.

"Actually, do you mind if I take her to your place?"

"Why?" Eliot looked suspicious.

"I want to talk to her about your theory about her being the target," Derrick lied smoothly. "I can do it during the car ride."

"Why don't you just ask her now?"

"I ... I," that lying thing comes and goes for my whole family apparently.

"He's actually going to drop me off at the office," I interjected.

"Why?"

"I have a story to file."

"I can take you there," Eliot said stubbornly.

"I thought I would text you to pick me up when I was done."

Eliot still looked unsure.

"I'll walk her into the building," Derrick offered.

"And you won't leave until I come up to the building to get you?" Eliot asked pointedly.

"I promise," I placed my hand over my heart with as much sincerity as I could muster.

"That means you can't even go outside and have a secret cigarette," Eliot instructed. "I don't care how stressed you are."

"You still do that?" Derrick looked disgusted.

"Mind your own business," I grumbled. "I promise."

"Fine," Eliot agreed. He stepped forward and dropped a kiss on my forehead. "I've got a few errands I need to run anyway."

"See, it works out well for everyone," I said.

"Remember your promise," Eliot cautioned me.

"I remember," I muttered.

Once Eliot was gone and I was safely encased in Derrick's car I turned to him. "I don't like being treated like a child."

"He likes you," Derrick said calmly. "I have no idea why, because you are like a really annoying child a lot of the time, but he does."

"I still think they're grasping at straws." I said the words but wasn't sure I actually believed them.

"They could be," Derrick agreed. "Or they could be right."

"I need you to keep this to yourself," I said. "I don't need my mom freaking out."

"I'm going to agree to keep this quiet for now," Derrick said. "But only because I think it's too thin to actually be a legitimate lead right now."

"I'll take it," I said.

Once we got back to The Monitor, Derrick took his promise to Eliot seriously. He made me stay in his car until he could walk around to the other side of the vehicle and open the door for me. His dark eyes were busy surveying the parking lot.

When I got out of the car, I started toward the front door, but I paused when I saw that Derrick's eyes were trained on a vehicle out in the adjacent second parking lot. "What?"

"That truck is moving."

I realized what truck he was referring to rather quickly. "I wouldn't worry about that."

"There's someone in there," Derrick started moving toward the vehicle with a purpose, his hand on the weapon at his hip.

"Yeah, but that's not a sniper in there, trust me." I started to follow Derrick in a vain effort to keep him from seeing what was in the truck. "The only weapon in there is a really little pistol."

When we got closer, Derrick pulled up short. "There are two people having sex in there."

"I know."

"Are they interns?"

"No," I shook my head. "It's the sports paginator and his girlfriend, Chelsea," I replied grimly.

Derrick continued to watch the scene as if mesmerized by the horror of it for a few more minutes. Finally, he peeled his eyes from the truck and turned back to me. "That's the whitest ass I've ever seen."

"I'm more horrified by the hair."

"On his ass or hers?"

"They're both equally appalling," I said.

"Newspaper people are freaks," he grunted and turned back to the building. "Freaks."

Eighteen

Since I had worked so late Monday night, Fish told me to take my time on Tuesday – even take the day off if I wanted to.

"You don't need to come into work if you don't want to," he said when he called me. Since I was still in bed, I didn't have a problem with his suggestion.

"What about the follow-up on Lance Plimpton?"

"I'm sending Marvin."

"Marvin, not Duncan, right?"

"Yeah, Duncan has some dirty jobs thing he wants to do," Fish replied.

"Dirty jobs? I don't get it."

"I don't know," Fish sounded irritated. "He wants to do some series where he follows people around on some disgusting jobs and then writes stories about it. He's all proud that he thought of it himself."

"He did not think of it himself," I corrected Fish. "It's a television show."

"It is?"

"You need to watch more than C-SPAN some time," I said.

"I'm going to bust his ass," Fish grumbled.

"Have fun. If he suggests growing a beard and going hunting, that's a television show, too. Just FYI. So is searching for Bigfoot."

When we disconnected, I rolled over and snuggled into Eliot's side. "Fish is letting me set my schedule today."

"What does that mean?"

"It means I can go to work if I want, but I don't have to."

"Does that mean I can keep you in bed all day?" Eliot asked suggestively.

"Maybe," I hedged.

Eliot sighed. "What are you going to do?"

"I was thinking ... ."

"Always a scary prospect," Eliot grumbled.

I ignored him. "I thought I would buy you breakfast."

"I could live with that," Eliot answered easily, but suspicion lurked in his eyes.

"And then, I thought you might know some gun nuts that might be able to give me some insight into the sniper and whether or not those shots were really hard or just coincidences."

Eliot considered the request for a second. "I might know a few people."

"You're agreeing to this?"

"Yes, because I'll be going with you," Eliot said firmly.

"Fine."

"Good." Eliot pulled me close to him for a second and then released me. "I'm going to want to work up an appetite before my breakfast."

I pulled back far enough to see his face. "Fine," I blew out a sigh. "But you're going to have to do all the work. I'm still tired from last night."

"I think I'm up for that."

"I noticed."

TWO HOURS later, Eliot and I finally made our way into the local Coney Island for breakfast. After the exertion of my morning, a plate full of greasy hash browns and eggs sounded like just the rejuvenating meal I needed. I would add a glass of tomato juice so I could get some vitamins, too. Eating healthy is chore for us all.

Eliot walked into the restaurant before me and, since I wasn't paying attention, I slammed into his back when he paused in the doorway.

"What the hell?"

"Maybe we should go somewhere else for breakfast," Eliot said carefully.

"Why?" I peered around him and frowned when I found who he was looking at. It was Jake, and he wasn't alone. Christine Brady was sitting in the booth across from him. "Why would he be having breakfast with her?"

"Maybe he's trying to play nice," Eliot shrugged.

"You can't make nice with a snake."

"Maybe he likes her."

"You can't like a snake."

"She's kind of attractive," Eliot mused after a few seconds. "In that dirty librarian kind of way."

"Men are sick."

Eliot laughed and the sound caused both Christine and Jake to turn their attention to us in the doorway. We had no choice but to enter now – otherwise we would look like idiots. I was no stranger to that particular look, but I refused to lose face in front of Christine.

The hostess led us to a booth that, ironically, was just across the aisle from Jake and Christine. Once we were seated, Eliot glanced over at the two of them and nodded. "Good morning."

"Morning," Jake replied smoothly.

"Do you live around here?" Christine asked. Small talk obviously wasn't her forte.

"Why?" Eliot asked coolly.

"It's just a weird coincidence that we would all end up at the same diner."

"I live down the street," Eliot said.

"Above your pawnshop?" Christine said pawnshop with the same amount of enthusiasm as one would say diaper genie.

"Yup."

The waitress filled our coffee cups and took our order and then it was just the four of us – again.

"I read your story this morning," Christine said after a few minutes.

"I'm glad you can read," I replied. "That probably comes in helpful in your line of work."

Christine ignored the barb. "I find it interesting that you were the only reporter in the area that managed to get the name of the victim."

"I'm good like that," I agreed, not rising to the bait she was lazily dangling in the water.

"She has a special gift," Eliot agreed. "It's like magic."

I glanced at him and raised an eyebrow. That was laying it on a bit thick.

"How did you get the name?" Christine pressed.

"I had a source," I sipped from my coffee cup dismissively.

"A police source?"

"No," I said carefully. "It was not a police source. It was a source within the school." That's totally plausible. I've done enough fluff pieces for that school that someone could've easily tipped me off. She couldn't prove I was lying.

"How would the school have known?"

"My guess is that, once the mother was informed, she told a friend and then the kids found out." I can lie when I want to – and sometimes the lies come smoother than they should.

"And if I were to ask the school, would they back this up?" Christine obviously didn't believe me.

"I don't know," I said evasively. "I guess it depends on whether or not you get the right person at the school."

"What if I told you that I planned on spending my morning over there asking if anyone tipped you off?"

What an idiot. Like that was going to trip me up. "I'd say you have a lot of time on your hands and to have a good time. Kids today are great. Especially teenagers. They're great little reflections of what is good and pure in this world today." FYI,

I hate teenagers on general principle. Still, watching a group of them hassle Christine sounded fun. Maybe I would take my flip camera and videotape it for YouTube.

Christine frowned. "You don't have a problem with me going to the school?"

"Not in the least."

"You don't think they'll be angry about being hassled?"

I angled my body so I could talk to Christine face on. "I think that Roseville has a new basketball floor because of the story I did. I think that the band has new uniforms because of another story I did. I think that the photo diary of their Christmas pageant that I set up brought a lot of money into their drama program. So, no, I don't think one annoying woman questioning them in an incessant and unnecessary way will make them stop talking to me."

Eliot smirked from across the table. He liked it when I went full on bitchy – as long as it wasn't with him. Even Jake looked amused with my response.

Christine looked agitated. "Well, I'm still going."

"Knock yourself out," I said, smiling at the waitress as she slipped my breakfast in front of me. "I think that the task force would enjoy a morning away from you."

And the three-pointer at the buzzer is all net.

"What are you doing today?" Jake changed the subject.

"I have the day off."

"Really?" Jake looked surprised. "I thought you would be talking to the family of the victim."

"Marvin is handling that."

"Why?" Christine asked. "Where will you be?"

"Eliot and I are spending the day together." That's not technically a lie.

"You don't have to work? Isn't this your big story?" Christine was baiting me again. Actually, it was more like she was tossing chum in the water and circling like a Great White to see if I would come in for a nibble.

"Since I technically worked a double shift last night, my boss gave me the day off."

"He sounds like a nice boss," Christine said dubiously. "I think it's more likely that he can't stand being around you any more than I can."

So much for playing nice – or even faking it.

"You'd have to ask him about that," I replied, dunking my toast in my eggs enthusiastically. "I can set up a meeting if you want."

"I already have a meeting with him set for tomorrow," Christine said smugly. "I have a few concerns regarding your coverage that I want to discuss with him."

If she thought that was going to bug me, she was wrong. Fish was many things, but loyal was at the top of the list – right above trapped in the 1970s fashion cycle. "I think that's a great idea."

"You do?"

"I do," I said. "I think you'll find that Fish might have a few things to tell you about how a newspaper and the coverage he selects work."

"That sounds like fun," Eliot agreed.

It wouldn't be fun for Christine. I could pretty much guarantee that.

Nineteen

Christine made a polite – if hasty – retreat when she realized I couldn't be goaded in the way she initially thought. I took the move as a way for her to regroup. I knew she wouldn't give up, but I figured she'd plan a different tactic for our next meeting.

Once she was gone, Jake let loose a genuine sigh of relief.

"Why are you having breakfast with her?"

"She thought it would be a good idea if we spent some time together in a casual atmosphere," Jake said. "She thinks we got off on the wrong foot."

"There is no good footing for a spy."

"Yeah, she doesn't seem to get that," Jake agreed. He watched me down my glass of tomato juice while grimacing. "That's gross."

"It's good," I countered.

"It's the only way she eats anything even remotely healthy," Eliot said. "I encourage it."

"So," Jake said after a few beats. "What are you really doing today?"

"I'm taking her to the gun range," Eliot said. "She wants to get a feeling for the shooter."

"Don't let her shoot a gun," Jake cautioned. "That could be dangerous."

"I'm the one that taught her to shoot a gun," Eliot reminded him.

Jake frowned at the memory. "That's how you guys met. I forgot. She bought a gun in your store."

"Yep," Eliot agreed. "It's all been downhill since then."

I kicked him under the table.

"What happened to that gun?" Jake asked suddenly.

"It's in a safe place," I said evasively.

"Locked up? Some place Lexie can't find it?"

"I said it was in a safe place," I said irritably.

"It's in a Darth Vader cookie jar in her office," Eliot explained.

"That sounds safe," Jake said sarcastically.

"Lexie is about all things yoga now," Eliot shrugged. "She can't be all Namaste with a gun."

"Yeah, but she has terrible taste in men," Jake said. "That hasn't changed, has it?"

"Not in the least."

After breakfast, Eliot drove us to the gun range. This was only the second time I had been there and I was no less amazed to see the amount of people that managed to congregate there instead of at work.

"Don't these people have jobs?" I asked Eliot when we entered the building.

"I don't know," he shrugged. "Maybe they can just set their schedule like you can."

"That seems unlikely," I glanced around. "It's like a *Duck Dynasty* convention."

"You like *Duck Dynasty*."

"I did at first," I corrected him. "Now they're setting up too many scenarios."

"It's a television show."

"Yeah," I said. "It's supposed to have some basis in reality, though. Everything on the show is scripted now."

Eliot led the way to the front desk, greeting the clerk with a familiarity that didn't exactly surprise me but did catch me a little off-guard. "Hey, Randall," he said to the fortyish man in Army green behind the counter. "Is Terry around?"

"Yeah, he's in the back," Randall answered, glancing in my direction. "Who is this? Is this the girlfriend we've been hearing so much about?"

I saw that Eliot had reddened a little at Randall's question. "This is Avery."

"What does he say about me?" I asked Randall curiously.

"He says you're a wonderful woman," Randall said stiffly. He clearly realized he'd made a mistake.

"I'm sure," I said, rolling my eyes at Eliot. "I bet he told you what a great cook I am."

"Yes," Randall agreed. "Said you made him dinner every night."

Eliot groaned behind me. "And that I was an immaculate housekeeper, too, right?" I pressed on.

"He said you're a cleaning dynamo," Randall said energetically. "There's no toilet you can't scrub."

"And that I'm a total honey in the sack, too, right?"

"Oh, yeah, you're very bendy. Wait. No. No. He didn't say anything like that." Randall was getting flustered now.

"It's alright, Randall," Eliot sighed. "She's just messing with you."

"That's that weird sense of humor you were talking about," Randall laughed hollowly.

"We'll be in the back." Eliot grabbed my arm and led me toward the gun range. "You're just mean sometimes."

"I can't help it," I shrugged. "He looked like such an easy mark."

"Just keep in mind, everyone isn't as easy as Randall," Eliot cautioned as he paused at the door that led from the store to the gun range. "And don't call them gun nuts. They're not going to like that."

"I'm not stupid."

Eliot cocked an eyebrow.

"Fine. I'm not that stupid."

"Let's hope."

A gun range, I've decided, is just like a spa for men. Instead of getting pedicures and steams, though, it's a place where they can boast and be manly together. It's just a gossip session – with firearms – for men.

Eliot led me to the far end of the range where a tall man, dressed in black pants and a USMC shirt was loading his weapon. Eliot was in good shape – built – but this guy looked like he could pop Eliot's head off his shoulders without breaking a sweat. His neck was as wide as my thighs (which aren't dainty, mind you) and the veins in his arm were pronounced.

The man looked up when he caught the hint of movement we provided out of the corner of his eyes and then his face, which has previously resembled a pissed off Doberman, broke into a wide smile. "Hey, Kane. What are you doing here? Getting in some target practice?"

"Not exactly," Eliot said, clasping hands with the behemoth in a friendly manner. "I'm actually helping Avery."

The man looked me up and down, never losing his smile. "This is her, huh? You didn't say she was so cute."

"What did he say?" I asked curiously.

"He just said you were blonde and sassy. I'm Terry Sherman, by the way."

I shook his hand. "Avery Shaw."

"Yeah, I know. Ever since I heard you were dating Eliot here, I started reading your stories in The Monitor."

"Oh yeah? What do you think?"

"I think you're good," Terry said.

He didn't strike me as a literary critic, so I let that slide. "Well, I'm always glad to have a fan." That was kind of an awkward statement. I wanted to take it back the minute I said it. Terry didn't seem bothered by it, though.

"Well, I'm definitely a fan then."

"We're actually here for your help, Terry," Eliot said.

"My help?" Terry looked surprised. "On what?"

"Have you heard about the freeway shootings?"

"Yeah," Terry nodded. "You don't think I had anything to do with them do you?"

"No," Eliot shook his head quickly. "We're more interested in your take on the difficulty of the shots."

"I don't know enough about them to offer an opinion," Terry said honestly.

"I know," Eliot said. "That's why I brought some visual aids."

Eliot opened the file he had been carrying and placed a series of aerial photos on the table next to Terry. The bridges were highlighted on them – and the location of the cars when the shots were believed to be fired was also circled in red. I was surprised.

"Where did you get those?"

"I told you I had errands to run last night."

"Where does one run an errand that garners them these? And at night?"

"I've got a whole network of people you don't know about little miss busybody," Eliot said.

Terry picked up the pictures and considered them for a few minutes. "This is the one on the Cass Bridge?"

"Yeah."

"How busy was the traffic pattern?"

"Fairly busy," Eliot said. "It wasn't rush hour, though. There were still cars around."

"And it wasn't dark, right?"

"Right."

"What about this one?"

"That's the 12 Mile overpass," Eliot said. "That one was during rush hour and it was dark. Not really dark at the time of the shooting, but it was dusk."

"Do we know if specific cars were targeted?" Terry asked.

Eliot slid a sidelong glance in my direction. "We believe, at least in the 12 Mile shooting, that a specific target was probably in mind."

"We don't know that, though," I corrected him.

"I'm not going to get into that right now," Eliot said firmly.

Terry glanced at both of us but didn't acknowledge our little exchange. "I would say that the 12 Mile shot was actually relatively easy."

"Really?" Eliot looked surprised.

"It's a straight shot without any curves for at least a mile. And, even though it was dark, that whole area is lit up pretty well because of all the billboards and the big stores on either side of the freeway."

"I hadn't thought of that," Eliot mused.

"The Cass shot was also pretty easy," Terry continued. "It was broad daylight. If it wasn't a specific shot and just a crime of opportunity, that puts it in the simple realm."

"What about the Oakland shot?" I asked.

"I'm not as familiar with that area," Terry admitted. "Off the top of my head, though, that's a pretty open area."

"So, you're saying that whoever is doing this doesn't necessarily have to be a pro," Eliot said.

"That would be my guess. Do you know what kind of weapon is being used?"

"The cops aren't releasing that," I replied.

"Figures." Terry continued studying the pictures. "If you're thinking military, I think you're overreaching."

"Why?"

"Because, if this was a military trained sniper, I think he'd be going for harder targets," Terry said simply. "This is like an adult playing Candyland."

"So, you're thinking someone with reasonable gun knowledge but not the ability to take the hard shot?" I asked.

"Pretty much," Terry said.

"Like a hunter," Eliot mused.

"Exactly like a hunter," Terry agreed. "Exactly like a hunter. Only his prey is people."

Twenty

Once we were done at the range, I had Eliot drop me off at The Monitor with a promise that I would call him for a ride back to his place when I was done. I hadn't planned to go into the office at all, but I wanted to run some things by Fish.

"This mother hen thing is starting to get old," I told him as I jumped out of his truck.

"Yeah, well you wouldn't be saying that if you were dead on the street," Eliot shot back.

"If I was dead on the street, I wouldn't be saying anything," I pointed out.

"Knowing you, you'd still find a way."

When I got into the office, I found Fish first and told him what I had found out. He took in the information like he always did, like he was bored and only half listening. "So, we're looking for someone that doesn't necessarily have military experience but knows their way around a gun?"

"Pretty much."

"Unless someone is trying to cover up that they have military experience and they're doing it by going for easier shots," Fish suggested.

"That's a possibility," I ceded.

Fish turned to Brick, who was leaning against the cubicles watching us. "What do you think, Killer?"

Killer? What a fun nickname. Or not.

Brick smiled at Fish and flashed an impatient glance in my direction. "I think that people are always eager to blame the military. I think it's like a sickness with some people."

"Except, I just said it probably wasn't someone with military experience," I shot back.

"Unless it's someone with military experience trying to pretend they don't," Brick corrected me.

"He said that," I pointed to Fish.

"You agreed with him."

"You just don't like women," I grumbled.

"What's that supposed to mean? I like women fine."

When he was nailing them in the parking lot. I didn't say that out loud, though. As much as I disliked Brick, I wasn't about to tattle on him to the boss – unless he really pissed me off and I was backed into a corner.

"Why do you think he doesn't like women?" Fish asked curiously.

"I just heard he was on his second divorce," I explained quickly. "And he didn't have anything nice to say about his soon-to-be ex-wife."

"Why should I?" Brick challenged me. "She told me she wanted to smother me in my sleep."

"I've met you," I replied. "I can see the inclination."

"She also took my kids from me and none of them are talking to me right now," Brick charged on. "She's got them drinking the Kool-Aid. Do you think that's right?"

"I don't know," I shrugged. "Are any of them girls? And what kind of Kool-Aid are we talking about? That blue stuff is pretty good."

"Two of them are girls. What's that's supposed to mean?" Brick looked like he was on edge – and I had a mad desire to push him over it to see what happened.

"I wouldn't let young, impressionable girls hang around you either."

I glanced at Fish; he looked distinctly uncomfortable with the conversation. He wasn't telling me to shut my mouth, though, which meant he was also interested in hearing Brick's response.

"I'm a good father."

"Then why would she want your kids away from you?"

"Because she's a vindictive bitch," Brick snapped back.

"Why would she be vindictive?" I was trying to get him to talk about Chelsea.

"She thought I was cheating on her," Brick said, regaining some of the calm he had momentarily displaced. "Which I wasn't."

"Why would she think that?"

"Because she was spying on my Facebook account."

"If you didn't have anything to hide, why would you call it spying?"

"Do you want your boyfriend – or girlfriend, I guess, given your attitude – going through your Facebook account?"

"I don't think my boyfriend – why would you think I'm a lesbian, by the way – would give a crap about the gossiping I do with my cousins," I replied tartly.

"You're a mean woman," Brick said. "I just assumed that meant you were a lesbian."

I glanced at Fish to see what he thought of the statement, but he was steadfastly studying his computer screen and pretending the conversation wasn't happening. Coward.

"Have you ever considered women are only mean when they deal with you?" I asked pointedly, turning my attention away from Fish and back to Brick.

"That's what my wife said, but she's not too bright, so I didn't really believe it."

She would have to be slow to marry him. "Well, I would revisit the statement and do some soul-searching."

"Or maybe it's you."

I cringed when I heard the voice. Duncan. Of course he would get involved in this conversation. "Duncan, don't you have something else you should be doing? Like a dirty job or something?"

Fish lifted his head. "Speaking of that," he started. "Avery said that's not an original idea and you saw it on television."

Duncan flashed me an irritated look. "That doesn't mean it's still not a good idea and I would be tying it to jobs in the county."

"It sounds like a waste of time to me," I said airily. "This is a community newspaper. These stupid features you keep dreaming up are just a drain on manpower."

"They get a lot of hits on the website," Duncan countered, his weasel-like eyes narrowing in my direction. He thinks he looks like Tom Cruise, but it's more like he looks like Tom Cruise's cousin – the one that's been locked in a basement to keep him away from people for a decade.

"Your family clicking on your stories doesn't count," I shot back.

"I got a thousand hits on my last extreme sports column," Duncan said. "Tell her, Fred."

"He got a thousand hits on his last extreme sports column," Fish mimicked Duncan.

"Wasn't that on in-line skating?"

"So?"

"How is that an extreme sport? Little kids learn to do it when they're five. Your extreme ego column was nothing a joke," I continued. "We all thought it. We talked about it all the time."

"That's not true." Duncan looked to Fish for confirmation.

"It was pretty stupid," Fish said finally. "And I can't help but agree that we need you to start covering more community news. I'm going to let you do the dirty jobs thing, but you only get one day a week to do it. That's going on the job with them and writing the story. No overtime."

"That's not enough time," Duncan whined.

"Yeah? Well you took an entire week to write each of those extreme ego – I mean extreme sports – stories," Fish countered. "It was a total waste of time. That's the offer, take it or leave it."

"It got a thousand hits," Duncan repeated the number, in case we hadn't heard it the first three times he said it.

"Yeah? And Avery's story on the freeway shooter got a hundred thousand," Fish replied. "You see the difference there?"

"Yes, I see how great Avery is," Duncan snarled. "She's wonderful and great and we should all bow down to her."

"Only when I'm wearing a tiara," I shot back.

Duncan turned to Brick. "It's good to have someone here that sees the kind of person she really is."

Brick didn't look impressed with Duncan's statement. "I don't like her," he said. "I definitely don't like you, though."

"What?" Duncan's mouth dropped open in surprise.

"There's a reason they call you the office douche," Brick said. "The name fits – although you don't smell like a summer's eve."

Duncan closed his mouth and then opened it again. No sound came out. I wondered if Brick had rendered him speechless – which sort of made me like him. "I'll be down in human resources," Duncan said finally. "Filing complaints against all three of you."

"What did I do?" Fish asked.

"You let her talk to me that way."

Fish shook his head. "Whatever."

"I'll be running this place one day," Duncan announced. "And you'll all be sorry about the way you treated me when I am."

"Ah, a newspaper of one," I replied.

Duncan flounced out of the room, making a deliberate right down the hallway to prove that he really was going to human resources. Fish turned to me when he was gone. "Do you have to send him over the edge every time you're in a room with him?"

"It's so easy."

"Yeah, well he's crazy and you know what crazy people do when they're challenged," Fish said.

"Act crazy?"

"Exactly."

I turned back to Brick. "I have to say, while I find you to be an absolute pain, the way you poked him was pretty funny."

Brick smiled at me, the first real smile he'd ever sent in my direction. "You're not bad yourself."

"Do you need something, Brick?" Fish turned to him.

"Just to tell you that I am going to take tomorrow off," Brick said. "I'll work Sunday, but I'm going to take tomorrow and get some hunting in."

"What are you hunting?" I asked.

"Guinea hens."

"What's a guinea hen?"

"A really loud and obnoxious bird. My neighbor has a gaggle of them."

"You're not killing your neighbor's guinea hens, are you?" I asked suspiciously.

"Who knows?" Brick had a mysterious smirk on his face. "Who knows where I'll find them."

When he was gone, I turned back to Fish. "Do you ever think that this whole newsroom is just one big psych experiment?"

"You would be one of the biggest experiments," Fish said, waving me off. "Now either do some work or leave. I think you've been enough of a distraction for the day."

Yep, my work here was done.

Twenty-One

Since there was no one left to irritate at work, I texted Eliot and waited for him to pick me up. When I slid into his truck, I plastered my best "you want to do me a favor" look on my face and waited.

Eliot didn't immediately take the bait.

"What'd your boss say?"

"He said that I need to stop irritating Duncan to the point of no return."

"What?" Eliot blinked hard – twice. "You had time to irritate Duncan?"

"And Brick."

"Who – or what – is a Brick?"

"He's the new paginator in the sports department."

"And his name is Brick?" Eliot looked doubtful, like I had given him the nickname or something.

"I guess is name is actually Brandon Richard – or something like that – and he shortened it to Brick himself."

Eliot considered my explanation for a second and then shook his head. "You're surrounded by crazy people."

"Do you count yourself in that statement?"

"I'd have to be to put up with you," he teased.

"Speaking of that," I started, yeah, segues aren't my strong suit. "I have something I need to do tonight."

"What?" Eliot was immediately suspicious.

I squirmed under his pointed stare. "You see, I'm getting this, 'I don't know,' vibe from Brick."

"Vibe?"

"Vibe," I confirmed.

"And what is this vibe telling you?"

"That he's a really angry guy," I replied.

"Are you sure you just don't bring it out in him?"

"That's what he says," I agreed. "I think it's more than that, though."

"Be specific."

I told Eliot about Brick's two failed marriages and the fact that he was happily humping his current squeeze in the parking lot of the paper whenever the mood struck. Eliot looked more amused than agreeable when I finished.

"So, just because he's going through his second divorce and having sex in a car, you think he's a freeway shooter?"

When he said it like that it sounded ridiculous. "He's also an avid hunter with a military background."

"So are millions of other people," Eliot pointed out.

"His girlfriend just happens to be the secretary at the insurance office where the first victim worked," I added.

Eliot opened his mouth to unleash another retort and then closed it. "Well, that is kind of a coincidence," he conceded. "You still need to connect the dots for me, though."

"Well," I started. "Chelsea told me that her boss was always hitting on all the women at the office."

"Who is Chelsea?"

"The girlfriend."

"Okay, continue."

"You should see all the women there," I explained. "They all look like fashion models, not insurance agents."

"Maybe I should switch my coverage," Eliot mused.

"That's not funny."

"No, I'm being serious," he said. "I've been thinking about it for a while."

"You're a tool."

Eliot smirked at me and pinched my hip as he turned onto Mount Clemens' main drag. "So, what? You think the boss hit on this Chelsea and Brick went ballistic – there's a sentence I never thought I'd hear myself say – and shot him for revenge? And, what, he got a taste for the killing and now he's just killing random people?"

"Maybe," I shrugged.

"That seems like a stretch," Eliot said pragmatically.

"There has to be some tie," I pushed on. "I just have a feeling, in my bones, that something isn't right about him."

"Is that feeling propelled by anything more than the fact that you don't like him?" Eliot questioned me seriously.

"I never said I didn't like him," I retorted.

"That's written all over your face, honey," Eliot said easily, pulling into a parking spot in front of his pawnshop. "Let's say, though, just for the sake of saying it at this point, that I agree with you. What does that have to do with whatever you have planned for tonight?"

I smiled at him – widely this time. I knew I had already won. Despite himself, Eliot was curious about both Brick and Chelsea. "Well, once he gets off work tonight, he says he's going hunting and I want to follow him and see if he's really hunting guinea pigs or people."

"Guinea pigs?" Eliot wrinkled his brow. "Who hunts guinea pigs? They're in cages."

"Or, a guinea hen, I guess he said. Is there a difference?"

Eliot broke in to a wide smile. "That, right there, is why I find you so fascinating. Even when you're a dumbass, you're cute when you do it."

"I think I've just been insulted."

AT A QUARTER to midnight, we were ready. And by ready, I mean dressed all in black. Eliot had initially balked when I suggested getting dressed up for our little excursion – something Carly never would've done. Once I promised to let him play *G.I. Joe* —in bed -- when we got back, though, he reluctantly agreed.

"I feel stupid," he said when we were parked in the restaurant parking lot across from The Monitor.

"You look great," I countered. I actually meant it. There was something about the tight black shirt and black cargo pants that was giving me a little thrill.

Eliot cast me a sidelong look. "We could have sex in the parking lot, if you want?"

"That would be hard to do while we're following him," I said.

"I think I could manage both," Eliot offered.

"Let's focus on one task at a time," I suggested.

"Fine. How long are we waiting for this guy?"

"He's supposed to get done at midnight."

"Are you sure he'll actually leave at midnight?"

"No," I answered honestly. "Why would he hang around, though?"

We sat in silence a few more minutes. I could feel Eliot getting irritated. "I'm not waiting here all night."

"I'm not asking you to."

"You better be ready to yell *Go Joe* at just the right moment," he grumbled.

"That's a really weird fantasy."

"You wanted me to dress up like Han Solo and pretend to get frozen in a block of carbonite."

"I did not."

"You did, too."

"I did not."

"You did, too."

"I didn't really ask," I finally said. "I just said it might be fun."

"Is that him?"

I followed Eliot's gaze, scrunching up my eyes in the dark until I could get a clear view. "That's him."

"He's little."

"He's small but solid."

"He looks like an angry little koala bear."

I thought about it a second. "That kind of fits."

"Put your seatbelt on," Eliot instructed as he followed Brick onto the freeway. "Do you know where he lives?"

"Somewhere in the northern communities," I said. "Marysville or something."

"Marysville?" Eliot whined. "That's like a half an hour away."

"We don't know that's where he's really going," I reminded him.

"Fine."

We followed Brick north, two cars back the entire time, until I-94 narrowed to two lanes. "Maybe he is going home."

"You're still going to be a soldier of fortune for me," Eliot grimaced.

"A deal is a deal," I said. "You're building this up so big, it's bound to be a letdown now."

"Oh, it won't be a letdown."

Once Brick exited the freeway, Eliot followed him. Instead of heading into a residential area, though, Brick was driving toward a strip mall at the north end of the town. "Where is he going?" Eliot mused.

"There's no access to the freeways around here, is there?"

Eliot shook his head. "I don't think so. I'm not really familiar with this area, but the freeway is back behind us. I don't think he's hunting people tonight."

"Do they sell guinea pigs at a strip mall for him to hunt?"

Eliot fixed me with a hard stare. "You don't know anything about hunting, do you?"

"I know a lot," I protested.

"What do you know?"

I opened my mouth to answer.

"What do you know that you haven't seen in the movies?" Eliot asked hastily. "Or from reruns of *Duck Dynasty*?"

I snapped my mouth shut. He was such a know-it-all.

Eliot continued to follow Brick into the parking lot, purposely shooting down three stores before he parked. We sat in the truck quietly for a few moments, just watching Brick's truck. The lot was relatively busy for this time of night, but I figured most of the cars were there for the sports bar at the corner of the strip mall. After about five minutes, another car pulled into the parking lot. It was too dark to see who the driver was, but I could make out a dark figure exiting the driver's side door of a small white Escalade and climbing into the passenger side seat of Brick's truck.

"What do you think?" I asked Eliot.

"It's weird."

"Besides that? You think it's some sort of drug deal or something?"

"Now he's a drug dealer?" Eliot looked dubious.

"He might be," I said primly.

Eliot blew out a frustrated sigh. "Stay here. I'll try to get a closer look."

"Don't you think that will be obvious?"

"It will be less obvious if I do it than if you do it. At least he won't recognize me."

"Be careful."

Eliot fixed me with an icy look. "I'm always careful."

I watched as Eliot carefully slid between several vehicles as he made his way toward Brick's truck. He was using the other vehicles to hide his approach, I realized. The fact that he was dressed in black – my idea, mind you – was helping him hide in the shadows.

I let my attention momentarily drift from Eliot and land back on Brick's truck. I couldn't be sure but it looked like it was moving. No way. Here, too?

I jumped out of Eliot's truck with the intention of stopping him. I took a more direct route toward Brick's truck and pulled up short when I saw Eliot was staring into the truck's window from about three feet away.

"I don't think it's a drug deal," I hissed.

"They're having sex." Eliot looked disgusted. "You have me following people that are meeting up in a parking lot – in fricking Marysville – to have sex."

"Well, how was I supposed to know?"

"You knew he liked to have sex in parking lots?" Eliot's voice raised an octave. "This wasn't exactly a surprise to you."

"Like I could've known this would happen," I shot back.

The rocking in the truck had abruptly stopped and the occupants – both in various stages of undress – were in a sitting position and glaring at Eliot and I from inside the truck. I gulped when I met Brick's hard gaze. This wasn't going to be good.

Brick opened the driver's side door and jumped out of the truck, slamming it hard behind him as he did. His shirt was unbuttoned – good grief he is hairy – and his face was alive with a furious shade of red that I didn't even know existed. "Are you following me?"

Brick was only about two feet away from me when Eliot moved in between us. "It was a mistake."

"What was a mistake? That bitch following me? Getting into my personal business?" Brick was clenching his fists at his sides.

Eliot extended his hands and physically pushed Brick back a few feet. "She's sorry. We're leaving."

"You don't put your hands on me," Brick erupted. "I'm a veteran. You don't put your hands on me. No one puts their hands on me! I'm a bloody veteran, for crying out loud!"

Eliot narrowed his eyes. "So am I. You're being a dick, though. And I'm not going to let you touch her."

Brick was seething, his chest heaving as he fought to catch his breath. "Are you her girlfriend?"

Eliot didn't rise to the bait. "I said we're leaving."

"I knew she was a lesbian. I just didn't know her girlfriend would have such long and pretty hair."

Eliot clenched his jaw, but he didn't turn around. He grabbed my arm and started to lead me away.

I heard another door slam shut and turned around to see that Chelsea had exited Brick's truck and was watching us. "That's the girl that came to the office to ask questions," she said to Brick.

Uh-oh. "Hey, Chelsea," I offered lamely.

"Are you following Brick?"

"No, we were just at the bar," I lied.

"He seems to think you were following us," Chelsea said dubiously.

"He's a little paranoid." Eliot was steadily trying to pull me away so I waved half-heartedly at Chelsea. "Sorry to ruin your night."

"You better protect your little girlfriend there," Brick shouted out. "She's not going to live long after something like this. She's got a whole shitstorm that's going to come down on her – and she deserves it."

That was it. That was Eliot's breaking point. He swung around and smashed a fist into Brick's face. The look of surprise that registered on Brick's features might have been comedic under a different set of circumstances. When the punch was followed by a steady stream of blood dripping from Brick's nose, though, I realized that I really had pushed this one too far.

Chelsea looked horrified and rushed to Brick's side. "Oh, honey, are you okay?"

"I'm going to kill you both," Brick howled from the ground, where he was busy trying to staunch the flow of blood that was covering the front of his shirt.

Eliot glanced down at me. "You're a lot of work."

"This might have gotten out of hand," I admitted.

"A whole lot of work."

Twenty-Two

The next morning I woke up with a crick in my shoulder – from pretending to be an international spy for Cobra Command, something that turned out to be more fun than I initially envisioned – and a pain in my head that had more to do with the embarrassment I would be facing once I had to see Brick again than anything else.

I texted Fish, telling him I would be checking some stuff out on my own today, and then rolled over to meet Eliot's warm, chocolate eyes. He was laughing.

"What?"

"Don't want to see Brick?"

"Not really," I hedged. "I just thought a day to cool down would do him good."

"You do realize that he'll probably tell everyone at the office what happened, and you're going to come off as a crazy stalker in this scenario?"

"Actually, I don't think he'll tell anyone," I said smugly.

"Why?"

"Because then he's going to have to admit what he was doing in a parking lot at one in the morning," I explained. "And, if he somehow leaves that part out, he knows I'll tell everyone what he was doing – and I'll probably make up stuff to make it worse. He still thinks we don't know he's been doing the same thing in The Monitor's parking lot."

"You can't prove that," Eliot reminded me.

"That's not entirely true," I said. "The night Derrick dropped me off at the paper – after the kid in Roseville was killed – he personally witnessed them going at it."

Eliot lifted himself up on one elbow. "You didn't tell me that."

"I forgot."

"Liar," Eliot laughed, throwing himself back against the pillows again. "You just didn't want me to say 'no' to your little adventure last night."

"That's an ugly lie."

"Whatever."

My cellphone rang from the nightstand and I reached over Eliot to answer it. I cringed when I heard the voice on the other end of the phone.

"While you're not exactly my favorite person to talk to, I do have a few things to remind you of."

"Mom?"

"No, it's Harriet."

"I know it's Harriet," I sighed. "I was just being ... never mind, you'll never get it. What do you want?"

"I want to remind you that Carly's shower is tonight."

I froze; the phone cradled next to my ear, and turned to Eliot with a hint of panic in my eyes. "No, the shower isn't until next week," I said.

"Why would the shower be after the wedding?" Harriet's voice was clipped – she was obviously still angry from our conversation the other day.

"Her wedding is this weekend?" That couldn't be right.

"Yes, this weekend."

"I forgot," I admitted.

"Carly knew you would, that's why she told me to call and remind you."

"Why didn't she have you call yesterday?" Or the day before would've been even better.

"She might have told me to, but it slipped my mind with all the unrest over here in the past few days."

"What unrest?" I narrowed my eyes.

"Well, since you purposely created unrest between Carly and I, it's been a tense few days," Harriet replied primly.

"I didn't purposely create unrest between you and Carly," I corrected her. "Carly told me to be a bitch to you on the phone so I was."

I could feel Eliot shaking with silent laughter on the bed beside me.

"Carly says it was your idea."

She would. "Fine, it was my idea."

"I knew it!"

"When is the shower? And why are you guys having a shower on a Wednesday again?"

"We wanted to have it over the weekend, but you said that Carly had to have a bachelorette party on the weekend so that meant moving the shower to the middle of the week." Harriet was clearly enjoying the conversation now. "The bachelorette party you're supposed to organize."

"I have it under control," I sniped, grabbing Eliot's phone and using it to send a quick text to Lexie – one that informed her she would be in charge of planning the bachelorette party. I was relieved when she immediately texted back and said she'd handle it.

"The party is at 8 p.m. this evening," Harriet reminded me.

"I got it."

"Presents are mandatory."

"I bought a present months ago."

Harriet disconnected and I turned to Eliot. "What do you get someone for a bridal shower?"

Eliot started laughing. "How should I know?"

"Well, I've got to figure something out between now and 8 p.m. tonight – and it's got to be something that doesn't look like I just picked it out today."

Eliot thought about it a second. "We could go to the mall, I guess." He didn't look thrilled with the prospect.

The mere thought brightened my day, though. "That's a great idea," I said. "I want to swing by that shoe store by the food court."

"You don't need any more shoes," Eliot grumbled.

"I want to see those Black Sabbath Converse in person," I said. "They look cool online, but that doesn't always mean they'll still be cool in the store."

Eliot sighed. "I thought we were just looking for a present for Carly?"

"You don't need to go," I said pointedly. "I am more than capable of going to the mall myself."

Eliot frowned. "I would feel better if I went with you."

I sighed dramatically. "I can't take much more of this."

"You weren't saying that when I stepped between you and the angry koala last night."

He had a point. "If you want to watch me, you're going to have to go shopping with me."

"Isn't that what I just said?"

"No," I shook my head. "You said you would pick out a gift for Carly with me. That's not shopping."

"Fine," Eliot gritted out.

"And lunch at the food court."

"You're pushing it."

"It will be fun," I lied.

"Sounds like hell to me."

TWO HOURS later we were at the mall – and Eliot's mood hadn't improved.

"Why are we in a toy store?"

"I just want to see if they've came out with any new *Star Wars* Lego sets that I want."

"Really?"

"It will take two minutes."

Eliot watched me peruse the shelves for a few minutes and then he pointed. "You don't have that one."

"You remember my Lego sets? And you say I'm juvenile."

Eliot ignored the comment. "Is there a reason you don't want this one?"

"It's from the prequels."

"And the prequels sucked," Eliot nodded his head knowingly.

"There were some decent moments in *Revenge of the Sith*," I countered.

"Yeah," Eliot agreed. "The profound suck that was Jar Jar Binks, though, still brought the entire franchise to its knees."

I couldn't argue with that.

Once we left the store, I started leading Eliot toward a shoe store at the end of the ell when he stopped me. "Aren't we supposed to be shopping for Carly?"

"Yes, and we will."

"When?"

"Soon."

"Define soon."

"You're so anti-shopping."

"I don't have a problem with shopping," Eliot argued. "I have a problem with meandering around a mall and buying things you don't need."

"Define need."

Eliot rubbed the bridge of his nose. "You make me tired."

"Fine," I huffed. "I will bypass the shoe store for the day."

"Good."

"Let's go buy Carly's gift."

"What are you going to get her?"

"I've been thinking about that," I replied. "I think I'll just go with the standard sexy underwear."

"Won't that be embarrassing for her to get in front of her future mother-in-law?" Eliot asked dubiously.

"Of course," I said with a small smile. "That's what she deserves for sacrificing me to that witch."

"That doesn't sound like something you should do to your best friend."

I considered the statement for a second and then shook my head. "No, it's a great idea."

I led Eliot to the second floor and headed in the direction of the Victoria's Secret that I knew was sandwiched between The Body Shop and Gap. When I rounded the corner, Eliot started slowing his speed until he was a few feet behind me.

"What are you doing?" I asked curiously.

"Maybe I should wait out here." Eliot was glancing around to make sure no one he knew was loitering in our direct vicinity.

I pursed my lips. "I'm disappointed."

"About what?" Eliot was suddenly defensive.

"You're the big, strong man that is supposed to keep me safe and yet you're scared to go into a store that sells women's underwear?"

Eliot squared his shoulders. "I'm not scared. I just don't want to."

"That's scared."

"It's not scared. It's reluctant."

"There's a difference?"

"Can't you just go in without me?"

"Fine," I blew out a sigh. "However, if I get shot by a freeway sniper in there because you were scared to look at women's underwear, you're going to feel really stupid."

Eliot didn't look like he believed me. "If you were to get that black thing," he pointed to a lacy teddy ensemble on one of the headless mannequins. "I wouldn't complain."

I glanced at it, considering. "Maybe – if you're a very good boy. I'm a little worried it will give you nightmares, though."

Eliot's face brightened as he turned to the walls that overlooked the lower level of the mall. "I could put up with a few nightmares if you wore that."

It took me about a half an hour to pick something out for Carly. When I told the sales clerk I needed a size two she gave me a suspicious look. "It's for a friend."

When I bought the ensemble in the front window that Eliot liked – in a size eight – she looked relieved. "This will look great on you and it's much more realistic."

When I left the store, I found Eliot standing exactly where I left him. I couldn't help but notice that two women were sitting on a nearby bench staring at him – staring and gossiping – but he seemed oblivious to them. They obviously liked what they saw, but whatever he was fixated on was of more interest to him.

"You have two fans," I said when I sidled up to him.

Eliot didn't turn to acknowledge me. "Isn't that Christine Brady?"

"Where?" I asked curiously, following his line of sight.

"Right there, at that kiosk in the center of the mall."

I squinted my eyes and followed his finger. "Yeah."

Eliot watched me, waiting for me to react. "What am I not getting?"

"Do you see what she's buying?"

I shook my head and focused more on the scene below us. It took me a second but then it registered. "Is this a gun and knife show?"

"Yep."

"In the middle of the mall? Can they do that?"

"Apparently."

"What do you think she's buying?" I asked finally.

"Looks like ammunition," Eliot replied carefully.

We exchanged a furtive glance. I think he was worried that I would jump to conclusions and I think I was worried that I would, yes, jump to conclusions.

"It could just be a coincidence," I said finally.

"It could," Eliot agreed.

"What are the odds of that?"

"I don't know. I'm not a mathematician."

"Crap. This day just keeps getting worse."

Twenty-Three

"What do you wear to a bridal shower?"

Eliot was working on his laptop in the kitchen and watching me through the doorway to his bedroom as I tossed various outfits onto his bed as I mentally considered (and then ruled out) them. "Right off the top of my head, I would say clothes."

"But what kind of clothes?" I ignored the sarcasm. I wasn't really in the mood. "I don't have a lot here. Just a couple *Star Wars* T-shirts and a few pairs of pants that I've left here over the past few weeks."

"Where is it again? At a restaurant?"

"Yeah."

"How nice is the restaurant?" Eliot seemed distracted by whatever he was looking at on his laptop.

"Casual."

"Then just wear jeans and a plain shirt – and then pick up all those clothes you just tossed on the bed and put them back in the closet."

"Yes, Dad," I muttered under my breath.

"I heard that."

"I meant for you to." Not really.

I got dressed in simple jeans, my *Mischief Managed* T-shirt with both Fred and George Weasley on it – and then sat down in the middle of Eliot's living room to wrap Carly's present. Eliot glanced up at my shirt and smiled. "You think that's going to make Harriet happy?"

"That's why I wore it," I said. "Plus, it's virtually promising that I won't get into any trouble tonight."

"Yeah, a shirt is going to do the impossible."

I ignored the jab. "What are you doing?" I asked.

Eliot glanced at the sexy camisole and tap pants I held up and then folded. He raised his eyebrows a second and then glanced at me. "Where's my outfit?"

"In the bedroom waiting for you to put it on."

Eliot stuck out his tongue in my direction.

"I'm starting to rub off on you. You're getting more and more immature."

"That's a terrifying thought."

He always said that – but I'm not sure that he believed it.

I went back to wrapping, which wasn't exactly one of my gifts, and then turned back to Eliot. "You never answered me. What are you doing on your computer?"

"Trying to see if I can track down some information on Christine Brady."

"I thought I was going to do that tomorrow," I pouted.

"Does it really matter who does the leg work?"

"No, I guess," I conceded. "As long as I get credit for taking her down."

"The credit is all yours."

"Where are you even looking?" I asked curiously.

"Public records."

"So, just general digging?"

"Pretty much," Eliot nodded, never taking his eyes off his computer screen.

"You think you'll find something?"

"I've got some people I want to check with while you're at the shower. It will give me something to do," Eliot explained.

"You mean you're not going to sit here and cry because you miss me?"

"No."

"How about sitting here and imagining me in that black thing?"

Eliot cocked his head. "I can do that while you're at the bridal shower."

"You know," I said slyly. "You could text me early in the shower and I could leave for an emergency. That way, I could still say I went to the shower, but that I got inexplicably called away. That wouldn't be my fault."

"Not going to happen," Eliot replied succinctly.

"Why?"

"Because, my errands are going to take a few hours and at least I know you'll be stuck inside at a bridal shower for hours," Eliot smiled. "That makes me feel better."

That made one of us.

AT FIVE minutes before eight, I was standing outside the passenger door of Eliot's truck making my last-minute plea for him to save me. "You said you were here to protect me."

"From a crazy person with a gun, not your best friend and cake."

"I'll be your sex slave for a night," I offered.

Eliot paused, considering my offer, and then shook his head. "I can pretty much talk you into anything I want. Besides, you'll be safe here for the night, and that's the most important thing."

I really shouldn't argue with him when he was saying sweet things like that, I reminded myself. It didn't stop me. "You're being really mean to me and I won't forget it."

"Get your ass in the restaurant."

Once inside, I spent as much time slipping my jacket off in the coatroom as I possibly could before my absence would become noticeable and then I slunk into the designated party room off to the left of the facility.

Carly was sitting at the head of the table, surrounded by a bevy of women I had never seen before. The level of chatter was idling at headache-inducing. I seriously considered trying to hide in the bathroom – but that thought was fleeting. "There you are!"

I glanced up when I heard Carly's voice. She'd obviously been waiting for me.

"Sorry I'm late," I said earnestly. I knew Carly would be the only one at the party to know I was lying.

"I was worried you weren't coming," Carly said pointedly as she slipped away from the table and firmly planted herself at my side.

"Of course I was coming," I said soothingly. "Like I would forget your bridal shower. Who are all these people?"

"Harriet said you did."

"Harriet is a filthy liar."

"Hello, Avery," Harriet said stiffly, trying to sneak around me and join the other women at the table.

"Hello, Harriet." If she wanted me to be embarrassed by my statement, and the fact she had heard me say it, I was beyond it at this point. "Who are all these people?"

"I was seriously worried," Carly lowered her voice. "I thought you would use the freeway shootings as a way to get out of this."

"Well, luckily for you, the one place I want to be even less than this is at the office."

"Why?" Carly asked suspiciously.

I told her about making Eliot stalk Brick the night before. My humiliation was apparently worth it, though, as Carly cracked the first real smile I'd seen in weeks. Before I realized what was happening, she was bent over at the waist and laughing so hard her whole body was shaking. "I can just see you trying to convince Eliot that wasn't your fault," she sputtered. "And that chasing a guy named Brick around was a good idea."

Harriet was watching us from the table irritably. "What are the two of you talking about?"

"Avery's crazy co-workers," Carly said, wiping tears of laughter from her eyes.

"Yes," Harriet nodded primly. "I've heard you work with a lot of colorful people."

"What does she do?" One of the women at the table asked.

"She's a reporter for The Monitor," Harriet responded, although she looked like she wanted to be talking about anything but me.

"Ooh, that sounds exciting," the woman said. "I bet it's always something new."

"Like the freeway shootings," another woman piped in. "Are you working on that story?"

"I am," I nodded obliquely and then turned to Carly. "Who are these people, really?" I whispered the question.

"They're friends of Harriet's."

"So there's no one here that we know?"

"No," Carly shook her head. "Harriet said that, since you planned a bachelorette party that didn't include her, that she got to pick the invite list to the shower. My sister was supposed to come, but her kid got sick so she conveniently got out of it."

"Then why was I invited?" I complained.

"Because she thought she could make you look like a fool," Carly shrugged simply. "She didn't think her friends would actually like you."

"And I dressed up for her and everything," I said sarcastically.

Carly glanced at my shirt and frowned. "You better not wear anything *Harry Potter* to the wedding."

"I thought I had to wear that ugly dress?"

"You probably shouldn't piss me off since I'm the only friend you have here right now," Carly warned me. "Nothing *Star Wars* either," she reminded me.

"That goes double for me," I told her.

"What goes double for you?" Carly asked, confusion etched on her face.

"That no pissing me off thing."

Carly considered the statement and then nodded reluctantly. "You're right. We're stuck here together."

"You want a beer?"

"How about a keg?" Carly shot back.

I glanced at the women, two of whom were exchanging knitting patterns, and then bit my bottom lip resolutely. "A keg it is. You're going to need it when you open the gift I got you in front of these women anyway."

Carly narrowed her eyes suspiciously. "Why? What did you get me?"

"Sexy underwear."

Carly giggled. "That should be enough to end the party. We'll save it for just the right moment."

"Half way through the keg?"

"That sounds just about right," Carly agreed.

Twenty-Four

"What's that noise?"

I had been in the middle of a glorious dream. You know the one. It's the one where Chris Hemsworth and Chris Pine are battling for your affection with great big swords. Oh, and they're shirtless. Unfortunately, I didn't get to see who won because this really annoying beeping sound had interrupted the dream – and woken me up.

"That's your phone," Eliot muttered sleepily from beside me.

"My phone? My phone. My phone." Maybe if I kept repeating it that noise would just cease and desist.

"Answer it." Eliot threw the phone onto my chest and rolled over onto his side, wrapping his pillow around his head grumpily as he did.

"What?"

"Is that how you answer a phone?"

I knew I should have checked the Caller ID before I answered. "Mom? Why are you calling at the ass crack of dawn?"

"It's 7:30 in the morning. Why aren't you up?"

"I had a late night."

"If Eliot is holding you back from getting a full night of sleep, maybe I should have a talk with him," my mom mused.

"I think that's a great idea, Mom," I said. "I think Eliot would love to talk about our sex life with you."

Eliot groaned from beneath the covers.

"Don't get fresh," my mom admonished me. "You know I don't like that."

"Sorry, Mom," I muttered. "Why are you calling at 7:30 in the morning?"

"We have a problem."

"We have a problem? What we?"

"Our family. We're the we."

"Oh, right. Go on. We have a problem."

"Your grandfather has been arrested."

I felt the air whoosh out of me, followed by the absurd need to laugh. The laughter won out. "What do you mean he's been arrested?"

"The police came to the house about a half hour ago, put him in cuffs and took him away."

"What did he do? He hasn't been skinny dipping and resting out on the trampoline naked again has he? It's too cold."

"No, that's not it."

I could hear my mom frown over the phone. "Are you going to tell me why he was arrested or is it some big secret?"

"He refused to show up for jury duty."

"I already knew that."

"Yes, well, the situation was a little worse than we were led to believe."

"How so?"

"Apparently he just didn't not show up at the courthouse. He also ignored two notices from the court."

"Shit," I sighed. "You're kidding me?"

"No."

"What did the cops say when they arrested him?" I glanced over and noticed Eliot was now up and in a sitting position. He could only hear my end of the conversation, but it clearly amused him.

"They said that he was going to be put in front of a judge at nine sharp. You need to come home and handle this," my mom said in her best pouty voice.

"How am I supposed to handle it?"

"You have connections."

"That doesn't mean I can bully a judge."

"I thought you said you could bully anyone?" My mom reminded me.

"I was five and I was trying to get a new *Star Wars* toy out of the hands of that little snot who didn't even know what a Millennium Falcon was. He just wouldn't give it to me."

"Are you coming or not?"

"I'm on my way."

YOUR FAMILY should be studied."

I glanced over at Eliot and frowned. "You didn't have to come. I don't need to be babysat." This constant surveillance was starting to grate. Okay, really, it was starting to bug the shit out of me.

"Like I'm going to miss this." He said the words, but I knew he was really sticking close because he was convinced I was in some sort of danger. It should have been sweet, but it was really annoying instead.

"Turn here," I directed Eliot grumpily.

"You act like you don't think this is going to be fun," Eliot teased.

"I think this is going to be unpleasant."

"Why?" Eliot looked surprised.

"It's not unpleasant for me," I said hurriedly. "I'm more worried about Derrick."

Realization washed over Eliot's face. "You think it will reflect badly on him?"

"I don't think Jake would take it out on him," I explained. "I do think it couldn't have come at a worse time, though."

"Because of Christine Brady," Eliot supplied knowingly. "You really think she would use this against Derrick?"

"I think she wants to get at me and she'll be willing to use Derrick to do it," I said. "And I think she'll definitely be willing to use our family to get at Derrick."

"She probably thinks that your grandfather can be used against you," Eliot mused, half to himself. "She doesn't realize that when your family acts out you actually get off on it."

"I don't get off on it," I scoffed. Mostly.

"You do enjoy it."

"Well, they're funny."

"They are that."

Eliot pulled into a parking spot and killed the engine. He glanced over at me. "Are you ready for this?"

"No, but let's go."

After making our way through what little security the rural courthouse had, we found ourselves in the only courtroom, which was, not surprisingly, packed with members of my family. I looked for Derrick first and, when I found him, he looked furious.

"I figured they'd call you."

He glared in my direction. "This is unbelievable."

"Hopefully the judge will give him a choice of serving on a jury instead of jail," I said.

"Do you really believe that?" Derrick asked thinly.

"The judges are different up here than down by us," I said. "The judges aren't such hard asses."

"Let's hope," Derrick said grimly.

Eliot slid onto the bench next to Derrick, offering his companionable silence to help bolster my cousin. I appreciated the gesture.

"All rise."

Everyone stood up and waited for Judge Peter Watros to take his seat. He glanced up when he was settled and seemed surprised by the full house. "Bring in the accused," he said warily.

The side door to the courtroom opened and I saw that a police officer was ushering my grandfather, who was still in his pajamas (thank God he wasn't naked) to the front of the courtroom. One look at my grandfather, his robust belly, his thinning hair and the murderous expression on his face and I knew things were about to get very ugly.

"Sir," the judge turned to my grandfather. "Are you aware of why you're here?"

"Because we're apparently fascists now," my grandfather shot back.

Derrick groaned.

"No, we're here because you were sent not one, not two, but three different jury summons and you ignored them all."

"I didn't ignore them," my grandfather countered.

The judge looked down at the file in front of him again. "Oh, no, I see you sent the summons back to the court with a message written on each one. I believe it said 'go fuck yourself.'"

I rubbed my face tiredly as I tried to hide the smile that was flirting with the corner of my mouth. It wasn't funny, I reminded myself. The problem was, if I were in any other court, I wouldn't have tried to hide my smile.

"Was that wrong?" My grandfather didn't look like he cared either way.

"Sir, it is your duty to show up for jury duty when so ordered," Judge Watros said patiently.

"I didn't have time. I run a business."

"That's not my concern, sir," Judge Watros said. "You have to show up for jury duty. It's the law."

"Jaywalking is a law, and that's bullshit, too."

This time, I couldn't stifle the laugh that bubbled up – and neither could a couple of my cousins. My mom shot me a withering look.

"Sir, you do realize that if you don't show up for jury duty, that I'm going to have to put you in jail."

My mom and grandmother gasped while I cast a look in Derrick's direction. His face was unreadable.

"Fine, then put me in jail. If you want to be a dick, be a dick. Nothing is going to stop you."

I rolled my head back and cracked my neck. I knew this was going to be unpleasant. There was no way around that now.

"I'm not being a dick, sir," Judge Watros said, and I could tell he was fighting the urge to laugh, too. That was actually a good sign. "I'm trying to appeal to your sense of community."

"Oh, you're one of those," my grandfather said dramatically.

"One of those what?"

"A faggot-loving imbecile that preaches about community instead of getting a real job. You're a Democrat, aren't you?"

Derrick bit his lower lip. It was a surreal situation, but I swear he was fighting the urge to laugh, too.

The judge, however, didn't look quite as amused as he had a few minutes before. "Sir, I'm not going to put up with another outburst."

"Your honor, if I could have a moment?"

I turned in surprise at the new voice that had piped up from behind me, turning to see Jake – in his sheriff's department best – standing in the doorway. He spared a glance in my direction and then moved forward.

"Sheriff Farrell?" Judge Watros looked surprised.

"Yes, sir," Jake stepped forward. "I apologize for being late. I just got news of this ... situation a little while ago."

"And what do you have to do with this situation?" Judge Watros asked.

"I have been very close to this family for a number of years, including Charles here," Jake said smoothly. "I think this situation is just a big mistake that has gotten out of hand."

"You think that calling me a faggot-loving imbecile is a mistake?"

Jake swallowed hard and then turned to my grandfather incredulously. "Really?"

"Well, he is," my grandfather shrugged.

"Sir, I don't know if you're aware that Mr. Baker here is a fine and upstanding citizen. He's just having an ... off day."

"Sheriff Farrell, you have a great reputation in this state," Judge Watros said. "You're well known and respected. However, the defendant has had a litany of complaints against him. Do you know what they are?"

"I'm afraid to ask," Jake grumbled.

"Well, let me enlighten you," Judge Watros picked up the file in front of him. "Mr. Baker has been seen on no less than ten occasions walking in his yard naked."

"It's my yard," my grandfather piped in.

"He has killed a fly and purposely told a customer to open up and say 'ah.'"

"She was a bitch," my grandfather said. "And she knew it was a joke."

"He has threatened customers in his eating establishment when they order poached eggs," Judge Watros continued. "Including screaming that if they wanted poached eggs, they should tell him to his face they want poached eggs and, when they do, he has lobbed loaves of bread at them."

"Well, poached eggs are just stupid."

"He drove a car into the river and just left it there," Judge Watros went back to reading from his list after a brief quelling look at my grandfather.

"Lexie actually drove the car into the river," Mario piped up from his seat. "My grandfather just took credit for it."

Judge Watros ignored Mario's outburst. "He terrorized the mailman by putting rotten eggs in his mailbox because he wouldn't stop putting junk mail in it. Then there was the time he put the handset of a pay phone through the wall at the super market because he couldn't make a collect call. And, my personal favorite, he planted a series of six lilac bushes – all stolen from a public lot – and placed them in his neighbor's yard so he wouldn't have to, and I quote, look at her ugly face again. Now, I ask you, Sheriff Farrell, is this an upstanding citizen?"

Judge Watros turned to Jake expectantly.

Jake looked down at his shoes uncertainly. "No, sir, it doesn't. Mr. Baker is a colorful character, and there's no crime in that."

Jake was grasping at straws now. I had to admire him.

"I think a few days in jail might be just what the doctor ordered," Judge Watros said. "And it's definitely what this judge is ordering. So, Mr. Baker, you are hereby remanded to the city jail until you agree to show up for jury duty."

My grandfather didn't look impressed. "Go ahead, drag me away. I'll always know, though, that I was right. Because this is America and I am an American and I will fight to the death my right to call that judge a faggot-loving imbecile!"

And that was all she wrote.

Twenty-Five

"Well, that was a nightmare," I grumbled when Eliot, Jake, and I made our way out to the parking lot. I had been careful to avoid my mother as I slipped out of the building. Thankfully, she had been too busy to even look for me after my grandfather had been carted off.

"I can't believe he did all of those things," Jake rubbed the bridge of his nose tiredly. "How does one person even think of doing all those things?"

"What are you even doing here?" I turned on Jake curiously. The question came out more hostile than I had initially envisioned.

"Don't you mean thank you?" Derrick grumbled as he joined the three of us, casting a dark look in my direction. Derrick extended his hand to Jake. "I don't know what to say."

"It's not a big deal," Jake said uncomfortably, shuffling his feet.

"No, it is a big deal," Derrick replied. "How did you even find out?"

That was a good question. "Didn't you tell him?" I turned to Derrick curiously.

"No," Derrick shook his head.

"There was a memo on my desk," Jake said. "I assumed it was from Derrick."

"I would never have asked you to come out here," Derrick said hurriedly. He was obviously embarrassed by the whole situation.

"I know," Jake said, averting Derrick's gaze. "I know that you wouldn't try to manipulate me that way."

"Good grief," I muttered. "Why don't you guys just hug and get it over with?"

Eliot smirked, but Jake merely shook his head in disgust. "You're enjoying this far too much. I saw you laughing in the back."

"I couldn't help it," I protested. "I had forgotten about some of that stuff."

"He's in jail," Derrick countered. "I hardly think it's funny."

"He's not going to stay in jail," I argued. "He'll give in. Eventually."

"Have you even met him?" Derrick asked scathingly.

He had a point.

"Well, Grandma will guilt him into it eventually. He won't be able to say no to her forever. Especially when our mothers start in on him, too."

Derrick considered it for a second and then blew out a sigh. "You're probably right."

"I'm just glad he was wearing pajamas last night so he wasn't arrested naked." I was going for levity.

"Oh, he was naked," Derrick said. "The cops let him get dressed."

"Let him?" Somehow that scenario wasn't ringing true in my head.

"I think they insisted," Derrick conceded.

Jake and Eliot snickered at the visual.

Something else was nagging at me, though. I turned back to Jake. "Who would have left a memo on your desk?"

Jake shrugged and glanced at Derrick. "Who did you tell?"

"No one," Derrick said. "Trust me, I wasn't broadcasting this."

Jake turned to me. "Who did you tell?"

"No one," I said. "I got the call and came right here."

"You obviously told Eliot," Jake said, inclining his head in Eliot's direction.

"He was there when my mom called," I said. "He's convinced I'm going to be shot every time I get in a car so he insisted on coming."

It wasn't until Jake frowned that I realized he was irked by the admission that Eliot and I had been together this morning. His reaction wasn't lost on Eliot either. Before Eliot could say anything snide – and help this situation devolve any further – I jumped into the thick of things with both feet.

"I bet it was Christine."

Jake and Eliot, who had been eyeing each other distrustfully just seconds before, both turned to me and fixed me with twin piteous looks.

"What are you babbling about?" Derrick asked.

"I bet it was Christine that put the memo on his desk," I said hurriedly.

"Why?" Jake didn't look convinced.

"Because she's out to get me."

Derrick rolled his eyes. "She's out to get you so she puts a memo on Jake's desk to help me? That makes perfect sense."

"No need to be sarcastic."

"Yeah, that's your weapon of choice," Derrick shot back.

"She might not be wrong about Christine," Eliot said carefully. "There's definitely something up with that chick."

I shot him a grateful look for the backup.

"Just because she doesn't like Avery that naturally means she's up to something?" Derrick looked dubious. "If that were true, half the population of Michigan would be up to something nefarious."

"Good word," I piped in. "That word-of-the-day toilet paper is really working out for you."

"Who told you about that?" Derrick turned on me. "Did Devon tell you about that?"

I took an involuntary step back, running into Eliot as I did. "It was a joke."

"Oh," Derrick's face flushed. "I was just joking, too."

Jake rolled his eyes. "You two are like kids when you get together, squabbling over your favorite toy."

"Are not," I stuck my tongue out at Derrick.

Jake glanced at me, trying to collect himself. "Why do you think it was Christine?"

I exchanged a quick look with Eliot, deciding on the spot not to tell Jake about seeing her buying ammunition the day before. If I was wrong on that front, I would never hear the end of it and it could just be a coincidence. "You saw her at breakfast the other day," I said hurriedly. "She's clearly got it out for me."

"I don't see how that translates to Derrick, though," Jake prodded. "You have different last names."

"She knows he's my cousin."

"How?"

I shrugged. "She told me the day at that press conference."

Jake looked surprised. "She did?"

"Yeah, she basically inferred I was getting preferential treatment from you and Derrick."

"She's never even mentioned Derrick to me," Jake mused, a far off look in his eyes. "She never even brought up his name."

"I think the fact that we're related is common knowledge," Derrick said. "No matter how much I've tried to distance myself from her."

"Thanks," I muttered.

"You're welcome."

"Ludington knows, though," Jake sighed. "And this is all stemming from him."

"Because of me," I said triumphantly.

"I wouldn't be proud of that," Eliot whispered in my ear. "That just means you're to blame for all this because you drove the guy around the bend."

"I didn't drive him around the bend," I scoffed. "He was already there when I met him. I just didn't know it."

"You didn't help matters," Derrick countered. "He's still trying to dig out from that little press conference snafu you designed where you basically got every media person in the area to call him a racist for weeks."

Yeah, that was kind of fun.

"And there was the time he tried to launch his own house for wayward teens and you posted the video you had of him – from years ago – where he said that at-risk teens were all prostitutes and drug addicts," Derrick reminded me. "Where did you even get that footage from?"

"He really said it," I protested. He just didn't know I had been filming him when he'd been talking to one of his aides.

"Yeah, but you kept it," Jake replied. "That was just weird."

"I keep all the video I take of him," I said honestly.

"Why?" Eliot asked curiously.

"Because he's like a walking gaffe machine," I shrugged. "He's always going to say something that will come back to haunt him at some point." And I was always going to be happy to use it.

"Yeah, but you fixate on him," Jake said.

"He has it coming," I whined.

"Well, now he's going after you and we all have to pay for it," Jake sighed, shaking his head. "Anyway, I need to be going." He shook Derrick's hand, nodded at Eliot and then moved toward his vehicle.

"Just a second," I muttered to Eliot and then followed Jake over to his black truck.

He heard me coming and turned around. "I'm not in the mood to fight."

"Well, I am."

"Well, let's table it until I've had some breakfast – or at least some coffee."

"I don't appreciate you blaming this on me," I said.

"I'm not blaming it on you. We all helped create this situation," Jake said tiredly. "You're just the tip of it."

"Excuse me?"

"I did give you favoritism. I did step in when you were scrapping with Ludington – several times. I did let you get away with whatever you wanted pretty much whenever you wanted."

That's not exactly how I remembered it. "That's bullshit."

"Really?" Jake turned on me. "I found you at a crime scene where you disturbed evidence and I just let you go."

"That's beside the point," I said guiltily.

"I know that you blackmail Derrick for information whenever you can and I don't do a thing about it. I find it funny sometimes, mostly because he's so straight-laced at work and you lighten him up," Jake seemed like he was half talking to me and half talking to himself.

"I wish you wouldn't do this," I started earnestly. "I did this. I'll find a way to fix it. I'll fix it."

"Yeah?" Jake raised his eyebrows. "How, exactly, are you going to do that?"

"I've already started pulling Tad's financials."

Jake looked nonplussed. "So, you're going to fix this by going after the guy that's going after us because he already can't stand you? And you think that's going to make things better?"

"Pretty much."

"And you think that will work? You think you'll magically find something that will make all of this better?"

"I'm a vindictive bitch," I said simply. "I'll do what I have to do."

"Or, maybe, you could just grow up and apologize" Jake suggested.

"That's not going to happen," I said immediately.

"And that, right there," Jake pointed at me angrily. "That's why you create enemies wherever you go."

"And that's why I always win," I countered.

"Are you winning now? Because it doesn't look that way to me. It doesn't feel that way to me. Who here is winning? Because it's not us."

"Well, you just need to calm down," I said angrily. "Just take a step back and relax. I'll fix this."

"You keep saying that and yet you have no idea how you're going to do that."

"I'll figure it out."

"Yeah, you do that," Jake said bitterly, opening the door of his truck and climbing in. I'd obviously been dismissed. I moved out of the way as he started to pull out of his parking spot.

"I'll fix this!"

Twenty-Six

Eliot was waiting for me in his truck when I turned around. I trudged over to the vehicle dejectedly and climbed in. "That didn't go well."

"What?"

"I tried to tell him I would fix things, but he seems to think I'm incapable of doing just that."

Eliot was quiet as he focused on the road and finding his way back out to the freeway.

"What? You don't think I can fix this either?" I turned on him.

"I don't know," Eliot shrugged. "I guess anything is possible."

"Tad is a pain. He's always sticking his nose into something. I will find a way to get my way. Heck, for all we know, Christine is the freeway shooter and it will be a moot point," I said, glancing outside of the truck as the foliage sped by.

"Do you really think Christine is the freeway shooter?"

"I don't know. Why was she buying ammunition?"

"Maybe she likes to shoot a gun. There are people out there that find it relaxing," Eliot reminded me.

"It's just too much of a coincidence."

"What's her motivation?" Eliot asked.

"Maybe she's crazy," I replied flippantly. "Maybe she's trying to purposely set up a case that she thinks is impossible to solve and that will make

Jake look bad? Maybe she has a multiple personality and one of her personalities is a sociopath?"

Eliot raised an eyebrow. "A multiple personality?"

"I watch a lot of soaps," I grumbled.

"Maybe that's it."

"What?"

"The reason you're so dramatic."

There was a grim – and cold – tone to Eliot's voice.

"What's your deal?"

"I don't know what you're talking about," Eliot said evasively.

"Why are you being so ... cold?"

"I'm not being cold," Eliot countered. "I'm concentrating on driving."

"You're mad about something."

"Why do you say that?"

"I don't know," I replied. "You're just different. You weren't this way a few minutes ago before I ..." I broke off.

"Before what?" Eliot prodded me.

"Before I went and talked to Jake," I said succinctly.

"You mean before you raced after him and left me just standing there watching you chase after you ex-boyfriend?" Eliot's tone was biting now.

"I didn't race off," I challenged him. "I just wanted to tell him that I would fix things."

"No," Eliot shook his head. "You didn't like him being mad at you so you felt the need to race after him to make sure he still loved you just as much as before."

"That's just ... not true." I was flabbergasted. "I don't even know what to say to that."

"Because you know it's the truth," Eliot charged on. "You know that you were so worried that poor Jake might have had his feelings hurt because we spent the night together – yeah, don't think I didn't notice that little reaction – that you couldn't wait to run over there and make sure he was okay."

"That is not true," I said angrily. "I went over there because I didn't appreciate him blaming this all on me."

"It's your fault, Avery," Eliot slammed his hand down on the wheel of the truck. "You didn't do it on purpose and you didn't do it with malice, but you did do this. You did."

"That's not fair," I argued wanly.

"Why was Christine Brady hired?"

"To spy on Jake."

"That's being both simplistic and evasive. Why was she hired?"

"Because Tad felt I was getting special treatment and he wanted an inside person in the sheriff's department," I admitted reluctantly.

"That's still too simplistic," Eliot snapped. "Ludington hates Jake because of you. He wants Brady in there because it makes Jake uncomfortable. Jake has taken up your cause in front of Ludington at least once that I know of – and

I have a feeling there have been a lot of other times. He did it one too many times and now, here we are."

"You act like I did this on purpose," I pouted.

"No," Eliot shook his head vehemently. "I know you didn't do this on purpose and, sometimes, I don't even think you realize what you're doing. It's innate in you."

"What is?"

"This need to always be right."

"I don't always need to be right."

"Really?" Eliot rolled his eyes. "When was the last time you were wrong? Wait, let me rephrase that, when was the last time you admitted you were wrong?"

I wracked my brain for an answer. Unfortunately, I couldn't think of one off the top of my head. Instead of admitting that, though, I decided to make the fight worse – which was further proof of just what Eliot was accusing me of. "You're just jealous of Jake, and you have no reason to be."

Eliot's face had turned red. "I am not jealous of Jake."

"You're mad that I went over and talked to him instead of staying with you. Just admit it."

"You admit that you were more worried about poor Jake's feelings than anything else."

"No, because that's not true," I said angrily.

"And it's not true that I'm jealous of him," Eliot retorted.

"You're acting jealous."

I was frustrated. Days of Eliot watching my every move and early morning phone calls from my mother had collided with Eliot's irrational anger and now things were spiraling out of control. I could see it happening. I could feel things slipping away from me. I did nothing to stop it, though.

"Avery, you are insufferable!"

Any semblance of the cool that Eliot emitted so effervescently on a normal day was gone. He was enraged – and I was the only one in his orbit to target with that rage.

"You're not so easy to deal with either," I sniffed obstinately.

"Shut up," Eliot raged. "Just shut up for the rest of the drive. Do you think you can do that?"

I ignored Eliot's statement and turned my full attention to the scenery speeding by along the freeway. I couldn't figure out why he was so mad. I was having trouble figuring out why I was so mad. All I knew was that my gut was balled into a small knot of irrepressible anger – and it was, quite literally, making me sick to my stomach.

I endured the ride back to Eliot's pawnshop in uncomfortable silence. I was hopeful that things would blow over once we got a little space from each other. When I jumped out of Eliot's truck and headed straight for my car with just that in mind, Eliot was around the truck and his hand was on my arm in an instant.

"Where are you going?"

"Home," I said. "I need some air. You've been smothering me for days. It's not cute anymore."

"You're not just leaving."

"You're not the boss of me," I reminded him. "You're not my father."

"And you're not a child, so stop acting like one," Eliot shot back.

"Eliot," I took a deep and steadying breath. "You don't want to be around me anymore than I want to be around your right now. If I stay here, we are going to say terrible things to each other – and we might not be able to take them back."

"That doesn't change the fact that you're in danger," Eliot countered.

"You think I'm in danger," I corrected him. "I think it could've just been a coincidence. Even if it wasn't, though, I'm in no danger as long as I stay off the freeways. I'll take Gratiot back to my house." I thought it was a reasonable compromise.

"I said no!" Eliot said stubbornly.

"Well, I say yes!" I shot back. "And of the two people here, I'm the one that's the boss of me."

"You're just doing this because you know I'm right," Eliot bellowed.

I glanced around the street and noticed we were starting to draw a crowd. Theater in the street is amusing for everyone – except those directly involved. I lowered my voice when I spoke again. "You're jealous of Jake, and I don't know what to do about that. You're acting out because of that."

"Maybe I am."

I was shocked by his admission.

"Maybe I'm jealous because you're always worried about Jake's feelings. Maybe I'm jealous because Jake is always rushing to your rescue. Maybe I'm jealous because Jake looked like he was going to blow an artery when he found out we spent the night together even though we're adults and that's what adults do."

"I can't do anything about Jake's feelings," I said helplessly.

"And what about your feelings?" Eliot turned the conversation around on me.

"My feelings? What feelings?"

"Don't," Eliot took a step toward me angrily. "Don't sit there and pretend that I'm imagining all of this."

"Imagining what?" Now I really was lost.

"There's still something there between you and Jake," Eliot said. "I see it. I keep telling myself I'm imagining it. I see it, though. I'm not oblivious. It's in the way he looks at you. It's in the way you look at him."

"I'm not with Jake," I said. "I'm with you."

"Yeah, but for how long? Just until you and Jake stop playing games? Am I even a real person to you? Or am I just the guy you're going to play house with until Jake gets his head out of his ass and you grow up?"

I was stunned by the question. "How can you even ask that?"

"It's how I feel," Eliot said darkly. "Every time I see the two of you together it's like a punch in the gut. I know you have feelings for him."

I decided to try a different tactic. "He's always going to be part of my life," I said. "We grew up together. We spent years together. Every dumb teenage thing I ever did was with him and Derrick. He's my past, though. I can differentiate between the past and the present. I'm with you."

"He's in your present, though," Eliot said bitterly.

"I can't do anything about that," I said cautiously – yet firmly. "Our jobs overlap. It is, what it is."

"Well," Eliot blew out a long and shuddering breath. "Maybe I need you to cut him out of your life."

I felt as if the air had been knocked out of me. "You know I can't do that."

Eliot's dark eyes weren't angry anymore. They were just tired. "Well, I think you have a choice to make."

"I've already made that choice," I said shrilly.

"Then why does it feel that you haven't?"

"You're just overtired," I said desperately. "You just need to sleep and recharge and then everything will be fine."

"It won't be fine," Eliot argued. "I'm not just going to sit here and pretend that this isn't a real problem. I'm not going to pretend that my feelings don't matter."

"And I'm not going to be dictated to," I said quietly.

"Then I guess we both have some things to think about," Eliot replied sadly.

I guess we did – and boy was Tad Ludington going to pay for this fight. I was really pissed now.

Twenty-Seven

Once I got in my car, I thought I knew where I was going. I was so frustrated, though, that I meandered throughout the middle of the county for a full hour – just daring someone to take a shot at me in my car – before heading home.

When I got to the house, I realized I hadn't been there in days. Eliot's irritation with Lexie had basically had me ceding my home turf to her – and that just roiled up my anger anew. I couldn't understand why Eliot was being so ridiculous.

The truth was, as much as I thought Eliot was overreacting, I also thought there might have been a germ of truth in his statements. I was still tied to Jake. I did still care about him – enough that I didn't want him to get his feelings hurt. Did I love him, though? I searched my heart for the answer. I kept coming back to the same answer: Eliot was a jerk and Jake blaming me for this situation was completely unfair.

I slammed into the house and found Lexie lounging on the couch watching *General Hospital*. "Why didn't you go up to grandpa's court hearing?" I barked the question in obvious anger and I felt instant regret when the confused – and hurt – look washed over Lexie's face.

"I didn't have a ride," Lexie said. "I don't have a car, remember?"

I had forgotten. "Well, you could've ridden with Derrick."

"He left before I found out. I called him. I called you, too."

I pulled my cellphone out of my pocket haughtily. I would've heard my phone if it rang. I realized I had it set to silent and that the screen was showing three missed calls – all from Lexie. "It's set on silent," I grumbled, throwing myself onto the couch next to Lexie.

"What crawled up your butt and died?" Lexie asked curiously.

"Eliot."

"What did he do? Does he want you to kick me out again?"

"When are you finding a place of your own?" I turned to her. If I was going to be spending more time at my own house, then Lexie was going to have to go.

Lexie didn't look thrilled with the change in conversation topic. "What did Eliot do?"

"He thinks I'm still in love with Jake."

Lexie tilted her head to the side as she considered the statement. "You love him; you're not in love with him."

I pursed my lips at her attempted psychology. "What does that even mean?"

"It means that you love him, like you love me," Lexie said simply. When she caught sight of the look I was shooting in her direction, she decided to expand. "Well, not exactly like you love me. It's more of a friendship love."

"Why do you think that?"

"You guys were together for a long time," Lexie said. "You have a lot of history. Eliot should be aware of that. It shouldn't threaten him."

"He says that I'm worried about hurting Jake's feelings – and he did have a weird reaction when he found out Eliot and I had spent the night together," I said.

"Jake isn't stupid," Lexie said. "He knows he can't be with you. You have careers that aren't compatible – and lifestyles."

"Meaning?"

"Meaning that you're perfectly happy spending a night with your Xbox and a Lego game and he's got four nights a week of dinners and public appearances," Lexie explained calmly. "You're not fit for that lifestyle. Getting dressed up, making small talk with people – that's just not you."

She had a point.

"Jake knows that in his head, his heart just might be lagging a little bit," Lexie continued sympathetically.

"He dates women all the time," I pointed out.

"He does," Lexie said. "Jake is happy with the direction his life has taken. Let's be honest, when we were kids, his life could've gone to the county jail via a different route."

That was definitely true.

"Jake made a decision to choose the life that he wanted," Lexie said. "He made that decision at a young age. He's happy with his decision and, at least for now, he's set with that decision."

"And I made a decision on how I wanted to live my life," I replied knowingly.

Lexie shook her dark head and snorted through her ski-slope nose. "You haven't decided what kind of life you're going to live yet."

"I own a house," I reminded her. "I'm a reporter."

"That's where you live and what you do," Lexie countered. "That's not how you want to live your life."

"What are you babbling about? Is this some spiritual crap from those yoga retreats you keep talking about?" She was starting to bug me.

"You're not a fully-formed adult yet," Lexie said. "I'm not either. Jake is a fully-formed adult earlier than most of us. There's a reason he's the youngest sheriff in Macomb County history. He's just more mature and more driven than us."

I wasn't exactly comfortable with her lumping the two of us in the same maturity bunch. "I still don't understand what you're saying."

"Jake knows who he is and he knows that you're not who he should be with," Lexie said. "That doesn't mean a part of him doesn't want that to be different. He's drawn to you. He's got a lot of feelings tied up in his past with you. His heart tells him he should be with you even though his head knows that it would never work – at least right now."

I opened my mouth and Lexie silenced me with a look. "You know that you want Eliot, but a part of your heart is always going to belong to Jake because he was your first love. That's not wrong. It's not a slap at Eliot. It's just human nature."

"Why don't you explain that to Eliot," I grumbled.

"Eliot knows it," Lexie said. "He's just worked up right now. He'll get over it. He's addicted to you – like a drug."

"That's a scary thought."

"The three of you are just going to have to find a happy medium that you can all coexist in," Lexie said. "Jake is going to, eventually, find someone that he's actually suited for. Someone that he can love. Someone that will make him realize that maybe it's time to let you go. You and Eliot will grow up and get a little more grounded."

"I guess," I sighed. "Then Jake will get married and Eliot will calm down." The thought of Jake getting married – even if it was in some amorphous future -- gave my heart a small twinge.

"Then, when everything is settled between the four of you, that's when things are going to get interesting," Lexie said.

"What do you mean?"

"Oh, once you're an actual adult, things are going to be a lot tougher," Lexie laughed.

"I still don't know what that means."

"Once you're an adult, once you've grown up a little bit, then you're going to realize that you can fit into Jake's world and that's when things are going to get difficult," Lexie said. "You're going to stop wearing *Star Wars* shirts everywhere and realize that being an adult isn't so bad after all."

"You just said … ."

"I said you're not an adult now," Lexie replied. "I didn't say you would never be one. I said you weren't mature enough for Jake now. I didn't say you never would be."

"You're making an awful lot of assumptions," I said. "And I'm always going to wear *Star Wars* shirts. How do you know all this?"

"I have the gift," Lexie cracked a smile. "I can see the future."

"Are you smoking pot again?"

"No," Lexie scowled. "I'm just saying that I can see your future. I could always see your future. Jake is always going to be in that future – one way or another."

"And how do you, oh wise one, see this all shaking out?"

"If I was a Magic Eight Ball I would read: Ask me again later," Lexie said. "I think your future could go either way, at this point, and both directions will be good for you. You'll be happy either way."

"And what does your future hold?" I asked curiously.

Lexie smiled. "I will be rich, famous and have a lot of sex."

"Good for you," I laughed.

"Good for me indeed."

"You're going to have your own place in this future, right?"

"Just let it go."

Twenty-Eight

I didn't sleep well that night. There were no comforting dreams of Captain Kirk and Thor having a flex-off in my subconscious. There weren't even any uncomfortable nightmares about Jake and Eliot squaring off for my honor. Instead, I woke up every twenty minutes and when I finally climbed out of bed the next morning I was more tired than I had been when I had first slid underneath the covers.

After showering, I decided that I had to talk to Eliot – whether he was ready to listen or not. I left Lexie slumbering on the couch and headed downtown with a purpose. When I got to Mount Clemens, though, the courage that I had been feeling all morning suddenly fled. Instead of storming into Eliot's store and demanding that he listen to me I opted to trudge into the neighboring coffee shop and build up some caffeine courage first.

When I caught sight of a familiar figure sitting at a window seat perusing a newspaper, though, my morning took a sudden swerve and my rage had a new – or old, depending on your point of view -- target.

"Tad Ludington."

Tad lifted his face in surprise and then plastered a forced smile on it when he realized a few people had turned in our direction when I had said his name. "Ms. Shaw, so good to see you."

Oh, he wanted to play it that way, did he?

"I bet," I replied coldly. I made sure to maintain an even tone while still projecting my voice loud enough for everyone in the small café to hear.

Tad ran his fingers through his greasy black hair which – I swear – was receding at a fantastic rate. It wouldn't be long before he would have to either go totally bald or start pulling a Donald Trump to cover up the bald spot. Tad sipped from his coffee and fixed me with an overtly friendly smile. It was one of those smiles that screamed oily politician and not genuine person. "Is something bothering you, Ms. Shaw?"

Two could play this game.

"Oh, no, Commissioner Ludington," I lied smoothly. "I'm just so happy to see you. It's like a happy coincidence. I was going to call you when I got to the office and set up a time for us to have an interview. I've got a lot of questions for you. This saves us both the trouble, doesn't it?"

Tad looked suddenly uncomfortable with my fake bravado. "I'm really only here for a quick cup of coffee and then I have to be at the county building for a meeting."

"What time is your meeting?"

"What?" Tad looked confused.

"What time is your meeting?" I repeated the question. Even though there were only six other people in the room I happened to recognize at least half of them. Two of them were gossipy court clerks from the county courthouse – and I knew Tad recognized them, too. He knew, just as well as I did, that our conversation would be broadcast throughout the entire political landscape within the hour. Unlike him, though, I was getting a little charge out of the situation.

"So, are you saying you don't want to talk to me about the fact that you spearheaded a move to give the sheriff's department a public relations liaison, even though Macomb County is facing a severe financial shortfall this quarter?"

I figured I might as well go straight for his jugular. He was the reason I hadn't slept – in a roundabout away – after all.

"The sheriff's department is a source of tremendous revenue in this county," Tad replied haughtily. "Are you saying the sheriff doesn't deserve a little help? He is a public figure that toils for this county, after all."

"Marvin Potts filed a FOI request for Ms. Brady's financial information," I ignored his secretarial pandering. "She's getting far more than any other public relations figure in the county."

Marvin had sent me an email with the financial information I had been looking for some time during the night. I was ready to push Tad on the subject of Christine's pay – and I was actually looking forward to it. I had been planning on phone stalking Tad all afternoon regarding the situation of Christine's salary. This made things easier.

"I believe, if you look at similar positions in other counties, you will see that Ms. Brady's pay is on par with them."

"Wrongo, pongo," I shot back.

"What?" Tad furrowed his brows.

"Oh, I mean, you're a filthy liar."

Tad leaned back in his chair and fixed me with a hard glare. "Are you calling me a liar?"

"That's what I just said," I retorted irritably.

"I don't have to listen to this," Tad made a big show of getting out of his chair.

"Sit down," I ordered.

Tad openly glared at me. "Last time I checked, Ms. Shaw, you're not the boss of me."

"Well, news flash, I may not be the boss of you, but you're about to be my bitch." Lack of sleep makes me speak before I think. Okay, genetics makes me do that, but lack of sleep makes me irritable so I'm mean when I stick my foot in my mouth on short sleep days.

Despite himself, Tad looked a little nervous. "Ms. Shaw, if you would like to make an appointment … ."

"I don't," I shook my head. "I want to know why Christine Brady, a woman with no background in public relations, got hired to be the public relations liaison for the Macomb County Sheriff – even though he didn't request a public relations liaison – and why she's making more than seventy-thousand a year."

Tad blinked several times and fought to make sure that his breathing remained equal. "Like I said, if you check with the other counties … ."

"Michael Stevens, the Wayne County spokesman, makes forty-thousand a year," I interrupted Tad's spiel. "Janet Chandler, the Oakland County spokesperson, makes fifty-thousand a year. They both went to school for public relations and had positions at various media outlets throughout the region over the last twenty years."

Tad met my gaze evenly. The gloves were off. "Just what are you trying to say?"

"Christine Brady went to school to be a teacher," I ignored him, but my icy blue eyes never left his rapidly reddening face. "She went to school for two years and then dropped out. Between 2007 and now I can't find where she's held any job. I'm not done looking, don't you worry about that. I have to wonder, though, since she never graduated from any state school and she doesn't appear to have any public relations experience, how is she tied to you?"

"What makes you think she's tied to me?" Tad was taken aback.

"You're the one that hired her," I countered.

"A hiring the board of the commission all voted and agreed on," Tad argued.

"Yes, but you're the one that submitted her name and pushed for her," I replied.

Tad narrowed his dark eyes in my direction. "Who told you that? The minutes of those workshops are supposed to be private."

I smiled triumphantly. "You just told me, you jackass," I shot back. "I know you're up to something and I'm going to find out exactly what it is." I took a few steps closer to Tad and lowered my voice so only he could hear me. "And, when I do find out what you're up to, I'm going to bury you so far that you'll never be able to crawl out."

Rage colored Tad's face. "Are you threatening me?"

"No, I'm making a promise." I straightened back up and took a step back.

Tad was trying to maintain at least the façade of control, but I knew he was struggling not to jump up from the table and throttle me right there. "Christine Brady is a professional and she's a tremendous benefit to the sheriff's department."

"Christine Brady is a spy that you've unleashed on Jake because you're jealous and you can't stop yourself from being a tool," I countered. "You want to somehow exert some control over Jake. I'm guessing you're going to try and make cuts at the sheriff's department. And then, when the county executive comes on board and you guys lose half of your board seats, you're going to run on a platform of cleaning up the graft in the sheriff's department. All thanks to your seventy-thousand-dollar spy."

Tad looked shaken by my bold pronouncement. I didn't have to look behind me to know that the courthouse secretaries were busily texting the gist of our conversation to other people in the courthouse. If I was lucky, the news would beat Tad back to his office.

"That is ridiculous," Tad sputtered. "I want Macomb County to be the best county it can be."

"Cut the shit," I replied. "You're looking for any angle so you can to hold on to your seat. I'm not an idiot, so do me the respect of not treating me like one."

"You're just mad that you're not the sheriff's department favorite now," Tad countered. "You're used to Jake and your cousin, Derrick, giving you exclusives and making your job easier."

"Tad, I have no problem doing the work when I want the information," I laughed. "You wouldn't believe where I'm focusing my attention right now. I think it's going to make you downright ... uncomfortable. I don't need anyone to help me do my job. You're just a petty little troll that wants to pretend you have some control over others in this county – including Jake. You don't have control over anything. You don't have influence over anything. You're a county commissioner, for crying out loud," I plowed on. "You're not even one of the popular county commissioners."

"You think I don't have any power?" Tad was on his feet. He had forgotten that we were performing for an audience – or maybe he was just beyond caring. "I have more power than you will ever have, little girl."

Tad was so angry that spittle was actually pooling in the corner of his mouth. I didn't give any ground, though. I wanted him to fly off the handle. I wanted him to go too far.

"You sit there in your little cubicle at The Monitor and you think you've got me running scared," Tad continued. "I don't run scared. I'm not just going to be reelected to the commission; I'm going to be the head of it. I'm going to be the most powerful man in the county."

"Wouldn't that be the county executive?" I asked dryly.

"Not after I manage to save the National Guard base," Tad shot back. He realized what he said the minute the words left his mouth. It was too late, though. They were out and I realized the importance of them even before he had registered the error in saying them.

"The National Guard base is in danger of closing?" My mind was racing in about seven different directions right now. This was huge.

"No," Tad protested quickly. "That's not what I said."

"How do you know the base is in danger?"

The courthouse secretaries were now watching the two of us with wide-eyed wonder. The National Guard base was a major employer for the county. If it left, the county's already precarious financial situation could become dire.

"I misspoke," Tad looked desperate. "That's not what I meant."

"How are you going to save the base?" I pressed him. "What's your plan?"

"I'm done talking to you," Tad's face had gone ashen. "If I see a word of this in the paper, I'll sue you."

"Good luck with that," I smirked. "You're going to have a lot on your plate in the next few weeks."

"What's that supposed to mean?" Tad challenged me angrily.

Unlike Tad, I wouldn't let anger rule me. I wasn't going to tip my hand that I was also looking into his financials. "Have a good week," I smiled brightly.

"You're going to leave this story alone, right?" Tad asked desperately.

I cocked my head to the side. "I don't know," I said sneakily.

"What do you want?" Tad sighed. "You want Christine Brady gone? Fine. I'll make her gone."

He was really trying to blackmail me. "Oh, Tad," I tsked. "Christine Brady is going to be gone because of public outcry. You know that. You weren't counting on me pulling her financials. That was just stupid on your part. You forgot how incredibly petty I really am. Once I find her tie to your past, that's just going to blow up in your face."

Tad clenched his jaw angrily.

"I'm going after the base story now, too," I continued. "I don't need you for that either and you know it. You don't have anything to offer me on that front."

Tad's eyes were icy as he regarded me. "I wouldn't mess with me, if I were you."

"You're not me," I laughed gaily. "And that's not even all I have on you."

"What? You're going to make me look like a racist again?" Tad looked bitter.

"I guess you'll have to wait to find out," I teased. The day was definitely looking up.

"I'll call Fred Fish and make him put a muzzle on you," Tad threatened.

"Try," I cajoled him. "See what happens."

"I'm not joking," Tad pushed on. "You'll be sorry you ever messed with me."

I took a step away from Tad, never letting the smile on my face falter. "May the best woman win," I challenged him.

"Avery, I'm not kidding. You'll be sorry you got involved in this."

I had already tuned him out, though. It was like Christmas and I was the only child opening all the gifts under the tree.

Twenty-Nine

I wasn't paying attention when I left the coffee shop. I had a café mocha in my hand, a smile on my face and malice on my mind when I felt two hands grip me and slam me into the wall outside of the coffee shop.

"What the hell?"

Tad forced me into the small alleyway between the coffee shop and Eliot's pawnshop. "You weren't expecting me, were you?" Tad looked far too pleased with himself.

"No, I wasn't expecting you to go crazy and attack me on the street. That's my bad."

"You and I are going to come to a little agreement," Tad seethed.

"Let me go you crazy ass," I slapped at Tad angrily. "Don't touch me."

"That's not what you said to me when we were in college," Tad leaned in with a predatory smile.

"I was stoned in college. I used to think potato chips on a peanut butter and jelly sandwich was a good idea, too," I countered. "You get smarter as you get older. Well, most people," I corrected myself. "You, apparently, just get dumber and dumber."

"You're not going to write about the base," Tad pressed me. "You're going to let it go."

"Do you think you're a Jedi Knight or something?" I scoffed. "This isn't the story you're looking for," I mocked him.

"I'm not joking with you," Tad said. "You're going to leave this alone."

"Did you just meet me? I'm not leaving this alone. I'm going to have this in the paper tomorrow. I can promise you that."

"No, you're not," Tad argued.

"Yes, I am," I replied. "You have nothing to threaten me with and you definitely haven't built up any good will with me that would make me look the other way for a few days. So, my friend, you are screwed."

"I said no," Tad grabbed my shoulders and shook me.

Without even thinking, I raised my knee and slammed it into Tad's groin. He grabbed his crotch and slipped to his knees, groaning in pain as he did so. "You bitch."

I took three steps backwards, thinking I was making my escape from the alley, but smacking into a surprise figure behind me. I gasped when I felt two hands grab my arms from behind to steady me. I swung around and felt relief wash over me when I saw Eliot standing there.

"What are you doing?" Eliot asked curiously.

I gestured to Tad. "He dragged me in here to try and scare me off from running a story." I was a little nervous to be around Eliot, but I was also anxious to settle things with him. I couldn't go another night without getting any sleep – and, apparently, he was fairly important to my efforts to achieve that goal.

Eliot eyed Tad angrily. "You put your hands on her?"

Tad was still cradling his groin and whimpering. He wasn't so far gone, though, that he didn't recognize the glint of anger that flashed across Eliot's face. "I didn't touch her," Tad lied.

"Then why are you holding your nuts like that?" Eliot queried.

"She kicked me for no reason."

"You liar!"

"I have trouble believing Avery found her way into that alley by herself," Eliot said calmly. "It's filthy and she's lazy. She wouldn't just wander in there."

"I don't think I like what you're accusing me of," Tad stood up straighter. I could tell he was still in pain but he was trying to hide it.

"I don't think I like you period," Eliot shot back. "Why don't you find your way to your job and leave Ms. Shaw here with me to take care of?"

"I'm not done talking to her," Tad replied sharply.

"Oh, you're done talking to her," Eliot took a step toward him. "You're definitely done talking to her."

Tad shrank back, smacking into the alley wall as he did. "I'm leaving," he grumbled, shooting me a death look. "You remember what I said. If you run that story, I'll sue you."

"You can't sue me because you're the idiot that told me about the base possibly closing," I countered. "That's your fault, not mine."

Tad cursed under his breath and then left the alley via the far exit on the next street over. Once he was gone, Eliot turned to me awkwardly. "Are you okay? Or do I have to chase that little ferret down and beat the shit out of him?"

"I'm fine," I replied, suddenly nervous to be alone with Eliot. "He was never really a threat."

"He's a dick," Eliot muttered.

"How did you even know we were over here?" I asked curiously.

"I didn't," Eliot said. "I was leaving to run an errand and I saw your car. I thought you might be in the coffee shop, so I was going to look, when I caught sight of you here. I didn't realize you weren't alone right away," Eliot admitted.

I couldn't hide the small smile that played at the corner of my lips. "You were going to look for me?"

"Don't get too cocky," Eliot smiled. "I was just curious. I thought maybe you were here to talk to me."

I thought about making him fidget, but then I put myself in his position for a second and thought better of it. "I was here to see you," I admitted. "I was trying to get some caffeine courage next door when I ran into Tad."

"And that obviously went well," Eliot said.

"Yeah, all the anger and lack of sleep kind of collided and then I let it explode all over him," I shrugged sheepishly.

Eliot ran his hands down the side of my face lightly, tracing the dark circles under my eyes and then pulled his hand away quickly. "Why didn't you sleep?"

One glance at his drawn and pale face told me that he hadn't had a restful night of sleep either. "I was upset," I replied honestly.

"I shouldn't have yelled at you," Eliot sighed heavily. "I was frustrated and you didn't deserve it."

"I deserved some of it," I countered. "I just don't think I deserved all of it."

Eliot grinned. "That's some roundabout thinking there."

"So I've been told," I laughed.

Eliot's face sobered after a second. "You were right about me being jealous of Jake."

"You were right about me being worried about upsetting Jake," I said. "But I'm not worried for the reasons you think I am."

Eliot raised his eyebrows to illustrate his interest. "What does that mean?"

"Lexie and I had a long talk last night."

"Well, right away, I know I'm not going to like this conversation," Eliot grumbled.

"She took your side," I taunted him.

"She did not."

"She did, too."

"Well, then she's back on drugs," Eliot grumbled.

"Eliot," I sighed wearily, the weight of my sleepless night hitting me hard. "I can't cut Jake out of my life, you know that. Our paths cross. It is what it is."

"I know," Eliot nodded tiredly.

"I can tell you that I'm not with Jake for a reason – and it's not just because of you," I said truthfully.

Eliot cocked his head as he listened to me. "I'm not sure how to take that."

"I'm with you and I like being with you," I admitted. "Even if I wasn't with you, though, I wouldn't be with Jake. Our lives don't mesh. There's too much water under the bridge. There's no going forward there."

Eliot nodded stiffly. "I know that."

"Then you've got to let it go," I cajoled him. "If we keep circling the same the fight then there's going to be no going forward here either."

Eliot considered the statement. "I can't promise that we're not going to fight."

"I know. Promising that you'll never get mad at me has no ring of truth to it."

"Oh, I can guarantee I'll be mad at you again," Eliot laughed. "Probably this week."

I frowned at him.

"You're a frustrating individual," Eliot continued. "Don't even try to act all wounded. You know you're a walking headache."

"Then why even bother," I muttered bitterly.

"Maybe the payoff is worth it," Eliot sighed, dropping his forehead to mine briefly. "No pain, no gain."

"So now I'm a walking platitude," I pulled away and searched his gaze.

Eliot gripped the front of my coat and pulled me toward him, dropping his mouth to mine possessively. I sank into the kiss, actually sighing sadly when he pulled away. "You're a walking platitude, a pain in the ass and I couldn't sleep without you snoring next to me last night," Eliot said softly.

I pulled away, horrified. "I don't snore."

"Then you do a really good impression of my father," Eliot laughed, linking his fingers through mine.

"I think I've been insulted."

"You're fine," Eliot led me from the alley and toward the stairwell that led to his apartment above the pawnshop.

"Where are we going?" I whined. "I have to be to work in an hour."

"That's plenty of time," Eliot laughed.

"Sex, sex, sex," I muttered. "That's all you think about."

"Who said anything about sex," Eliot winked in my direction. "I just want an hour for a nap. You can snore all you want."

Yeah, now I knew I'd been insulted. A nap did sound good, though.

Thirty

I walked into The Monitor with a huge smile on my face. Not only had I made up with Eliot, I'd managed to scare the crap out of Tad Ludington and get a quick nap in. The only way my morning could've gotten any better was if someone had given me a functioning lightsaber as a gift or if I could suddenly choke people with the powers generated by my own mind.

I dropped my coat and purse at my desk and then headed straight for Fish. He saw me coming, and he didn't look happy.

"Tad Ludington is insisting on coming in here and having a meeting with me this afternoon," Fish snapped. "Any idea why?"

Hmm, to lie or not to lie? That is the question. "I had a fight with him a little over an hour ago."

"I know," Fish replied. "I heard. Apparently the county courthouse is buzzing about you kicking him in the balls."

"He grabbed me first," I said defensively.

Fish narrowed his eyes. "I should have been a little more specific. The actual quote from the courthouse was that you verbally kicked Ludington in the balls. Is there something else I should know?"

"No," I said smoothly. "Not a thing."

"Is Ludington going to say the same thing when he gets in here?"

"I have no idea," I said honestly. "My guess is that he's going to try to threaten you first and then try to compromise second."

"Okay," Fish said resignedly. "What's he going to threaten me about?"

"He let it slip during our little tiff that there's been some talk that the National Guard base is going to be closed," I said conspiratorially.

Fish raised his eyebrows, interest knitting them together. "He told you that?"

"He didn't mean to," I said. "I was hammering him on Christine Brady and he was trying to divert my attention. Kind of."

"What do you have on Christine Brady?"

"Marvin got the financials on her," I said, rubbing my hands together excitedly. "She has no background in PR and she's making seventy-thousand a year."

"That seems like a lot," Fish said. "I thought they were slashing the county budget?"

"It is. The Wayne County PR flak is only making forty-thousand and the Oakland County chick is making fifty-thousand," I said.

"And what was his rationale for this?"

"He said she was qualified and that Jake deserved the help," I said loftily. "He seemed surprised that I would bother to dig into her past. He also admitted he was the one that suggested her – which means there's something sneaky there I'm going to dig up."

"He's met you, right?" Fish smirked. "He should have known the first thing you would do is dig."

"I know. I don't know what he thought would happen when he dropped that woman into my pool and told her to attack me," I responded bitterly.

"Are you going to write a story about that?"

"What do you think?"

"Are you going to write it today?" Fish clarified his question.

"Probably not," I admitted. "There's another press conference at the sheriff's department on the shootings this afternoon and I want to see if I can find anything out about the National Guard base."

"You should ask Bill if he's heard anything," Fish suggested.

I wrinkled my nose unhappily. Bill Crowder was our main political reporter. In addition to talking to me like I'm twelve – and constantly making fun of my shoes and clothes – he was also known for disappearing every afternoon. No one knew exactly where he was going, but he always came back smelling like the bottom of a whiskey bottle. He seemed to think meeting your sources at a bar was still a viable option – even though it was no longer 1980.

"I don't need him to follow up on this," I said carefully.

Fish fixed me with a hard stare. "He's a good reporter, and that's technically his beat."

"I thought he was chasing around one of the local mayors because he thought he was banging an underage girl?"

"You have such a way with words," Fish lamented. "I think he has time to do more than one story."

I couldn't help but wonder if Fish would ever get around to telling Bill that he had time to work on more than one story at a time. I was pretty sure that Bill didn't know that.

"Can't you ask him?" My voice sounded whiny, even to me.

"I find it funny that you've been held at gunpoint, threatened at knifepoint and someone has tried to run you over – and that's all in the past six months – and yet you're scared of Bill," Fish taunted me.

I glanced over my shoulder and into Bill's cubicle. Most reporters at The Monitor decorated their cubicles with funny photos – *Star Wars* and Rafael Nadal for me, Shania Twain and female wrestlers for Marvin – and yet Bill had decked out his cubicle with a variety of photos of old, white men.

"I don't like those pictures of the old, white dudes," I said. "I think that's weird."

Fish rolled his eyes. "Those are politicians."

"How do you know?"

"I recognize Bill Clinton and Bill Huckabee."

"Well, that's sad on you," I said. "I might be able to respect him if he had pictures of female politicians, but since he asked me to type up labels for him the other day I'm guessing he thinks women have a place – and it's not in politics."

"You think, maybe, you're just stalling because you don't want to deal with him?" Fish asked pragmatically.

"That's an ugly thing to say."

"Do what you want," Fish sighed.

Yes! I knew I'd wear him down.

"He has the lead on the base, though," Fish added. "He knows the players better."

Dammit!

I trudged back to my desk and threw myself into my chair dramatically. Marvin peeked around the corner when he heard me sigh. "What's wrong with you?"

"Fish is making me talk to Bill."

"Why?" Marvin asked. "You know he's a closet smoker, right?"

"Yeah, I also know he's been having special lunches with one of the interns," I replied.

"Which one?" Marvin asked curiously.

"The tall one with the big … ."

"Boobs? Yeah, she's hot. I think her name is Chloe."

"I was going to say big mouth," I said dryly. "She told me I dressed like a teenager the other day."

Marvin glanced at my Rogue Squadron hockey jersey and Wonder Woman Converse and raised his eyebrows dubiously. "She has a point."

I raked my gaze over his "uniform" – black polyester pants, faux leather shoes from K-Mart, a white button-down shirt and an abstract tie that could've only been found in the free bin at

Goodwill – and shook my head. "Like you have room to talk."

Marvin ignored the jab. "What do you need to talk to Bill about?"

"Ludington let it slip that someone is looking at closing the National Guard base," I said. "He realized what he was doing right away, but it was too late. Fish said I have to talk to Bill about it because it's technically on his beat – even though it's my discovery."

"You should probably talk to him now," Marvin said sagely. "If you wait until later this afternoon he'll be bombed."

"How come we're the only ones that notice that?" I asked incredulously.

"Everyone notices," Marvin replied. "We're the only ones immature enough to point it out."

He probably had a point. "Fine," I grumbled. "I'll go talk to Bill. I'm not going to like it, though."

"No one does."

"The intern does," I shot back. "Although I don't think they're doing a lot of talking. I wonder if his wife knows."

"And that's why most of this newsroom thinks we're assholes," Marvin said.

"I can live with that," I shrugged.

"Yeah, I don't care either," Marvin agreed.

I wandered down to Bill's cubicle and made a show at knocking on the fabric-covered wall. "Knock, knock."

Bill looked up from his computer screen, quickly minimizing the email window he had been typing in just a few seconds before. He was quick, but I was quicker. I saw the intended recipient – and I think Chloe had a special lunch date in her future.

"What's up?" Bill asked distractedly.

"I had a news tip cross my desk this morning," I started.

"You weren't here this morning."

"I didn't literally mean my desk," I said.

"Then why did you say it?"

"I don't know," I shook my head. "I was actually in a coffee shop."

"Is this where you made a scene with Tad Ludington?" Bill asked pointedly.

"It wasn't a scene," I lied.

"I saw it," Bill argued. "It was definitely a scene."

"How did you see it?"

"It's on YouTube," Bill said.

Those secretaries were good. I knew they had been watching, but I'd totally missed them taping us. That actually made my job easier. I'd send them a fruit basket later. "Oh, well, then you're aware of the National Guard base thing he said?"

"There have been rumors about the base closing for weeks," Bill waved off my question. "There's nothing to it."

"You've made calls and checked it out?"

"I've talked to some people," Bill said. "They said there's nothing to it."

"Who are these people you've talked to?" I pressed. I had a feeling they were sitting on a bar stool in some dark dive when he asked the questions. "Was Tad one of them?"

"I don't have the antagonistic relationship with Commissioner Ludington that you do," Bill said. "He doesn't feel the need to toy with me. He tells me the truth."

"You've never slept with him," I said bitterly. "If you'd slept with him, you'd be bitter, too."

"I guess I'll have to take your word for that," Bill said. "Maybe you shouldn't be holding a grudge from college. It's not very becoming. It makes you look petty."

"I am petty."

"Well, then I guess you're doing a good job of showing that."

"Yeah," I agreed. "I'm awesome that way."

I glanced up and saw Fish watching our exchange curiously. I guess slamming Bill's head into his computer monitor was out of the question – at least for as long as Fish had me in his sights. That was going to limit my options.

"It's just a rumor," Bill repeated. "Trust me, if there was any truth in it, I would know."

"Well, I guess I'll leave it to you," I said with faux defeat.

"That's probably best," Bill agreed. "I think this is just a little above your pay grade."

I stalked away from Bill and back to my cubicle. Marvin was standing next to it waiting for me to return. "What did he say?"

"He says he's a dick."

Marvin smiled. "We already knew that."

"He says it's a rumor and he has it under control so I should just mind my own business."

"Are you going to do that?"

"I said I would."

"Yeah, but are you really going to do that?" Marvin looked doubtful.

"Of course not," I scoffed. "I'm going to go at the story my way, get all the credit for it and then do a dance around his cubicle when I'm the big hero and he looks like a schmuck."

"That's my girl," Marvin laughed. "I've trained you well."

Thirty-One

Marvin and I had lunch together to strategize. I agreed to include him on the National Guard base story – mostly because I knew my plate was pretty full right now and we had to jump on it right away. Thanks to the YouTube video, we weren't the only people to know about it.

Marvin was going to hit up some local politicians he knew and I was going to head to the press conference at the sheriff's department. We were going to keep in touch via text and email this afternoon.

"Don't tell Fish what we're working on," I warned him outside of the restaurant.

"I'm not an idiot," Marvin complained.

"Don't tell Fish what we're working on," I repeated.

"Just go," Marvin muttered.

I wasn't really worried that Marvin would tell Fish what we were doing on purpose. He's a good reporter, the best I know. He was a little kooky, but that worked for him. Like most reporters, though, he has a huge mouth and he speaks before he thinks. I needed him to keep our investigation between us for as long as possible. If Bill actually found out we were making headway on this, he would sweep in and take the credit – and I'd be damned if I let that happen. I wasn't lying when I said I was petty.

I was a half an hour early when I got to the sheriff's department, so I decided to make use of my time. After I was buzzed into the back offices, I made my way down to Jake's office.

I hesitated outside his closed door. I didn't want to do this, but things couldn't go on the way they were. We had to come to some sort of compromise. Not just for him and me, but for Eliot, too. I squared my shoulders, took a deep breath and then knocked.

"Come in." Jake's voice was muffled.

I opened the door and slipped into his office, shutting the door behind me when I was safely inside. Jake looked up in surprise. His tired eyes washed over me and I felt guilt well in the pit of my stomach.

"What are you doing here?"

"There's a press conference," I replied nervously.

"That's in the conference room."

"I know. I thought we could talk first."

Jake blew out a weary sigh. "I'm sorry I yelled at you yesterday. This isn't all your fault."

"Thanks," I replied honestly. "I don't believe you, though. I didn't come for an apology anyway."

Jake leaned back in his chair and watched me as I nervously fidgeted on the other side of his desk. "Why did you come? Because I've known you long enough to know that you really do want an apology, no matter what you say."

He was right, I did want an apology. I didn't want to trick him into one, though. Well, at least not yet. "I wanted to make you aware of some information I stumbled upon today."

"About the shootings?" Jake looked surprised.

"No, not about the shooting," I said hurriedly. "I feel bad about getting you into this situation but not bad enough to risk my story."

"Of course," Jake said. "I should have known that. So, what information did you stumble on?"

I told Jake about my run-in with Tad, including his accidental tip about the base. Jake listened as I recounted our encounter. His face had turned an ugly shade of red by the time I was done. "He grabbed you and dragged you in an alley? That asshole needs a butt kicking."

"I kicked him in the nuts," I said easily. "It's fine."

Jake's face split into a wide grin. "You kicked him in the nuts?"

"Yeah," I said. "Then Eliot showed up and threatened him some more. I don't think he's going to be a problem. At least for a few days. Although," I mused. "He did set a meeting with Fish for this afternoon. He's going to try and threaten him to put a muzzle on me. His words, not mine."

"Will Fish fall for that?"

I shook my head. "Fish hates him. He's going to play nice because of the politics involved, but he won't bow down to the little king."

"Well," Jake breathed in deeply, considering the new information. "What do you think?"

"I have Marvin trying to feel out some contacts about the base," I said. "I think that Bill is lazy and just believes what people tell him because he doesn't want to do the work to dig. Tad is freaked out, that I know. There has to be some truth to those rumors."

Jake pursed his lips. "Do you think this somehow ties to the shootings?"

"I don't know," I admitted. "I can't rule it out, but I don't think we have all the pieces yet."

"Let's say it does tie into the shootings, how would that work?" Jake asked.

"Maybe Turner is trying to prove that the base is important to the area for more than employment," I suggested. "Maybe he's set it up so someone from the base can swoop in and save the populace from the shooter?"

"That's a reach," Jake said. "There are other ways to prove the worth of the base."

"I'm not sure the base has anything to do with the shootings anyway," I admitted. "I talked to a guy, and he told me that the shots weren't particularly difficult. That doesn't sound like someone that has military training."

"You talked to a guy?" Jake asked dubiously.

"He was at the gun range."

"Ah, a friend of Eliot's," Jake said stiffly.

"He was a nice guy," I protested. "He said that the shots were on a flat plain and that doesn't necessarily mean that the shooter has military training."

"I know," Jake said irritably. "We have experts of our own. How come you haven't printed that yet?"

"It's just one man's opinion," I said pragmatically. "I need more than that."

"Have you considered that the shooter really is a trained sniper and he's trying to cover up that fact and picking easy shooting perches as a counter measure?"

"I have," I said. "I've been following other leads on that front."

"What leads?" Jake asked suspiciously.

"That's for me to know," I said. "It has nothing to do with you."

"Fine," Jake grunted.

"Fine," I agreed. There was no way I was going to tell him about my suspicions regarding Christine and Brick. I would either look really smart or really stupid – and I wasn't sure if either of them were really involved. Since I disliked them on a personal level, I was afraid that was clouding my judgment. "What do you think about the Christine information?"

"I had no idea how much money she was making," Jake admitted.

"It's not coming out of your budget?"

"No. I haven't received her paperwork yet. I was told that I wouldn't have to worry about covering her salary until the next quarter and that the planned retirements from the sheriff's department would easily cover it."

Hmm. "Do you have any authority over her?"

"I am the sheriff," Jake replied blandly. That wasn't really an answer, though.

"I'm going to do a story on it."

"Ludington isn't going to talk to you on the record," Jake said.

"He doesn't have to," I smirked. "One of the court clerks from circuit court was in the coffee shop. She taped our fight and uploaded it to YouTube. It's already all over the place."

"No one told me," Jake said.

"Maybe the gossip mill hasn't hit over here yet."

Jake raised his eyebrows doubtfully.

"Maybe no one wants to tell you because you're so grumpy?"

"That's probably the truth," Jake sighed, running a hand through his hair. "Do you think this is enough to get her canned?"

"I think that public outcry over paying a woman to do nothing when you could be paying law enforcement to keep the public safe is going to be too much for Tad," I said smugly.

Jake smiled. "You do have a knack."

"And I didn't even have to use the Giannone money stuff I found," I said. "I can hold onto that for the next time he pisses me off."

"He's going to put up a fight," Jake warned me.

"He's more worried about the National Guard base," I said. "He's pinning his reelection hopes on that. He wants to get me, but he wants to keep his cushy job more."

"You're probably right."

"When are you going to learn? I'm always right."

Jake considered the statement for a second and then laughed. "You're persistent. I'll give you that."

Jake slowly got up from his chair and walked around the desk, stopping in front of me. "I am sorry," he said finally. "I jumped all over you and this wasn't really your fault."

"It was partially my fault," I argued. "I keep going after Tad. He was bound to go after me. I just didn't realize he'd use you to do it."

"He'll go after you again," Jake said.

"He will," I said. "Hopefully he'll leave you out of it next time, though."

"Well," Jake blew out a relieved sigh. "I am sorry."

"You don't have to be sorry."

"Just accept the apology," Jake growled.

"Fine, you're sorry."

Jake reached for me awkwardly, pulling me close to him and hugging me. It wasn't a romantic hug, but it was one that encompassed decades of friendship and intimacy. I sank into the hug, relieved that the immediate crisis seemed to have passed. I knew that I would piss him off again – and probably soon – but, for right now, we were okay. That thought quickly fled, though, when the door to Jake's office popped open.

We both glanced up in surprise. When Jake recognized that it was Christine standing in the doorway, he took a step back from me and fixed her with a hard glare. "You don't knock?"

Christine frowned at the two of us. "I was under the impression you were alone, not feeding information to a reporter before a scheduled press conference."

"He wasn't feeding me information," I argued. "We were talking about something personal."

"And what would that be?" Christine raised her perfectly manicured eyebrows speculatively.

"I said it was private," I shot back. "That means it's none of your business."

"The trail of information from this office to the media most certainly is my business," Christine argued.

"We weren't talking about the case," I lied. "We were talking about a family matter."

"Your family or his?" Christine asked pointedly.

"Does that matter?" I challenged her.

"It matters because I don't believe you," Christine said. "I think you were getting inside information. Something that has been strictly prohibited since my hiring."

Jake looked incensed. "I'm the sheriff," he said stiffly. "I don't answer to you. You're my employee."

"The county is paying my salary," Christine said haughtily. "I'm their employee."

"Not for long," I snarked.

Christine glanced at me warily. "What is that supposed to mean?"

"Go on YouTube and type in my name and Tad Ludington," I suggested. "You're going to find several videos, we have a long history. The newest one, though, is going to be of particular interest to you."

"And why is that?"

"Well, it shows me questioning him about your exorbitant salary and lack of public relations background," I replied honestly. "I'm going to want a statement from you, on the record, about why it's appropriate for a financially struggling county to be paying you $70,000 for an unnecessary job that you're not even remotely qualified for."

Christine visibly blanched. "Who told you that?"

"I pulled the financial documents," I said smugly. "That's public record. You can't hide that."

"And you think you can bully Commissioner Ludington into rescinding my contract?" Christine looked doubtful.

"I think that Tad has bigger things on his mind now," I replied snottily. "I think the Christine Brady experiment is going to be something he's going to be happy to end pretty quickly."

Christine shook her head angrily. "You're so smug. You think you're always going to just get your way, don't you?"

"I think, in this case, the best possible outcome for everyone involved – with the exception of you, of course – is going to be getting rid of the sheriff's department public relations liaison," I replied snottily.

Christine turned to Jake incredulously. "Are you going to let her dictate your office labor policies?"

"No," Jake shook his head. "I'm going to handle that myself."

Christine turned to me with a triumphant look on her face. I cast a sideways glance at Jake. I wasn't sure where he was going with this.

"Christine," Jake said quietly.

She turned to him expectantly. "Yes, Sheriff Farrell?"

"You're fired."

This really was turning into a magnificent day.

Thirty-Two

I excused myself from Jake's office after he lowered the boom on Christine. I could still hear her screeching from beyond the closed door when Derrick came out of his office across the hall a few minutes later.

"What is that about?"

"Jake just fired Christine." I was trying to be subdued, but I couldn't hide the whiff of glee that was emanating from me.

Derrick raised his eyebrows in surprise and then ran a tired hand over his jaw. It took me a second to realize he was trying to cover up a smile. "That's terrible," he said finally.

"I know," I agreed, averting my gaze from his. "It's awful when someone loses their job." If our eyes connected, I knew we would both burst out laughing.

Derrick cocked his head as he listened to Christine's shrieks from Jake's office. "Were you in there when she was fired?"

"I was."

"How did she take it?"

"Not well."

"Huh."

"Yep."

"We should probably go down to the conference room now and not keep loitering around out here," Derrick said thoughtfully.

"Yeah, we don't want to look like ghouls trying to pick apart her corpse when she comes out," I agreed.

"You need to stop watching so many horror movies," Derrick complained as we started moving down the hallway.

"I just watched the whole *Crystal Lake Memories* documentary," I said suddenly. "It was like seven hours of gossiping and backbiting – with special effects documentaries."

"Those movies are terrible."

"Bite your tongue. Those movies are awesome and, for some reason, I can't help but be reminded of Christine when I think about it."

"Ax in the face?"

"Female camper being beaten against a tree in her sleeping bag," I countered.

"Yeah, that was a great death. Those movies still suck, though."

AFTER the press conference, I returned to The Monitor to file a story and check in. Marvin was waiting for me when I got there, hopping up and down like a nervous bird as he did.

"Did you find anything?"

"I talked to the Harrison Township supervisor," Marvin said in a low voice. "He says that the base has been targeted before, but they've always managed to get out of it. He says that he hasn't heard anything recently about the base but he's going to make some calls."

"How would Tad know and yet the Harrison Township supervisor wouldn't?" That didn't make any sense.

"That's a good question. Maybe something else is going on?" Marvin looked thoughtful. He's goofy in general, but when he's sniffing out a story he's as professional as they come.

"Well, keep pressing," I said. "I don't know what else we can do besides that right now. I have to think that something is up. The more I think about Turner calling me into his office, the more I wonder if he was trying to sound me out."

"About what?"

"About the possible closure of the base," I replied simply. "He just used the shootings as a screen. Or, maybe, the shootings are all tied up into the base possibly closing and he was trying to get control of both stories."

"I know you like to fancy yourself the queen of the reporters, but there are more holes in that theory than a prostitute's nylons."

"What do you think then?"

"I'm don't think anything yet," Marvin replied. "We have to keep digging. Jumping to conclusions is just going to skew us off course."

I hate it when Marvin has more reason than I do. "Fine."

I cranked out my story and then left for the day. Tonight was Carly's bachelorette party and I had to check in with Lexie to see what we had planned. Back at my house, Lexie was a bundle of excitement and nerves.

"What are you up to?"

"Why do you assume I'm up to something?" Lexie asked innocently, smoothing down her lavender tank top.

"If you were any guiltier an inverted cross would've appeared on your forehead."

"You're always so suspicious," Lexie sighed.

"So, what's the plan?"

"I got a limo to take us to Ferndale," Lexie replied.

"Ferndale? Why?"

"We're going to Pompeii," Lexie said simply.

"The gay strip club?"

"Yup."

"Why there?"

"Because it's fun and safe," Lexie replied. "We can go wild and not worry about anyone hitting on us."

"They're male strippers, right?"

"Yes, they're male strippers," Lexie rolled her eyes irritably.

"So, we're going to be watching men get naked with a bunch of other men?"

"Yes," Lexie's voice was sharp. "If you don't like it, then you should have planned it yourself like you were supposed to."

"It's fine," I said. "It will probably be fun."

"It will be fun," Lexie grumbled.

"Who is coming?"

Lexie handed me a sheet of paper with a list of names on it. I perused the list curiously. "There's like twenty people here."

"You, me, Carly's sister, her sister-in-law, her mother, all your friends from college," Lexie nodded. "That's a normal guest list, isn't it?"

Oh, holy hell. "What is Harriet's name doing on this list?"

Lexie looked confused. "Isn't that her future mother-in-law?"

"Yes, Satan is going to be Carly's mother-in-law," I agreed.

"You can't not invite her. That's just rude."

"Since when do you care about being rude?" I asked honestly.

"I called Carly's mom for a list. She included Harriet. Take it up with her."

As much as I loved Carly's mom, I had no intention of fighting her on something like this. Not only did I think she could take me, I had once seen her get so drunk she thought the cement duck on her front porch was real. That was a whole level of crazy I wasn't in the mood to deal with.

"It's fine," I said forcefully. "We've got a limo. I can get falling down drunk. Maybe Harriet is fun when she's got some liquor in her?"

"Plus, we'll be at a gay bar," Lexie replied brightly. "Who doesn't love that?"

Given what I knew about Harriet, I had a feeling that going to a gay bar was the last thing she would want to do. For that reason alone, I was starting to warm up to the idea of going to Pompeii.

AT A FEW minutes after eight, a long black limo was parked at my curb. When Lexie and I climbed in, we were both surprised to find a pall over the inhabitants of the limo.

"What's up?" I asked Carly warily, casting a glance at her mother and Harriet worriedly.

"Nothing," Carly waved the duo off dismissively. "They just found out we're going to a gay bar."

I pulled a flask out of the small purse I had chosen for the night – one that I could slip over my neck and not have to worry about losing – and handed it to Carly. She didn't even ask what was in it before she took a swig. I had a feeling that fifteen-minute ride from her house to mine had felt four times as long as it really had been.

"It will be fun," Lexie said, sliding into the seat next to me and casting a dubious look in Harriet's direction. "We could drop you two off back at home if you want?"

I turned to Carly's mom and Harriet hopefully.

"Of course we're not going to miss the bachelorette party," Harriet said primly. "That would be unconscionable."

"You're just worried I'll get drunk and cheat on Kyle," Carly scoffed, handing the flask to her sister wordlessly.

"We're going to a gay bar," I said sagely. "You'd have to grow a penis for that to happen."

"Give me another drink," Carly instructed. "Maybe if I get drunk enough that will be possible."

Harriet ignored Carly's crass response and turned to me. "Who else are we picking up?"

I looked to Lexie expectantly. "It's just us in the limo," she said. "Everyone else is meeting us there. They all lived on the west side of Detroit and in Oakland County, so it didn't make sense to pick them all up."

It took about twenty minutes to get to Ferndale and, by the time we got there, my flask was empty. Harriet's dislike of our drinking had only propelled the three of us to keep doing it for the entire ride.

Once we got to the bar, I was relieved to see a lot of familiar faces waiting for us outside. I didn't know everyone there – Carly had been a member of an academic sorority at college, so a lot of the people in attendance were her friends and not mine – but there were enough former college comrades to keep me busy for the next few hours.

The hostess, a strapping young man in a white evening gown, led us to our table and told us someone would be by to get our drinks in the next few minutes. The bar itself was packed. I took the opportunity, once we were seated, to get a better look at our surroundings.

I don't know what I had been expecting, but this wasn't it. Television and movies had informed my knowledge of gay bars in an unfortunate way. There were no cages hanging from the ceiling – which was a relief – but it did look like a hundred glow sticks had exploded everywhere.

After ordering something called a Typhoid Mary – which I was assured was just a fancy

Bloody Mary – I turned to Carly. "Is this what you wanted?"

"This place looks fun," Carly enthused.

"I'm sorry about Harriet being here," I said ruefully. "I left Lexie in charge of the guest list."

"You know what?" Carly said saucily. "I don't give a crap about Harriet anymore. The wedding is almost here and I'm going to have a good time tonight."

"That's good," I laughed.

"We're definitely going to have to dance later," she said, motioning to the packed parquet area in the middle of the bar. I have negative rhythm, but I figured that no one would notice in a busy atmosphere like this one.

"I think they have a floor show first," Lexie said, settling into the seat on my right. "After that I've heard it's a free-for-all."

That should be fun. I was happily sipping my third Typhoid Mary when I heard the unmistakable sounds of YMCA start bellowing from the speakers. I turned to the stage behind the dance floor expectantly and was rewarded with about twenty Village People – and then some -- and they were all dressed in unique ways.

"So they've got a construction worker, a cop, a fireman, a Renaissance knight, a soccer player, a horse rider in assless chaps and a priest," Carly mused after a few minutes. "That's a group you don't see every day."

"I like the assless chaps, although I'm not sure they were designed for twerking," I added after a few minutes of watching.

"They've got unique rhythm," Lexie agreed.

"This is obscene," Harriet complained when the fireman came up behind her and wrapped his sparkly hose around her neck, gyrating behind her chair rhythmically.

"Put a dollar in his belt and he'll go away," Carly suggested helpfully.

Harriet looked doubtful, but did as she was told. This only caused the faux priest to come over and join the fray behind her back. I couldn't help but notice that Harriet's eyes kept widening as more and more bare-chested boys filed into the open area behind her.

The sudden flash of a cellphone camera surprised me. I looked to my left and watched Carly as she happily snapped pictures of her future mother-in-law. Thankfully, Harriet was too blinded by muscles, glitter, thongs and sweat to notice. A scantily-clad doctor was trying to get her to tie him up with his stethoscope at the present moment, and she looked a little less resistant than she had only moments before.

"What are you doing?"

"Blackmail material for after the wedding."

"Good thinking."

It was almost two in the morning when we finally left. Harriet and Carly's mom were both drunk off their asses – as were the rest of us – but everyone was raving about what a good time they had when we said our goodbyes on the sidewalk in front of Pompeii.

It took both Carly and I to shove Harriet into the limo; she was mostly dead weight at this point. I had no idea how Carly and her sister were going to get Harriet and her mom into the house once Lexie and I were gone – but I figured that was their problem.

Just as I was about to get into the limo, my attention was drawn to a group of guys smoking – either hand-rolled cigarettes or pot, I couldn't be a hundred-percent sure which – just outside the front door.

"Did you guys have fun?" One of the guys asked.

"Yeah, it was great," I replied honestly. "I wasn't sure a bachelorette party at a male gay bar was going to be a good idea, but they should offer that in the Zagat's guide for Detroit."

One of the guys, an attractive blond with an easy smile, barked out a laugh. "Make sure you tell your friends that gay people are more than the stereotype. We don't just want to sit around and play with each other's lightsabers."

What? I glanced down at my glitter Princess Leia shirt and smiled back at him. "I like the stereotype," I admitted.

"You go girl," the guy drawled, clearly pandering. His southern accent sounded real, even though he was clearly turning on the southern charm just for my benefit.

I smiled, despite myself. I turned to climb into the limo but was momentarily distracted by the sound of fireworks and a sharp breeze that moved past my left cheek when I tried to duck down.

I pulled back in surprise. "Is someone lighting off fireworks?"

I turned to the guys behind me and was shocked to see that they'd all hit the ground behind the limo. The wall where they had just been standing, though, had a big hole in the middle of it that I could swear hadn't been there a few minutes before.

"What's going on?" I started to straighten up, but the blond guy had crawled over to me and was dragging me back down on the ground next to him.

"They're shooting at us, girl! Get your fool head down."

Thirty-Three

The Ferndale cops were on the scene in less than five minutes. My level of intoxication had gone from a hundred to zero – okay, twenty – in that same amount of time. While, in general, I detest police officers on moral ground – they're usually jerks to me – I had to admit that the Ferndale cops were a different breed.

"Ma'am, you should really sit down. You've had a shock."

I glanced at the young police officer, who had insisted we go back inside of Pompeii for questioning, curiously.

"I'm fine."

"You were shot at," the officer corrected me. "You could've died. If you need to vomit, I'll understand."

I glanced around the bar, which had emptied out pretty quickly once the police had shown up. "I'm fine. I'll just keep drinking water. I don't think vomit will be an issue."

A different police officer, one who had a few more years on him, picked his way through the crowd and across the bar – which the cleaning staff were busily trying to scour – and headed toward me.

"I'm Detective Mohan," the officer introduced himself. "Can you tell me what happened?"

"I really didn't see," I said honestly. "I was getting in the car when I thought I heard fireworks. I felt something kind of fly by my face and then the next thing I know the guys behind us were yelling about being shot at."

"There's a slug in the wall," the officer said carefully. "What we're trying to ascertain is if you were the one being shot at or if they were?"

"It was probably me," I admitted.

"Why do you say that?"

I rolled my tongue in my mouth as I pondered the question. In the end, I told the detective everything – well, mostly everything. There was no sense of lying, I realized. My ties to the freeway shooter story were going to be pretty easy to dig up. When I was done, I waited for Detective Mohan's response. To his credit, he handled things a lot better than most of the cops I knew would have.

"You think this was the freeway shooter?"

"Who else?" I shrugged.

"Maybe the shooter was aiming for the men that were behind you? There are still people that dislike the gay lifestyle." I could tell Detective Mohan was trying to feel me out – to see if I was a kook or something.

"If this had happened in Macomb County, I might buy that," I said. "This is Ferndale, though. It's very gay friendly."

"And what were you doing at a gay bar?"

"Bachelorette party," I replied simply.

Detective Mohan nodded, like what I had just told him was normal. Maybe, for Ferndale, it was. "That would mean someone followed you here from Macomb County?"

"It's not like it's that far," I said.

"No but, if you're right, you would've been a specific target and not someone just randomly gay bashing."

I considered the statement. "Which one is worse?"

Detective Mohan just shook his head. "I have no idea."

I took a swig from the bottle of water on the table next to me and glanced around the room as Detective Mohan talked to another officer a few feet away. Carly was trying to calm her mother and Harriet down because both were near hysterics. Lexie was staying close to the far wall, suspiciously eyeing the cops that passed her. Even though I was fairly sure she wasn't holding tonight, I don't think she was going to look at law enforcement with anything but suspicion any time soon.

"Is she in here? Where is she?"

I swung around when I recognized the voice. Jake was here. He must have been notified as soon as it happened for him to get here so quickly. It had only been about forty-five minutes. Jake strode into the room like he owned it, authority swirling around him, despite the fact that he was in simple jeans and a sweatshirt. His eyes scanned the room with a hard purpose, only softening when he saw me sitting at the table alone. He moved toward me swiftly, Derrick close on his heels.

"Are you alright?"

I didn't answer him right away. The third figure that had walked into the room with Derrick and Jake was something of a surprise to me. Eliot.

"I'm fine," I said.

Eliot was by my side in seconds, his hands on my arm – gripping my elbow tightly. "Were you hit?"

"No," I shook my head. "I didn't even realize what was happening until it was over."

"Someone took a shot at you and you didn't notice?" Derrick's face was pale. If I didn't know better, I would think he had been worried. "Where's Lexie?"

I gestured toward the far wall and watched Derrick move toward his little sister. They had a torturous relationship, but Derrick loved Lexie – almost as much as he wanted to throttle her most days.

"Exactly what happened?" Jake asked Detective Mohan. He listened as Mohan recounted what he knew and then turned to me angrily. "I thought you were going to be careful?"

"It was a bachelorette party," I argued. "We went in a limo. How was I supposed to know that someone would follow me?"

"Because you're you," Jake shot back.

Eliot was being largely silent, but I could feel the anger radiating off of him. I squeezed his hand reassuringly and then turned on Jake. "You act like this is my fault?"

"Whose fault is it?" Jake challenged.

"We don't know that they were aiming at me," I said.

"We don't know they weren't," Eliot said quietly. "Odds are, you were the target."

"What odds? It could've been someone randomly gay bashing." I knew I was grasping at straws, but I didn't like the look of helplessness that was washing over Eliot's face. If he'd been intent on babysitting before, this was going to send him over the edge. And I'd been having such a good day before this.

"Do you believe that? Really?" Eliot's voice was calm, but I could tell he was straddling a precipice here. What he really wanted to do was sling me over his shoulder and lock me in his apartment until this was all over with.

"There were a group of men standing right behind her," Detective Mohan said. I could tell he was trying to help me.

"How close was the bullet to her?" Jake asked Mohan pointedly.

Mohan looked uncomfortable under Jake's scrutiny, so I answered for him. "Not close at all."

Mohan raised his eyebrows at my flagrant lie. Eliot didn't miss the gesture. "How close was the bullet to her?"

"She felt it breeze by her cheek," Mohan replied, averting his apologetic green eyes from my accusatory blue ones.

Eliot's grip tightened on my arm. "You felt it breeze by your cheek?"

"It was probably just the wind."

Jake shot me a disappointed look. "You must be tired. That was one of your weaker lies."

"I'm probably still drunk," I retorted. "Give a few more minutes to sober up and I'll come up with something better."

Derrick was back and he'd brought Lexie with him. "I'm sending Lexie back with Carly and everyone else."

Jake nodded in agreement. "Make her stay the night at Carly's house. Don't send her back to Avery's place."

"Why?" I asked curiously.

"Because someone might try again at your house," Jake said honestly.

Lexie's face was white and she didn't put up an argument when Derrick led her back to Carly. After a brief conversation, Carly glanced at me and then left with Lexie. I knew she had questions, but she was smart enough not to ask them now.

Once they were gone, Derrick turned to Jake. "So what do we do with Avery?"

"I think we should put her in a safe house," Jake said, never turning to me as he spoke.

"That's not going to happen," I scoffed.

Eliot glanced down at me. "If we all think that's the best way to do this, then that's exactly what's going to happen."

"If all three of you think that's the best thing for me then that's what's going to happen? I don't think so."

Jake ran his hands through his hair in frustration. "Do you want to die?"

"I'm not convinced I was the target." That was a lie, but there was no way I was going to go and sit in some safe house for God knows how long.

"Don't be a pain," Derrick ordered. "This is serious."

"You think I don't know this is serious?" I practically exploded. Jake and Eliot looked taken aback by my sudden fury. "I know this is serious. I also know I have a job to do and I'm not going to let you three – no matter how noble you think your intentions are – dictate how I live my life!"

"We're trying to protect you," Derrick countered. "Have you taken that into consideration?"

"Have you considered that, if someone really wants to hurt me, that they might hurt someone else if they can't find me?"

"Oh, so now you're doing this for the greater good?" Derrick shot back incredulously. "You're unbelievable. You've been like this since you were a kid. You're going to get your way, no matter what you have to do to get it. This is just like the time that you told grandpa that you saw news reports about a rabid yeti because you didn't want to go camping."

"You can't prove that there's not a yeti out there," I muttered. "And I was five. Pick a more recent example."

"Okay, how about the time that you were late for school because you were smoking pot with that town loser Johnny Frank and you told the principal that someone mugged you on your way to school and stole your book bag?"

"That could've happened, too."

"And yet you didn't want to file a police report because you believed in giving people second chances?"

I hated that Derrick knew all of my embarrassing secrets. I really hated that he announced them to everyone whenever the whim hit.

"Yes, fine, you got me," I rambled angrily. "I tell lies when I don't want to do something."

"It's a crime to tell a lie to a cop," Derrick said cagily.

"Well then, lock me up officer," I replied snidely, holding my wrists out in front of me. "Slap on the cuffs."

Derrick looked like he was about to do just that.

"Just remember, I know a few things about you, too," I seethed. "And not just about how you used to wear dresses in college."

"That was a fraternity prank!"

"Then why did you do it in high school, too?"

"I didn't do it in high school!" Derrick was enraged now. "You just told people that because you thought it was funny."

"You did, too, do it in high school. I have pictures. You were wearing that purple dress I had to make for home ec."

"That doesn't count," Derrick replied. "You had two hours to make that dress and my mom made me model it. It's not my fault that you made it so small that no one else could fit into it. I sat in that thing for two hours while you purposely poked me with needles every chance you got."

I smirked. That was a funny memory. "I'll put that picture up on the internet," I threatened him.

Jake decided to step in. "You don't have any pictures of me in a dress," he reminded me. "You can't threaten me."

"I know your secrets, too," I warned him. "I was there the night you got arrested for peeing on the big fish downtown."

"That story is public," Jake said. "What else have you got?"

Crap. He was right. "I know that you used to practice kissing on a stuffed frog," I said triumphantly.

Jake's cheeks reddened, while Eliot regarded him curiously. "You kissed a frog?"

"I was twelve," Jake answered. "She told me that everyone practiced kissing on stuffed animals – and I believed her."

Eliot shook his head, smiling despite the surreal nature of the situation. "You were really a mean kid, weren't you?"

"Mean? He was just an easy mark."

Jake blew out a sigh. "Fine. I'm not going to make you go to a safe house, but you're going to have to agree to some rules."

Uh-oh. "What rules?"

"You're not to go anywhere alone." I opened my mouth to protest, but Jake shut me down. "No exceptions. I'll throw you in jail. I will. Whether the charges stick or not."

"Then I'll write a story about wrongful imprisonment," I shot back.

"I don't care," Jake said. "Go ahead. At least you'll be alive."

I turned to Eliot for support, but one look at him told me he agreed with Jake. "Fine," I grumbled.

Jake turned to Eliot. "You'll take her to your place for tonight?"

Eliot nodded. "I'll take her to and from work, too."

"What about while I'm actually at work," I asked sarcastically. "Who is going to chauffeur me around town then?"

"I'll talk to Marvin," Derrick interjected. "He's not much, but he drives like a madman. No one will be able to get a clean shot at her if he's behind the wheel."

"I'm not driving around with Marvin," I protested. "He's more dangerous than a sniper."

"Then you'll stay at the office," Jake said forcefully. "I'll call Fish and clear that with him – and he'll agree with me. You know he will."

"Which one of you is going to go to the bathroom with me?"

It was meant as a rhetorical question, but all three men shuddered when I uttered it. Well, at least I won that point.

All of a sudden, there was a flurry at the back of the room. Jake looked up. "What's going on?"

"They've picked up a suspect," Mohan informed him. "A man was sighted several blocks west of here. He had a rifle with a scope with him at the time of his arrest. It was in his vehicle. Uniformed officers searched the vehicle when he ran a red light."

"Who is it?" I asked curiously.

"I don't know that yet, ma'am," Mohan answered curtly.

Jake glanced at Eliot. "Take her to your place. I'll call you when I know more."

Eliot nodded. "Good luck."

Jake cast a dark look at me. "You'll need the luck. She's going to be a pain in the ass until we're sure this is over. Watch her. She'll try to trick you."

"She'll have to think of a new bag of tricks to do that," Eliot replied. "I'm on to her usual ones."

Derrick shook his head. "If she tries something, call her mother," he said. "That will be enough to keep her in line."

Eliot's face brightened at the suggestion.

"I hate all three of you."

Thirty-Four

Eliot was quiet for the bulk of the ride home. I caught him giving me a series of serious looks during the drive, but whatever was on the tip of his tongue stayed there. I couldn't decide if he was fighting the urge to yell at me or tell me he was glad I was okay. Both scenarios irritated me, though, so I didn't encourage him either way.

When we finally pulled up in front of his pawnshop, I moved to climb out of his truck, but he stopped me with a hand on my arm. "Wait until I unlock the door and come to get you."

I rolled my eyes dramatically. "You really think someone is going to take a shot at me in downtown Mount Clemens?"

"No," Eliot said. "I didn't think anyone would take a shot at you in front of a gay bar in Ferndale either, though."

I was too tired to argue, so I waited in the truck until he pulled me out of the passenger seat and herded me toward the door that led upstairs to his apartment. I couldn't help but notice that he was plastered to my backside in an effort to use his body as a human shield. The gesture should have been construed as sweet, but it was the last straw for me. I had the good sense to wait until we were safely in his apartment, though, before I unloaded.

"I am not a child."

Eliot raised his eyes to my face briefly. "I didn't say you were."

"And yet you're treating me like a child."

"I'm not treating you like a child. I'm treating you like a woman that's been shot at twice in the last week," Eliot replied tiredly.

"Twice? I was shot at once."

"Not if you include that teenage boy that died in Roseville because he was driving a car that looked exactly like yours," Eliot challenged me. "I definitely count that, whether you do or not."

His verbal assault was enough to make me take a step back. I felt as if I'd been punched in the stomach. I felt responsible for that kid's death. I had forced the guilt down out of necessity, but exhaustion, anger, and emotional discontent had paved a road straight through to the center of my heart.

The feeling roiling through my blood was anger. I expressed it by promptly bursting into tears. Eliot looked stunned. He took a step toward me, but I pulled away angrily, swiping at the tears as they coursed down my cheeks.

"Don't cry," Eliot said quietly. "I can't take it. I shouldn't have said that. I'm tired. It's not your fault that kid died."

"It is my fault," I countered. "If he was shot because he was driving a car like mine then it is my fault."

"It was probably just a coincidence," Eliot offered lamely.

I shook my head. "You don't believe that."

"You want to know what I believe? I believe we're both so tired we don't know what we're saying. Now get in bed. We'll get some sleep and finish the fight in the morning."

"You promise?"

"That we'll fight in the morning? I can pretty much guarantee it," Eliot said tiredly.

"Good, because I hate to lose, but I'm too tired to focus."

"I think we both are."

I FIGURED that Eliot and I would only get a few hours of sleep before Jake or Derrick called us with an update. It was almost ten in the morning though when my phone rang. I was still wrapped up in Eliot's arms when my phone dragged me kicking and screaming into consciousness.

"Hello," I mumbled.

"Are you asleep? It's ten in the morning. Only drug abusers sleep this late."

"Good morning to you, too, Mom," I grumbled.

"Are you on drugs?"

"Not today," I replied tiredly. "I'm not ruling it out for the rest of the week, though."

"Do you think that's funny?"

"Maybe," I said. "I'm not fully awake yet, so my senses are still a little dull. I'll tell you in an hour."

"Well, it's not going to be funny in an hour either." God, she sounded like she was in a mood.

"What do you want, Mom?"

"Can't a mother just call to say 'hi'?"

"Not generally."

"Well, I just called to say 'hi.'

"Hi," I sighed. I could feel Eliot shifting next to me. He hadn't opened his eyes, but I could tell he was listening.

"So, your grandfather is getting out of jail today," my mom started.

I knew it!

"And we're planning on having a big family dinner tonight to welcome him home," my mom said. "I thought you would want to come."

"We'll see," I said noncommittally.

"We'll see?"

"I have a lot going on today, Mom."

"That man is your grandfather," my mother started. "He isn't going to be around forever."

"I think he'll still be around until family dinner next week," I replied dryly.

"Are you telling me you're not coming to family dinner?"

"No," I said wearily. "I'm telling you I'll try to make it to family dinner, but I don't know what's going on today so I can't promise anything."

"Avery Shaw, I don't ask a lot of you," my mother started one of her patented tirades. I pulled the phone away from my ear and turned to Eliot.

"My grandfather is out of jail."

Eliot looked at the phone curiously. He could still hear my mom rambling as I held the phone against the comforter. "And you're supposed to go to family dinner tonight?"

"Yeah."

"So? We'll go. What's the big deal?"

"Well, if they've got the freeway shooter in custody it's going to be a long day," I said pragmatically. "I'm not letting the big break in the story go so someone else can write it."

"You mean get the glory," Eliot replied sagely.

"No, it's my story. It's not about glory."

"Well, tell her we'll be at dinner and if things get out of control then you can cancel and blame me," Eliot said pragmatically.

"Oh, I'm definitely going to blame you." I picked the phone back up and pressed it to my ear. My mom was still going strong.

"You know what's right and you know what's wrong," my mom continued. "You do what you know is right in your heart."

"We'll be there, Mom," I interjected hurriedly.

"See, I knew you would see reason."

I disconnected wearily a few minutes later. "You don't have to worry about a sniper getting me. My mother is going to be the death of me."

SEVEN HOURS later, Eliot and I were on our way to the family restaurant. I had managed to file a story from Eliot's apartment after a series of phone calls that started with Jake and ended with the Ferndale Police Department.

Unfortunately, the individual in custody wasn't answering any questions and, since he hadn't been charged with anything, his name wasn't being released to the media. Eliot had been frustrated by the delay, but Jake didn't have any answers.

"I just don't know," Jake said. "I can't find a tie between him and any of the victims and it's going to be at least twenty-four hours until we have a ballistics match from the gun he was carrying and the bullets used in the shooting."

"What about on the preliminary level?" Eliot was pressing.

"It's the same caliber of shell, a twenty-two," Jake replied. Well, at least that was one new little tidbit.

"That could go with anything, though," Eliot said.

"It could," Jake agreed.

So that was where we were. A short story saying the police had a suspect in custody, but no charges had been levied and they couldn't be sure they actually had the real perpetrator off the streets. I had no reason to legitimately avoid dinner – so we were on our way to Oakland County and a night of hellish family conversation. I had offered to go by myself, to save Eliot the aggravation of my family, but he had declined.

"I like your family."

"They're still on their best behavior with you," I shot back.

"You mean it gets worse?"

"You haven't had the pleasure of seeing my grandfather naked yet," I reminded him. "You're not truly a member of the family until you've had that picturesque sight."

"Well, maybe tonight will be the night," Eliot mused.

"We can only hope."

When we got to the family restaurant, I jumped out of the truck before Eliot could make it to the other side of the vehicle. He gave me a dirty look, but let it go. He didn't want to create a scene with my family if he could help it – but he wasn't above using my close call from the night before against me if he had to. I knew that.

The first person I saw when I entered the diner was my grandfather holding court on a stool at the counter with a bevy of regulars congregated around him to hear about his county jail exploits.

"And then I told that judge that I would rather die than go to jury duty," my grandfather said, rubbing his hands together with obvious glee. "Now, sir, he had to save face so he threw me in jail. I decided to go on a hunger strike, though, and he gave in, like I knew he would."

I glanced over at Derrick, who was sitting in the family booth watching the spectacle with a frown on his face. "He went on a hunger strike?"

"He didn't eat the donuts they offered him in the morning."

"Oh, well, I guess that counts."

I slid into the booth next to Derrick, forcing him to slide over to make room for both Eliot and me. "So, anything else new?"

"Nope."

"Would you tell me if there was?"

"Nope."

He was obviously still angry from the night before. "Have you seen Lexie today?"

"No, but I talked to her. She says that Carly's family is crazier than ours," Derrick replied.

"They're not crazier," I countered. "They're just a different type of crazy."

"You mean they don't skinny dip and put on a show for the neighbors?"

"They don't skinny dip, but I've seen Carly's mom hold entire conversations with a cement duck on her front porch. It's just a different kind of show."

"I guess it takes all kinds," Derrick mused.

"Pretty much."

Derrick watched our grandfather with a cross of consternation and affection. "He likes being the center of attention."

"He does," I agreed.

"That must be where you get it from," Derrick said pointedly.

Eliot laughed quietly beside me. I didn't appreciate the comment, but I decided to let it go. I wasn't in the mood to throw down with Derrick at the moment. Thankfully, I was distracted by the arrival of more family members. Pretty soon, we were all wedged into the rectangular booth together.

"So, how does it feel to be out of jail?" Mario asked our grandfather curiously. "No one made you their bitch, did they?"

"He wasn't really in jail," Derrick countered, ignoring the "bitch" comment.

"The hell I wasn't," my grandfather challenged Derrick. "I was behind bars for days. I was on a hunger strike. I could've died for my beliefs – and I was ready to."

"Not eating donuts doesn't equal a hunger strike," Derrick retorted. "Plus, I heard you were allowed out of your cell most of the day to play cards with the other police officers because they needed a fourth for euchre."

"So?"

"That's not jail," Derrick said stiffly. "You got lucky – and apparently you cheated at cards."

"I had the law on my side," my grandfather argued.

"No," Derrick argued. "You broke the law. You did not have the law on your side."

"Are you calling me a liar?" My grandfather narrowed his eyes in Derrick's direction. The truth is, Derrick was his favorite grandchild – we all knew that – but that didn't mean he wouldn't cause a scene with his favorite grandchild if he thought he was in the right. And, here's a tip about my family: We always think we're in the right.

"A liar? No," Derrick shook his head ruefully. "I think you think you're telling the truth. That doesn't mean it's the truth, though."

Uh-oh.

"Listen here, son," my grandfather said with faux patience. "You should learn to respect your elders."

Derrick must have been spoiling for a fight. Any other time he would've backed down. That wasn't the case this time, though. "I do respect my elders," Derrick said. "I just think my elders should respect what I do for a living."

"What? Being a cop?" My grandfather was incensed now. "That was your decision. I told you to pick another career."

"I wanted to be a police officer," Derrick argued quietly.

I was starting to get distinctly uncomfortable. "I want the special spaghetti tonight," I announced.

Eliot eyed me curiously. I usually enjoyed a good family free-for-all. I wasn't the one that usually broke up a family fight, but I wasn't in the mood for a screaming match tonight.

"It's not on the menu tonight," my grandfather said stiffly.

"Isn't there sauce out in the back freezer, though?" I asked pointedly.

My grandfather nodded.

I grabbed Derrick's arm and pulled him out of the booth. "Why don't you help me get the sauce?" I suggested.

"I don't want spaghetti," Derrick grumbled.

"Yes, you do. You love the spaghetti."

I didn't give him a chance to continue arguing. Instead, I pulled him through the swinging double doors and through the kitchen, not slowing down until we were behind the restaurant. "What were you thinking?"

"What was I thinking? I was right," Derrick replied snottily. "I was right and he was wrong."

"He's never going to admit he's wrong," I pointed out.

"That doesn't mean I'm wrong," Derrick pouted.

"No, you're not wrong," I agreed. "This isn't a fight you can win, though. So why fight it?"

"Maybe I can win?"

"No," I shook my head, my blonde hair swinging vigorously as I did. "You're mad about something else and just picking a fight with him to get it out."

"And who am I mad at?" Derrick asked curiously.

"Me," I said simply.

"I'm always mad at you," Derrick scoffed. "Today isn't anything special."

I considered my next words carefully. "I saw your face last night. You were scared when you heard that I had been shot at. You were even more scared when you realized Lexie was there."

"She's finally getting her life together, or kind of," Derrick sighed in exasperation. "I don't want this to derail her."

"It won't."

"How do you know?"

"Don't you know? Our family knows everything. Lexie is a survivor. She's going to be fine. I'm going to be fine, too."

Derrick rolled his eyes but followed me into the detached shed out back. It was dark inside and I could hear Derrick fumbling for the light switch on the wall. "Oomph."

"What happened? Did you stub your toe? Find the light. It's freaky out here."

Derrick didn't answer. I turned around, trying to find his silhouette in the dark. It was hard to make out, but it looked like he was still standing in the doorway behind me.

"Dude, seriously, turn on the light."

After a few seconds, the light did switch on. It wasn't Derrick that flipped the switch, though. The figure in the doorway wasn't one I expected – or even remotely suspected, when this all started.

"Oh, crap, you've got to be kidding me!"

Thirty-Five

"Not who you expected?"

"Not exactly," I said carefully, glancing around the dimly lit shed cautiously. The figure in the door hadn't pulled a weapon yet, but it was only a matter of time. "Where is Derrick?"

"Is that the little guy who came in here with you? He's here on the floor. I had to hit him so I could get a chance to talk to you. He'll be fine, though. I need him to live through this."

I bit my lower lip as I regarded Chelsea – yes, Chelsea – as she stood in the doorway. I didn't know a lot about guns, but the one she was holding looked pretty big. "I didn't expect you," I said honestly.

"Don't try to talk your way out of this," Chelsea said. "I know you suspected me. That's why you followed Brick and me to that parking lot. That's why you showed up at the insurance agency."

"I showed up at the insurance agency to talk to employees of the first victim," I said firmly. "That's standard procedure."

"Then why did you focus on me and not the other women in the office?" Chelsea asked doubtfully.

"Because I knew you were the only one that was going to talk to me," I replied. "I read people. That's what a reporter does."

Chelsea rolled her eyes. "I don't believe you. You knew it was me the minute you came into the office. That's why you followed us that night."

"Actually, I was following Brick," I replied honestly.

Chelsea knit her eyebrows together. "That's what you said then, but I didn't believe you. Why would you be following Brick?"

"Because I thought he was a suspect," I said honestly.

"Brick? He's the most honest man I know."

"He's got a trail of angry ex-wives in his wake that would probably disagree with that assertion," I said.

"That doesn't mean he's a freeway shooter," Chelsea scoffed. "He would never. He has a code."

"I don't see how an insurance secretary becomes a freeway shooter either," I said honestly. I was trying to buy time. Hopefully, Derrick would wake up and handle this situation. Or, if I stalled long enough, Eliot would come looking for me. I didn't think he'd have a problem with a frumpy insurance secretary – even if her gun was bigger than my car.

"I didn't have a choice," Chelsea said. "Malcolm had it coming to him."

"Had what coming to him?" I was trying to infuse as much empathy into my voice as possible. If she saw me as a friend, maybe she would have a harder time shooting me. I pushed the thought of the dead high school student out of mind, for the time being, though. It was counterproductive.

"What I told you about Malcolm was true," Chelsea said. "He hit on everyone in the office. He thought we were all his personal property."

"You said he didn't hit on you," I prodded.

"He didn't, not the way he hit on the other women," Chelsea said. "I thought he would. I know this is going to sound weird, but I was a little insulted that he never even looked at me sideways."

"I get that," I said. "You didn't really want him to hit on you but it was hurtful that he didn't hit on you at the same time. I think that's a common reaction. I'm not sure that was a very good reason to shoot him, though."

"That's not why I shot him," Chelsea said hurriedly.

"Then why did you shoot him?" In addition to being a stalling technique, I really did want to know.

"I was back in the file room one day. It was late. I thought I was the only one there. Mr. Hopper let me work late and take half days on Fridays when my schedule worked out. That's what I was doing. I was looking forward to an extended weekend."

Chelsea's face contorted as she spoke. She was close to tears. I felt a certain level of sympathy for her, which surprised me.

"I had locked the front office, so I wasn't really worried about someone coming in. I heard a noise, though, and when I turned around it was Malcolm."

I had a feeling I knew where this conversation was going – and I didn't like it. I just let Chelsea tell the story at her own pace, though.

"At first I thought he just forgot something," Chelsea continued. "He was looking around the room, but he wasn't really focusing on anything. You know what I mean? It was like his eyes were vacant. He asked me what I was doing and I told him. When he got closer I could smell the liquor on his breath. He smelled like he had been drinking for hours."

Chelsea stopped telling her story long enough to wipe the stray tears that had started streaming down her face.

"Did he ... hurt you?" I asked finally.

"He told me that I was his property," Chelsea said. "He told me that he hired me because he knew that I would give him what he wanted. That I would like it when I gave it to him, too. I told him that I was with someone. I told him that I loved Brick that I was trying to make a life with Brick. He didn't listen, though."

"He raped you?"

"Right there on the filing room floor," Chelsea said bitterly. "He just lifted my skirt and put his hand over my mouth and ... he just did it right there."

Chelsea's voice was hollow – as hollow as her soul, I suspected. I didn't know if what Malcolm had done to her had emptied her out or if she'd always been that way. That wasn't my current concern, though.

"Did you go to the cops?"

"I was going to," Chelsea said. "When he was done, though, he told me the cops would never believe me. He told me that I was fat and ugly and that they would never believe me."

Malcolm Hopper was definitely an asshole.

"I tried to tell Melanie, one of the women at the office," Chelsea said. "She just laughed at me and told me to stop telling lies. She'd been sleeping with him on and off for the past six months, you know. She said there was no way he would have sex with her and then rape someone like me."

"You still should have gone to the police," I offered. "They would've helped you."

"I tried to ignore it," Chelsea pretended she didn't hear me. "I worked there for another two months. I did my job. Every day I went in there and I did my job. And Malcolm? He pretended nothing had happened. He never even mentioned it. He never apologized. He never did a thing."

"So, what was the tipping point?" I asked. "When did you decide to kill him?"

"When he gave every woman in the office except me a raise," Chelsea said honestly. "He said that he couldn't be successful without his staff and that's why he gave them a raise. He didn't give me a raise, though."

"If he had, would you have forgiven him?"

"No," Chelsea shook her head vehemently. "I wouldn't have forgiven him. It was the final straw, though."

"So you bought a gun?" A really big gun.

"It's not mine," Chelsea said. "It's Brick's. I don't even think he knows it's gone."

"Does he suspect you?"

"Of course not," Chelsea laughed. "He would never suspect me. I'm just the sweet little girl he used to date in high school. I'm just the woman that loves him for who he is and doesn't want him to change – not like those other women he married. I'm the woman that cooks him dinner and cuddles up to him at night."

"I thought you were having sex in parking lots?" Not one of my better ideas, I know. My Foot-In-Mouth Disease rears its ugly head at the oddest of times.

"We had to keep things a secret," Chelsea said. "I couldn't spend the night at his house in case his wife came home. If she had proof of an affair, even though they're separated, she could've gouged him for alimony in addition to the child support. We could stay the night at my house, but that was only once or twice a week – at least until the divorce papers were actually filed."

"I don't understand, Chelsea," I admitted. "Why didn't you just tell Brick what happened to you? He would've helped you." I didn't know a lot about Brick, but I believed that was true.

"And tell him that I was treated like a dirty whore? I don't think so. I couldn't stand the way I knew he would look at me if he knew."

"So how did you target Malcolm? Did Brick teach you how to shoot?"

"I've known how to shoot since I was a kid," Chelsea said. "My daddy taught me. I've always been good with a gun. It was just a matter of learning the way he drove home every night and making sure I had an easy escape route. I've always been good with a gun," she repeated. "I never thought I would use it on a person, though."

"You used it on three people," I corrected her. "If you were just looking for revenge on Malcolm, why do the other shootings?"

"I wasn't going to, not at first," Chelsea admitted. "I was only going to kill Malcolm. When the police were all over the insurance agency, though, I knew I had to point them in another direction. I was worried that Melanie would tell the cops what I told her about the rape and then they'd focus in on me. I thought, if there were other victims, they would just assume it was a random freeway shooter and pull their focus away from the agency."

"Didn't it bother you? Killing a mother? Killing a student?"

"I wasn't aiming at a student," Chelsea said. "I thought it was your car."

Even though Eliot had suspected it, even though I had expected it, the confirmation was like a bullet ripping through my heart. "God, Chelsea, he was just a kid."

"I thought it was you!"

"Why did you even care about me?"

"Brick told me that you were looking into the freeway shootings," Chelsea said. "I had no idea who you were the first time I met you. I didn't put two and two together then. That was my fault, I know. I told him about you coming by the office that night, though, and he told me to be careful about you."

"He told you about me?"

"He told me you were a snake in the grass," Chelsea said. "He told me that you were one of those women who didn't know her place, that you thought you should be in charge like a man. I wanted to think it was just a coincidence, but then I did a little bit of research on you and realized that you weren't going to give up on the story. I knew you would be back."

"So that's why you targeted me? Was I going to be your last?"

"I don't know," Chelsea shrugged. "I hadn't decided yet. I just knew I had to shut you up. When I hit the kid, though, I decided to back off. I figured that would be enough of a warning to you. If I went after you again, then it would tip the cops off that you were on to something. I thought hitting the kid was divine intervention; that God was looking out for me. That he'd led me in the right direction and now you would just give up."

God, she really was crazy.

"It didn't take me long to realize, though, that you weren't giving up," Chelsea continued. "That became glaringly apparent when you followed Brick and me that night."

"I was following Brick, not you," I corrected her.

"Because you suspected him?"

"I thought there was something weird about him," I admitted. "He was hardly the only one on my suspect list, though."

"Really?" Chelsea looked alarmed. "Who else?"

"Well, I thought it had ties to the National Guard base for a while," I admitted. "Commander Turner was acting weird. Then there was the new public relations liaison for the sheriff's department. I saw her buying ammunition one day."

"Lots of people buy ammunition," Chelsea pointed out.

"I know," I said hurriedly. "I just really hated her and it would've made things so much easier if it was her."

"So you really didn't suspect me?" Chelsea was flabbergasted.

"Not even a little."

"Well, this is a little embarrassing then," Chelsea said sadly. "I'm going to have to kill you now because you know. I really am sorry, though. I know your family is in there and this will probably upset them, but I have to protect myself and Brick. We have a future, and we deserve to be happy."

"Brick isn't liable for you stealing his gun," I said. I was starting to panic. I was running out of time.

"No," Chelsea agreed. "I'll be able to put the gun back now and no one will know. The case will just go unsolved. It will be one of those things people talk about after a while, like Jimmy Hoffa and the Oakland child killings."

"What about the guy in the Oakland County Jail?" I asked. "How is he tied to you?" I needed to continue stalling.

"I don't know him," Chelsea said. "That was just a stroke of luck."

"How did you get away so quickly?"

"It wasn't hard. I was up on the footbridge above the street. I fired and ran. I didn't realize I hadn't hit you until I saw the news coverage later.

Imagine my surprise when I saw they'd made an arrest?"

"Chelsea, they'll track it back to you," I said desperately. "When I'm found out here, they'll eventually track it back to you."

"How? You said yourself I wasn't on your suspect list. They'll never know."

"Derrick is here. He'll know."

"Then maybe I'll have to kill him, too, after all," Chelsea mused. "I was originally going to try and make it look like a robbery gone bad. Maybe even use his gun and try to finger him for it."

"Why would Derrick want to shoot me?"

"Family strife? Your family is notorious for infighting. Your grandfather was just in the news for calling a judge a faggot or something. Would it be that much of a stretch?"

"Chelsea, I don't think you've thought this through," I started. I had seen a hint of movement from Derrick's foot. I still couldn't see him, though. I had no idea if he was awake or not.

"What?"

"The police are going to match the slug in that gun to the freeway shootings," I said. "If you kill me, maybe they won't look for the culprit too hard. If you kill a cop, though, there's nowhere you'll be able to hide."

"What if I make it look like a murder suicide? Those happen all the time."

"Yeah, but we were just inside. People are going to know that Derrick didn't shoot me and then shoot himself over spaghetti sauce."

Chelsea glanced over her shoulder nervously. "You're messing things up," she said. "I shouldn't have even stopped to talk to you. You're just trying to scare me."

"You should be scared," I said earnestly. "This isn't going to end well for anybody if you go through with this."

"I don't see where I have a choice," Chelsea said firmly, raising the gun. "I might not get away with it if I kill you, but I'll definitely get caught if I don't. What's one more murder? We don't have the death penalty in Michigan and I'm already looking at life."

I squeezed my eyes shut. I knew what was coming and I didn't want to see it as it happened. For a second, my mind wandered to Eliot and the anger he would feel when he found Derrick and I – because I knew he would be the one to find us, for some reason – and I felt my heart clench with unexpressed angst at the pain I knew he would feel.

Then something I didn't expect happened and my whole world tilted anew.

"Avery! Derrick! What are you doing out there? Stop hiding and get back in here! You're both grounded if you don't get in here right now!"

Oh, holy crap, my mom was coming out here.

Thirty-Six

"Who is that?" Chelsea hissed, taking a step toward me.

"It's my mother," I said, fear gripping my senses. "You can't shoot her."

"Then you better get rid of her," Chelsea warned, moving away from the shed door. "You better get her back in that restaurant. If she sees me, it's over for you and her."

Great. Nothing like a little bit of guilt to make a life-and-death situation all the more distressing. My mother would never let me forget it if she got shot – or killed. I didn't believe in ghosts, but if anyone could come back for some vindictive haunting, it would definitely be my mother.

I stepped around Chelsea carefully, glancing down at Derrick as I did. He looked like he was out cold, but I couldn't be sure. I was hopeful that he'd regained consciousness and he was just playing possum – but that was probably the abject fear talking.

Once I was in the doorway, my mom stilled her approach halfway between the restaurant and the shed. "What are you doing?"

"We're still looking for the sauce," I lied.

"It's right in the fridge," my mom said. "I saw it in there the other day."

"Okay," I said. "I was just calming Derrick down before we go back in."

"Well, he should just let it go," my mom said wistfully. "Can't we ever just have a nice dinner?"

"Take that up with the rest of the family," I said briefly. "We'll just grab the spaghetti sauce and we'll be right in."

My mom looked doubtful. I was using all of my Jedi mind tricks to freeze her in place. Unfortunately, just like when I was a little kid, I realized that I didn't really have control of the Force and nothing was going to stop her from coming into this shed if she made up her mind to do just that.

"Well, hurry up," my mom said finally, turning back to the restaurant.

I waited until I knew she was safely back inside and then turned back to Chelsea. "They'll hear the gunshot," I said. "The kitchen staff will hear it. You won't be able to get out of here."

"I guess we'll have to see, won't we?" Chelsea's face had gone from sympathetic to sinister, like a switch had been flipped.

"Just kill me, Chelsea," I begged. "Don't kill Derrick. He doesn't deserve this. He finally got a girlfriend that's not only real but that sleeps with him on a regular basis."

"That's funny," Chelsea laughed. "I didn't think you two got along."

"We don't get along," I said honestly. "Family doesn't get along. We love each other despite the fact that we're all assholes. We love each other because we know the worst about each other and, yet, we're still fine with it."

"And what's the worst about him?"

"He's overcompensating for being short, that's why he became a cop," I said honestly. "He likes control and being a cop gives him that."

"And what's the worst about you?"

"I'm selfish and narcissistic and I'm obsessed with *Star Wars*," I admitted. "I sometimes wish I could turn into the *Incredible Hulk* and pound the crap out of random people – or you right now," I continued. "I always pretend that I want to be the hero of a movie and yet, right now, I'm really looking forward to Derrick tasing the shit out of you and just sitting back and watching."

"Huh?" Chelsea looked around confused. She was too late, though. Her focus had been on me. She hadn't seen Derrick roll to his knees and crawl toward her. She hadn't seen him pull his police issue taser out of his pants and push it to her ankle. And, when she finally realized what was happening, the only thing she had time to register was the smug look on Derrick's face when he pulled the trigger.

Chelsea's body went rigid as the volts rushed through her body. She squeezed the trigger on the gun instinctively, but it was pointed at the wall of the shed and not at me. I dropped to the ground anyway, waiting for her to drop, too. When she finally did, I met Derrick's eyes in relief. "Took you long enough."

"I wanted to see what else you could get her to admit," Derrick said. His eyes were slightly glazed over, making me believe he probably had a concussion. "You got enough to put her away for the rest of her life, though. So, good job, I guess."

I shakily got to my feet, falling back down immediately as the adrenaline I had been living on for the past fifteen minutes fled my body. I crawled over to Derrick, being careful to avoid Chelsea – even though she wasn't in a coherent state of mind at the moment. "Are you okay?"

"Are you?"

"I guess."

"Then kick that gun away from her hand – kick it, don't touch it -- and get the cuffs out of my belt and cuff her."

I raised an eyebrow in surprise. "You're letting me cuff her?"

"I think you've earned it."

THINGS got out of control pretty quickly after that. Eliot had rushed to the shed at the sound of the gunfire, panic and fury written all over his face. After the initial relief registered, he was overcome with irate anger, although there was no enemy left standing for him to fight. "I told you not to leave my side!"

"I went out to a shed with a cop," I replied earnestly. "I thought I was safe."

"Obviously not," Eliot scoffed.

"We're still alive," I countered.

"Only because your mother interrupted," Eliot said. "You should probably thank her."

Oh, great, I would never live this one down. She was going to haunt me in flesh and blood instead of spirit.

In short order, the family restaurant was invaded by the Oakland County Sheriff's Department, medical personnel for both Derrick and Chelsea, and Jake Farrell at his uniformed best.

"Are you all okay?" He asked worriedly when he caught sight of me.

"We're fine," I said. "I wasn't even hurt a little this time."

Jake shook his head. "Is that supposed to make me feel better?"

"Derrick was a hero," I changed my tactic.

"He got hit from behind by an insurance secretary," Jake said. "The guys at the department are going to give him hell for that."

"Yeah, but he regained consciousness and saved my life, that's got to count for something."

"It does. Dumb luck."

"It's not like we knew she was following us," I said. "How could we know that?"

"No, but we knew you were a target," Jake said.

My heart pinged at the thought of a dead high school student. I pushed the guilt away, though. I would deal with that later, when I was alone with my *Little House on the Prairie* DVD sets – so it wouldn't look as bad when I bawled my eyes out. I had a reputation as a hard ass to uphold, after all.

"She made a full confession," I said helpfully.

"Derrick told me."

"I feel a little bad for her," I admitted.

Jake shook his head. "And that's why you're you, I guess."

"What?"

"You feel bad for the woman that wanted to kill you."

"Her boss was a dick."

"But that student and that mother were innocent," he reminded me. "And she wanted to kill you, too. You're awful forgiving about that little fact."

"I didn't say she was right," I said. "I said I felt a little bad for her."

"Well, get over that," Jake said harshly. "You're going to have to testify in court and I don't want the jury to feel bad for her."

He had a point.

THE NEXT few days were a blur. I had managed to file a first-hand exclusive on the arrest of Chelsea and scoop the rest of my competition handily. Then, while they were playing catch-up the next day, Marvin and I had broken another huge story about the National Guard base: It was expanding, not closing.

Commander Turner had agreed to sit down for a one-on-one interview with me regarding the expansion – even being relatively pleasant during the process – and I managed to lay claim to two big stories in two days. No one could touch my Media Queen title for the foreseeable future. Sure, I knew Turner had only agreed to sit down with me because I was the current media darling, but I wasn't going to decline a story that I knew would turn the county on its head.

The political reporter, Bill, had tried to raise a stink about Marvin and me stealing the base story from him, but his constant litany of complaints had fallen on deaf ears. Fish didn't care that we had broken it, only that the two exclusives had caused The Monitor's circulation to soar over the past two days.

"She did the work, she gets the glory," Fish told Bill. "She was almost killed – again. I think she's earned all her accolades this time."

That was enough to constitute a great week at any other time. There was more, though. The best part of my week came when Clara Black, the head of the board of commissioners in Macomb County, took credit for the expansion and effectively cut Tad out of the announcement.

I had heard, through the grapevine, that he was currently plotting my destruction. I would deal with that when it happened, though. I had other things on my mind -- like a wedding – which was finally here.

Epilogue

"What are you doing?"

I had expected a lot of things when I entered the cry room of the church where Carly was being sequestered until the ceremony. Carly trying to climb out of the small window in the wall wasn't one of them.

"I can't do this!" Carly swung on me and I was taken aback by the frantic look in her eyes. "What was I thinking when I agreed to do this? You have to help me get out of here."

I considered Carly's request and then shook my head.

"You love Kyle," I reminded her.

"His mother is the devil, though."

"You're not marrying his mother."

"I think she comes with the package," Carly said wryly.

Even though Carly had been largely calm over the past two weeks, I had figured she had one last freak out left in her repertoire. I had come prepared. I dug into my purse and pulled out the full flask I had thought ahead to pack, taking a swig before I handed it over to Carly. I was a little nervous, too, truth be told.

"What is that?" Carly asked suspiciously.

"Do you care?"

"No," Carly shook her head and took a guzzle. She started to sputter, but I stopped her quickly.

"It's red, it will stain your dress."

Carly snapped her mouth shut quickly. The quiet interlude gave me a chance to look her over completely. "You look beautiful."

"Really?"

"Really," I nodded. "There's never been a more beautiful bride."

"Do you think I can do this?"

"I think you can do anything you set your mind to. The question is, do you want to do this?"

"I love Kyle," Carly admitted.

"I know."

"I love him more than anything."

"Then allow yourself the chance to be happy," I cajoled her.

"What if Harriet makes me miserable, though?"

"Harriet is going to try to make you miserable," I replied honestly. "You have the power to make her miserable too. You'll be the wife. You'll be more important than her." I took out "though"

"How do you figure?" Carly looked interested.

"You're the one that controls the sex."

"That's true."

Crisis averted, Carly wrapped her arms around me in a tight hug. "I couldn't do this without you."

"You could too," I said uncomfortably.

Carly shook her head vigorously. "No. You're my best friend. You're my family. It's you and me forever."

I was warmed by her comments, even though I felt a little sappy at the sentiment. "You're my family, too."

"Just you, though," Carly said hurriedly. "I can't take on the rest of your family. They're crazy."

I couldn't argue with that. Thankfully, we were interrupted by a knock on the door. When Carly's father entered, he looked more agitated than happy. "Do you know there are nuns out there?"

"It's a Catholic church," Carly said irritably. "What did you expect?"

"They're not wearing those outfits, what do you call them?"

"Habits?" I offered helpfully.

"Yeah, habits. I didn't realize they were nuns."

"What did you do?" Carly asked suspiciously.

"I didn't do anything. I thought the one was pretty and I just gave her a friendly pat on the ass. I would never have done it if I realized she was a nun," Carly's dad was properly chagrined – or at least he acted like he was.

I squelched the urge to laugh. Every family has a little bit of crazy in them.

"You grabbed a nun's ass? Where was Mom when you did this?" Carly looked incensed.

"Your mother doesn't need to know," her dad cautioned. "It was just an accident."

"What if the priest doesn't marry us now?" Carly wailed. "What if he thinks we're heathens?"

"I promised them another hundred bucks," her dad answered. "They'll do the ceremony. They think you need the service to keep you pure, at this point."

"Because of you," Carly grumbled.

"I didn't know she was a nun!"

Once the wedding processional started, I convinced Carly to push her father's transgression out of her mind. "You can yell at him at the reception."

"You're right," Carly said. "I'm about to get married. That's what I should be focusing on."

"Absolutely."

I started to move toward the door and then glanced back at her. "You're going to do great."

"Thank you."

Carly frowned as she looked me up and down for the first time, finally taking in the whole of my wedding ensemble. "Are you wearing Catwoman Converse? Where are your shoes? You get back here right now!"

I ignored the order and walked out into the church. I figured the shoes would piss off Harriet – which would be enough for Carly to forgive me once she thought it over. I just couldn't wear those awful satin shoes.

As I made my way down the aisle, I caught sight of Eliot as he sat alone in one of the pews. He smiled when he saw me. He smiled wider when he saw my shoes.

The truth is, there is no such thing as happily ever after. There is such a thing as happy, though, and that's how I felt today. The Force was with us this afternoon – and Carly was going to get the wedding she always wanted, despite the Catwoman Converse. And me? I was going to get lucky after the wedding, and that was more than enough for me today.

Author's Note

I want to thank everyone who takes the time to read my novels. I have a particular brand of humor that isn't for everyone – and I know that.

If you liked the book, please take a few minutes and leave a review. An independent author does it all on their own, and the reviews are helpful. I understand that my characters aren't for everyone, though. There's a lot of snark and sarcasm in my world – and I know some people don't like that..

Special thanks go out to Heidi Bitsoli and Donna Rich for correcting the (numerous) errors that creep into a work of fiction.

If you're interested in my future works, follow me on Facebook, Twitter or join my mailing list. I do not believe in spam. I only announce new releases or free promotions.

Made in the USA
San Bernardino, CA
10 March 2015